INDEPENDENT STREET AT WAR

by

Joan Wallace

Printed in Great Britain.

Published by Gowan Publishing Ltd., Nottingham

First edition 1988.

ISBN 0 947790 03 9

Typeset by Spectrum Graphics (Nottm.) Ltd., Nottingham.
Printed by Cempress Ltd., Carlton, Nottingham.
Cover design by Hilary Evans.

ACKNOWLEDGEMENTS

The author gratefully acknowledges permission for the reproduction of copyright material listed below:

Reproduced by permission of EMI Music Publishing Ltd., London WC2H 0LD
BEER BARREL POLKA © 1939 Keith Prowse Music Publishing Co. Ltd.
MAKIN' WHOOPEE © 1928 Keith Prowse Music Publishing Co. Ltd.
IT'S A LONG WAY TO TIPPERARY © 1912 B. Feldman & Co. Ltd.
KNEES UP MOTHER BROWN © 1938 Peter Maurice Music Co. Ltd.

Reproduced by permission of Carlin Music Corporation, 129 Park Street, London WIY 3FA
IF YOU WERE THE ONLY GIRL IN THE WORLD (Clifford Grey) © Redwood Music Ltd., 14 New Burlington Street, London WIX 2LR.

Reproduced by permission of Chappell Music Ltd., 129 Park Street, London WIY 3FA
SHE'S MY LOVELY (Vivian Ellis) © 1937 Chappell & Co. Ltd.

Reproduced by permission of Noel Gay Organisation, 24 Denmark Street, London WC2H 8NJ
RUN RABBIT RUN © Noel Gay Music Ltd.

Reproduced by permission of Anthony Sheil Associates Ltd., Literary Agents, 43 Doughty Street, London WCIN 2LF
An extract from a poem 'GOD KNOWS' in the anthology 'THE DESERT' © Minnie Louise Haskins 1908.
Popularly termed 'THE GATE OF THE YEAR', the extract was quoted by HM King George VI in his broadcast on Christmas Day 1939.

Reproduced by permission of Yates's Wine Lodges Ltd., 18 Ralli Court, West Riverside, Manchester M3 5FT
The trade name Yates's.

Also by JOAN WALLACE

Independent Street *(published in 1984)*
Two of Clubs *(published in 1985)*

About the Author

Joan Wallace has lived in Nottingham all her life and was educated at the
Bentinck Road Secondary and William Crane schools.

She has written over one hundred short stories — many of these have been
published in the *London Evening News*, *Nottingham Evening Post*, *Woman's
Own* and various other magazines. Her regional stories have been broadcast on
Radios Nottingham, *Trent* and *Derby*. She has won the Silver Jubilee Cup
presented by the Nottingham Writers' Club for the best radio story and has
won their Writer of the Year award three times.

To Shirley and Trevor Herbert
with my love

'INDEPENDENT STREET AT WAR' is Joan Wallace's third book and undoubtedly her best to date. Within these pages we are transported back in time to that lazy hazy summer of 1939.

As Nottingham's citizens set off on their annual holidays to Skegness, Mablethorpe or Cleethorpes, many outwardly presented an air of calm and cheerfulness, yet inwardly had already acknowledged the fact that Europe was drifting inexorably towards war.

When war finally came in September 1939, it was not greeted with the enthusiasm that had accompanied the declaration of war in 1914, but more with a sigh of relief that at least things were now out in the open.

Wartime Nottingham is vividly brought to life through the trials and tribulations of the residents of Independent Street in general, and through the Denbey family in particular.

It is all here — rationing, fire watching, Air Raid Precautions, those first contacts with the brave and dashing young flyers of the Free Polish Air Force, the Yanks and of course the air raids.

Joan Wallace has succeeded in recapturing something of the spirit of those terrible times, when, for a few terrifying years our nation stood united to defeat a determined evil enemy.

CLIVE HARDY
Author of bestseller —
'Nottingham at War'

'INDEPENDENT STREET AT WAR' by JOAN WALLACE

ONE

Jack opened his eyes and experienced feelings of apprehension and fear creeping slowly through his body as his brain signalled that it was time to awaken properly.
He pulled the bedclothes tighter around his shoulders and hunched down, his mind pitter-pattered over yesterday.

The takings on his pot stall down Sneinton Market had been quite good, although they had taken some hammering during the first couple of weeks in August when most of the big firms had closed for their annual holidays. People had scarpered off to Skeggy, Mablethorpe and Cleethorpes — Jack's eyes closed again and he imagined the trains chugging out of the noisy and grimy Victoria station, crammed full with families, suitcases, buckets and spades and baskets filled with sandwiches, flasks of tea, and flannels for wiping dirty faces and sticky fingers.

Jack pursed his lips and made a popping sound. It had been good last night, in the Royal Oak. Plenty of back-slapping and free ale from the other men who were still congratulating him on the birth of his daughter. His queasy stomach reminded him that he had drunk too much.

He turned to look at the new arrival. The cot was placed next to Vera's side of the bed, the baby was hidden from him, peek-a-booing from inside a hand-crocheted shawl.

"Elizabeth Rose Denbey," Jack said the name out aloud and smiled to himself. Trust Vera and her mother to come up with a handle like that. They had copied the names of the two royal princesses — Elizabeth and her sister Margaret Rose.

The baby stirred then whimpered, reminding Jack of the noises old men made when they were dozing.

That unexplained apprehensive feeling still lingered inside his stomach. Maybe the baby was the cause? Jack examined the possibility.

It had been almost two months since he and Vera had made love — and it would be five weeks more, he imagined, before Vera would consent.

It makes a man feel like exploding, he thought, makes you feel like jumping off the Castle-Rock, all that frustration trapped inside. Her royal-highness Elizabeth Rose was only fourteen days old — it would be well into October before Vera felt like 'having a bit of love' again.

No, he thought, it was not the baby and it was not frustration that was causing his depression. His mind switched to full power and he became wide awake. It was the threat of war hanging over the country that was getting him down. The stupid behaviour of the politicians that had taken England right up to the brink. What the hell was Chamberlain and his crew playing about at anyway? Pussy-footing around with that maniac, Hitler.

Jack's toes started to clench and unclench, something he always did when angry. "I'll bet there'll be a war," he murmured into the cotton sheet that smelled of fresh air and starch, "I'll bet we'll be in it before I'm very much older."

The delicious aroma of frying bacon spiralled up the stairs and aimed straight for Jack's nose. He sniffed appreciatively and threw back the bedclothes. If there's one thing that'll shift my miseries, he thought, it's tucking into one of Vera's Sunday breakfasts.

He pulled the crocheted shawl to one side and smiled down at Elizabeth Rose. Eyes screwed up tightly, rose-bud mouth pouting, she lay with fists clenched against her chest. Jack's melancholy mood took flight.

"Hello, me little flower," he said softly, his breath whispering over her face, "who's me little duck then."

Suddenly, nothing else seemed important. Here, inside his house on Independent Street, here was all he should be worrying about — his family.

He shrugged his body into dressing-gown, slipped his feet into slippers and slithered towards the landing at the top of the stairs.

"Got a bad head, Jack?" Vera peeped out from the tiny scullery, face pink from gas-stove heat.

"Bad head?", Jack feigned surprise, "why should I have a bad head then?"

"All that boozing you did last night in the Oak. You were talking all slurred when you got back home. Kept going on and on about what you'd like to do to Hitler . . . and what you'd do to the government if you got the chance. I nearly gave you a soap-box to stand on. They'd love you down at Hyde Park corner."

"Oh, you did listen to me then," Jack slid his arm around her waist. Vera slipped from his embrace and reached for the kettle.

"Go on with yer . . . mind what you're doing then. The bacon'll burn if you don't watch out."

"Give us a kiss then I'll behave."

"You daft thing, Jack." Vera kissed him on the cheek.

"Now hurry up and nip to the lav . . . I'll pour the water for yer wash."

She placed an enamel bowl in the sink and poured boiling water.

Jack walked along the garden-path towards the lavatory. He paused and looked across to the corrugated-iron shelter which he and his neighbours had erected.

What a monstrosity, he felt angry again, stuck right in the middle of the garden. They won't get me sitting in that damp thing — waiting for a bomb to blow me to smithereens, he thought, I'd rather die in bed.

He opened the lavatory door and decided if the worst did happen he would take his family down into the cellar. He hung cut-out squares of yesterday's *Daily Mirror* on a nail. Yes, there'd be a war all right, he was certain of it now, they didn't give you air-raid shelters to erect just for something to do in your spare time.

2

He shut the lavatory door behind him—his chest felt all screwed up inside. What a time to bring a new life into the world. Shove your kids inside air-raid shelters and pray that Hitler's flying jokers couldn't aim straight. Hope that they wouldn't be gassed. Huh, and people still went to church on Sunday and said that God was good — well all I can say is he's got a bleddy funny way of showing it, Jack's toes started clenching and unclenching again, a bleddy funny way.

Jack washed his hands and swilled cold water over his face. The delicious aroma of breakfast made his mouth fill up with saliva. He sat down at the table, smiled at Alex and nodded towards the sideboard.

"Happy birthday, me lad . . . you've had a lot of cards. When I was nine, do you know what I got for my birthday?"

"What, Dad? . . . tell us then."

"Bogger all . . . that's what I got."

"Jack . . . remember it's Sunday," Vera tut-tutted.

"Well, it's true." Jack grinned at Alex.

"Didn't you get any presents at all, Dad?"

"Few comics . . . and a bacon sandwich if you were lucky. We kids never got bacon . . . not as a rule . . . our dad had to have the bacon. We got the rinds to suck. A luxury it was . . . bacon rinds to suck. Never had any meat."

"Didn't you get any toys then, Dad?" Alex's eyes held pleading — sorrowful and yet wanting to know about his dad's poverty. "Didn't you get any presents?"

"We used to make our own toys in them days. Get a bit of wood . . . whittle it down into summat . . . we had . . . "

. . . "Come on . . . come on," Vera interrupted his monologue by placing a plate crammed full with fried breakfast in front of him, "don't start that again . . . going on about sucking yer dad's bacon rinds . . . Alex don't want to hear about that do yer, duck. Not on his birthday." She stroked Alex's hair and added, "You wait till you see what you've got for your birthday. No dog-eared comics for my lad."

"Come on now, Vera . . . I've seen the time we haven't had two ha'pennies to rub together." Jack dipped dry bread in his tinned tomato-juice. "Our dad had to have the best . . . he was the breadwinner . . . had to have good snap inside him . . . if he took bad we all suffered."

"Well you just get your snap inside of you and let's have bit of peace." Vera sat down at the table and poured more tea.

They ate their breakfasts and conversation waited in the wings until the plates were almost empty of food. 'Don't talk when you're eating' was Vera's favourite hand-me-down from her mother. And elbows on the table was also taboo.

Jack dabbed the remainder of his fried bread in the last of the tomato-juice. "That was lovely, Vera. If there's any more tea in the pot I'll take a cup outside with me. I'll read the paper in the sunshine." He smiled at Alex and added, "When we've had a dekko at all the birthday presents. Come on then . . . let's have a dekko at your cards and then you can open the presents."

Alex opened the envelopes. There were six cards, each with a figure nine on the front, and one from Auntie Jenny that had a boy holding a kite that was flying towards the clouds.

3

Vera went into the front-room and came back carrying a cardboard box. She placed the box in front of the fireplace.

"Go on then, duck . . . have a dekko what you've got."

Alex fumbled with the wrapping paper and string.

There was a pea-shooter from Uncle Bert, a neighbour who worked on his dad's pot stall on Sneinton Market, and helped to sell things from his barrow. A scarf and matching gloves from Auntie Jenny who lived in London.

Marbles in a string-bag from the old couple who lived next door.

A book called 'Mystery Stories for Boys', half-a-crown, and a bar of Fry's cream chocolate from grandma and grandad.

Mrs Cohen, the Jewish lady who lived on Connaught Street, had sent him a jig-saw puzzle with a picture on the front of cowboys and indians fighting each other.

The most exciting presents of all were a real football made of leather, a book on football, and red and white stocks — love from mam and dad said the writing on the fancy paper they were wrapped in.

"How d'yer like that then?" Jack looked as pleased as Alex. "You can go and kick yer football about a bit on Brassey if you like."

"Ah . . . and put your old trousers on." Vera chimed in. "And don't let anybody pinch that ball. It cost yer dad a lot of money, that did."

The breakfast scene disintegrated. Alex rushed upstairs to find old trousers; Vera switched on the gas-oven and slid a joint of beef inside; Jack tucked the *Sunday Express* underneath his arm and picked up his cup and saucer.

"I'm going to get a bit of sunshine," he called to Vera, "it's going to be a lovely day . . . look at that clear blue sky."

He sat down in an old deckchair with his face turned towards the warming rays of the sun.

Sunday morning sounds dived into his head and the smells tingled their way into his nose.

Dogs barking excitedly as they followed the milkman's horse and cart as it clip-clopped its way slowly down Independent Street.

Little girls screaming, pretending to be frightened as boys chased them all over the waste-ground known locally as 'Brassey'.

The jingle-jangle from Raleigh bikes as men went on their way to the allotments to gather flowers and fruit to sell in the pubs at dinner-time.

And then there was the pungent aroma of allotment bonfires as men stoked up leaves and rotting wood — the smell of autumn that Jack remembered from his boyhood days — the excitement of grabbing an apple or pear from a tree and the thrill of biting into the juicy sweetness — so long ago — his mind traced the years to when he had been that ragged arsed kid, sucking on those bacon rinds and dreaming of becoming rich. Jack smiled to himself, so rich that he would be able to have whole rashers of bacon all to himself. Jack rubbed a hand over his stomach, the stomach full of breakfast, and he was grateful.

Jack lit a Woodbine and flicked the spent match over the wooden fence which surrounded the tiny back-yard. He held out the *Sunday Express* it was all bad news.

"I want to listen to the wireless, Vera," he reached down for his cup of tea, "see if they say owt about the Germans."

4

"Huh . . . who wants to know about Germans!" Vera frowning and looking anxious. "We've enough to do worrying about ourselves."

"They're just asking for another war." Jack's eyes skimmed over the front page of the newspaper.

"They ought to have more sense . . . after the last lot." Vera stood on the doorstep, arms folded across her pinafored bosom. "Pass us yer cup and saucer . . . I want to get the pots washed before Betty starts howling for another feed."

"I thought her name was Elizabeth?" Jack's mouth quivered into a smile.

"Yes, well it will be later on . . . when she's a young woman. But Betty sounds much daintier for a little baby."

"Women! I'll never understand them." Jack turned the pages of the newspaper, the news made him solemn. He had the last drag out of his Woodbine and coughed to clear his throat.

"Those coffin-nails'll be the death of you." Vera shook crumbs from the tablecloth.

"If Hitler has his way, he'll be the death of me first. Look at this, Vera . . . the Germans have gone into Danzig . . . and you know what that means."

"No . . . and I don't care. I've never even heard of Danzig."

"We promised the Polish people if Hitler's lot march into Danzig we're going in to help them. We'll have to join in now."

"Oh, the government say all sorts of things they don't mean. You exaggerate everything, Jack . . . you always do."

"Listen here, Vera . . . listen to this bit then." Jack held the newspaper out in front of him. "Hitler's planes bomb Warsaw. That was on Friday . . . only two days ago. Now then . . . Chamberlain warned if they didn't pack it in, we'd go in and help the Poles. We'll have to get involved, Vera . . . an Englishman's word is his bond. Hitler's got to be stopped and sharpish."

Elizabeth Jane yelled down the stairs for her mid-morning feed.

"Huh . . . I've got more important things to worry about." Vera undid her pinafore as she hurried upstairs to offer a milk laden breast to her hungry baby.

The wireless crackled to life — Jack fiddled with the knobs and found the Home Service. A man's voice, solemn and emotion filled, gave the nation their eleven o'clock news. Jack sat in an armchair — looked at Vera with the baby at her breast — he felt like a coiled up spring, wanted to leap into the air and shout his head off. Now Chamberlain began to speak and Jack shouted, "Listen, Vera . . . it's old Chamberlain."

"I'm listening, Jack . . . I'm listening."

"Ssshhhhh . . . oh, I knew it, I knew it."

"Ssshhhhh yerself, then."

Chamberlain's voice droned on, "Everything I have worked for . . . everything I have hoped for in public life has crashed into ruins this morning. If an assurance has not been given by the German government by eleven a.m. to His Majesty's government in London, a state of war between the two countries will exist from that hour."

The wireless crackled and Chamberlain's voice faded away into the air-waves.

"I told you . . . I knew it." Like the coiled up spring, released at last, Jack leapt from the armchair and rushed outside.

Neighbours had gathered into groups. They were all there, standing about doing nothing, faces portraying anxiety, the children sensing danger made extra noise, pushing each other and shouting and squealing.

Jack could feel his heart beating faster — adrenalin charged with fear.

"Good job we've got the air raid shelters built."

"Yer right there, Jack. Built 'em just in time, mate."

"It'll all be over in a week."

"Wait till our lads get stuck into the Germans."

"You'd think they'd learnt their lesson from the last good hiding we gave 'em. Bloody krauts . . . I hate the boggers, I do."

"Yes . . . all that gas . . . and the terrible loss of life. I hate them an' all."

"I knew we'd had it . . . when they made us fetch those gas masks. They'll try to gas us all. Been planning this lot for years. There'll be a lot of lives lost again, you mark my words."

"I'll join up, Dad. Germans don't scare me."

"Nor me . . . I fancy the Navy."

"Oh . . . it's the Air Force for me, mate. Blow the bastards out of the skies. Let me get behind a gun . . . I'll shoot the boggers down."

"We don't want no war." It was Vera's voice, piercing, saturated with fear. "What does it prove? What does it solve?" Vera turned to face her neighbours. "I'll tell you what it solves . . . nothing. And in the meantime, thousands of innocent people get killed. People like me dad . . . and young lads like me brothers . . . just out of short trousers and all used as gun-fodder."

"But we can't just let Hitler walk in and take Poland, Vera." Jack leaned against the garden fence. "He's got to be stopped."

"What's it got to do with us what's happening in Poland?" Vera would not be placated.

"Yes . . . what's it got to do with us?" Florence Wilkins, the attractive young widow from number forty three, tucked her arm inside the milkman's arm, "nothing to do with us . . . it's thousands of miles away."

"And what would you say if it was the other way round, then?" Jack aimed the question at Vera. "What if Hitler invaded England? You'd expect somebody to help us, wouldn't yer? Poles . . . Americans . . . Russians . . . you'd expect them to get over here sharpish."

"We don't want any wars here." Vera's mouth stretched tight and a defiant look loitered in her eyes.

Jack knew it was a waste of time arguing with her.

"Better put some bottles of ale in the air-raid shelter . . . just in case." Jack decided the tense atmosphere needed lifting a bit. "Good drink of Shippo's ale and a load of Sanderson's pork-pies and I'll be as happy as a sand-boy in there . . . like a day at the seaside," he lied.

"You talk daft, Jack," Vera's taut mouth relaxed, "you won't get me in that damp, smelly thing . . . not with Betty and Alex, you won't."

"The cats pee in it," Florence Wilkins giggled up into Danny the milkman's face, "it smells awful, it does."

"You'll be all right in there with me, Florence." Danny put a protective arm around her shoulders.

6

"Ooh . . . I can think of better places to be," Florence leaned against him, "fancy a bottle of Stout, me duck?"

"Now you're talking." Danny's face wrinkled into a grin.

"He looks just like a cheeky lephrechaun," Jack whispered to Vera, "I know what's going on there. I'll bet he gets more than a bottle of Stout."

"Well . . . they're both free agents," Vera relaxed a bit more.

"Come on everybody," she addressed her neighbours, "if you'd like to come to our house I'll make us all a nice cup of Camp coffee made of milk. Bring me three extra bottles please, Danny . . . put it on next week's bill."

Jack ushered them through the back-yard. Tension seemed easier to handle when shared with friends and neighbours, Jack decided. He helped Vera with the cups and saucers and told a joke or two. Keep their minds off that bastard Hitler, he thought, and then imagined he could hear the cry for help from the Poles — it echoed across mountains and oceans in one almighty scream, and he could not bear to turn his back on them. He would join the Army and do his bit. "Have you heard about the old bloke of ninety who married a young girl of twenty?" Jack turned to face his neighbours. "It could mean death I'm afraid, said the old bloke's doctor. Well, said the old bloke, if she dies . . . she dies."

Everybody laughed and sipped coffee — experienced the communal bonding together that only seemed to come to the fore during a crisis, thought Jack.

"Owd Hitler'll have his work cut out if he picks on the English." Jack handed round his packet of Woodbines.

"Not 'arf, Jack . . . you're right there." Danny accepted a cigarette.

"Ey . . . have you heard the one about the vicar who had eleven kids?" Jack perched himself on the edge of the sofa. "It's not yer collar you want to wear back-to-front, said his wife, it's yer trousers."

Everyone laughed and Vera looked over to where Alex was sitting reading a Comic Cuts. "Jack . . . behave yerself . . . little pigs have big ears." But she also laughed and the atmosphere in the room gently slid into party mood.

Neighbours had drifted reluctantly back to their own homes. Jack sat in the deckchair and cleaned his best brown shoes until the toe parts shone like polished conkers.

Chimes from the Council House clock told him it was twelve o'clock — pub doors would be opening in unison all over Radford.

Jack went indoors, stood in front of the sideboard mirror and flattened his hair down with Brylcreem. He placed his George Raft trilby on his head and cocked the hat to one side just like the film-star wore his hat.

"Alex . . . take this half-a-crown," Jack held out the money, "and go to the Phoenix . . . on Denman Street . . . get a quart of their home-made brew seeing as yer Grandad Alf's coming to yer birthday party. Take the big jug so's you won't spill any." He tousled Alex's hair and added with a grin, "And don't get supping any, me lad."

"No, Dad . . . I won't. I don't like the taste. Shall I get a few packets of crisps for me party, Dad?"

"Yes . . . get some crisps . . . here's another shilling." Jack turned to Vera. "I'm off to the Oak then, Vera. I'll bring you a light ale and some lemonade . . . so's you can make a shandy."

"Don't be too long, Jack. Remember it's Alex's birthday party. You can't stay in bed all afternoon."

Jack slid his hands over her breasts, caressed her in a non-sexual, playful gesture and answered, "Pity about that . . . I thought we might have had half an hour this afternoon . . . While our Alex was at Sunday school."

"You just hold your horses." Vera turned to face him. "Be patient, Jack . . . let me get right first." She tugged on the brim of his trilby and added, "Give me time to recover and I'll make a right meal of yer."

"Oooh . . . you fast cat." Jack patted her behind and then sniffed loudly. "That beef smells a bit of all right, Vera. Do plenty of roast taters."

Jack walked with the jaunty step of a man who was happy with life despite his feelings about the war. All the way to the pub he whistled 'Keep young and beautiful' through his teeth without once pursing his lips.

Bert was already standing near the bar when Jack reached the Oak.

"Drink up, Bert . . . two pints of mild please, Gloria." Jack held out a ten shilling note. "Are you having one, duck?" He rustled the note between finger and thumb.

"No . . . it's the way me skirt hangs, love." Gloria pulled on a pump decorated with hand-painted flowers and laughed heartily. The laughter made her breasts bobble about.

Jack looked her up and down and felt generous.

"Have a drop of mother's ruin, Gloria." He lit a Woodbine and offered the packet to Bert.

"Oooh, I was ruined a long time ago, Jack." Gloria laughed again and placed two pints of mild on the counter. "By the way . . . me dad caught a few rabbits yesterday. Send your lad round if you'd like one. A nice rabbit stew'll put hairs on yer chest."

"Blimey . . . you'd better not eat any then, Gloria." Jack scooped up his change from the counter.

"Oooh, don't be cheeky." Gloria sucked on a slice of lemon then popped it back into her gin. She licked her lips making a sheen on her lipstick and it seemed to Jack, at that moment, no woman had ever looked more beautiful. Gloria radiated warmth, good humour and alluring femininity.

"What do yer reckon about the war then?" Gloria wiped the counter top with a dishcloth. "I'm frightened to death. And I'm not going to wear me gas mask . . . it flattens me hair down and smudges me lipstick. And they needn't think they're going to get me working on munitions. . . they're not going to stick me in a factory where I can get blown up."

"There's nowt to be frightened of, Gloria," Bert wiped beer foam from his lips, "come in the air raid shelter with me . . . give me a big kiss and I'll protect yer from the bombs and gas."

"Oooh . . . I've heard about you, Bert."

"What you heard then? Who's been talking?"

"I heard about that party you went to . . . when you lost yer false teeth in the garden."

"Blimey, Gloria . . . I only want to kiss yer . . . I don't want to bite yer."

Gloria's laughter pierced a way through Jack's thoughts and he joined in the fun.

8

"Ey up, Bert . . . better not let your Annie hear yer." He drained his glass and added, "Fancy 'owt in the Nottingham races tomorrer? I fancy Red Beauty if the races are still on. She's got good form and if she carries a good weight she'll walk it. Might be cancelled though, because of the war."

"Oh, that's a good omen if you ask me, Jack. It sounds like Gloria. She's got two red beauties in that tight jumper . . . and she's got a good form. Best form in Radford, I'd say, Jack."

"Ey . . . just watch it." Gloria prised the top from a bottle of Stout.

"We are doing, me duck . . . we are doing." Bert laughed heartily and the top set of his false teeth wobbled away from his gums.

"Watch them, Gloria . . . they're looking you over," an elderly woman winked at Gloria and smiled, "all men are the same yer know."

"That's all right, Clara," Gloria pulled her jumper down over her hips and stuck out her breasts, "I'd rather be looked over, than overlooked."

"That's what Mae West said in a picture I saw the other week. Oh, I do think she's glamorous. You should see the clothes she wears."

The landlord clattered empty glasses into a sink and asked, "Fancy helping with the washing-up again, Clara? I've got all me cellar work to do this afternoon and I've got to see to me pumps. I'll make it worth your while."

"Oooh . . . I'll see to your pump any time, Jim." Clara laughed raucously and added, "You come home with me and I'll get your pump working a treat."

"You're too old for pumps, Clara," Jim joined in the laughter, "now what do you say . . . will you help out again . . . the missis isn't feeling too good today . . . her screws are killing her."

"Yes, I'll help out . . . I might as well . . . "

WHOOOWWWWWWWWWWW . . . WHOOOWWWWWWWWWWW . . . WHOOOWWWWWWWWWW.

Clara was interrupted by a loud howling noise. It was the air raid siren screaming its terrible warning all over the city. Everyone panicked.

"Bleddy hell, it's an invasion."

"Quick . . . get down the cellar."

"Oh, I've left me gas mask on the sideboard."

"I'm sure I can smell gas."

"Lock the doors . . . lock the doors."

"No, leave them open, we'll be trapped."

"Here you are, Clara . . . put my gas mask on, love."

"I can't breathe in them things . . . not with me asthma."

"Come on everybody, down the cellar."

"I daren't go down there . . . I've got claustrophobia."

"You can sit underneath the grate where they roll the beer barrels down then. You'll be able to see the sky if you keep looking up, Clara."

"I'm sure I can smell gas . . . they've dropped some gas bombs."

Jack watched as everyone scrambled towards the cellar door and decided that he must get back to his house, check that his family was safe. To hell with German invasions, he thought, and I can hold me breath till I get home, in case they have dropped some gas.

"I'm going to see to Vera and the kids, Bert." Jack opened the pub door and looked up at the sky.

"I'm right behind you, mate." Bert was shouting in his ear, "Our Annie'll be frightened to death . . . I've got to get back to Annie."

WHOOOWWWWWWWWWWW . . . WHOOOWWWWWWWWWWW . . . WHOOOWWWWWWWWWWW.

The noise seemed to pound into Jack's senses — shattering his nerve ends and paralysing his thoughts. He kept as near as he could to the houses and ran towards Independent Street closely followed by Bert.

"Oh, Jack . . . I was so worried." Vera was standing near the back-door, Elizabeth Rose cradled in one arm and Alex sheltering underneath the safety of the other. "Is it an invasion? What's happening, Jack? Shall we all go in the air raid shelter? Will we be safer in there do you think Jack?" Her face was as white as the shawl. "Shall we put the gas masks on?" She could not decide anything for herself. Terrified for the safety of her children her mind had refused to function properly.

Jack looked up at the skies for signs of aircraft. Only a few white clouds drifting lazily — hiding nothing — the sun shone just as brightly as it had earlier but Jack was not reassured, the normality of it all made everything seem more terrifying somehow.

"We'll go down the cellar." He pushed his family gently towards the cellar door. "Down you go, Alex . . . that's right. Now you take care of your mam and baby sister . . . I'll be back in a minute."

"Jack . . . where are you going? Don't leave us, Jack." Vera's eyes were large against the paleness of her face.

"Just going to see if the neighbours are all right. Going to check on Florence and the old 'uns next door. I think they'd like to be with us. I think they'd rather be together, if they're frightened." He hurried out of the door.

Jack gathered neighbours together like a shepherd rounding up sheep. He rushed around without worrying about his own safety — a hero and not realising the fact.

When they were all down the cellar Jack sat on an upturned orange-box and looked at all the people congregated in his cellar.

Florence Wilkins and Danny her milkman boyfriend, perched on stools, arm-in-arm and quiet.

Bert and Annie, balancing on either side of the old armchair that Vera was sitting in, with Elizabeth Rose cradled in her arms.

Mr and Mrs Tate from the fruit shop also sitting on upturned fruit-boxes and the elderly couple from next door sitting in deckchairs, arms folded across chests as though they were on the beach at Skegness.

"Let's have a sing-song." Bert stood up and faced everybody.

"It's a long way to Tipperary
It's a long way to go
It's a long way to Tipperary
To the sweetest girl I know."
Everybody joined in the song.
"Goodbye Picadilly, farewell Leicester Square

It's a long, long way to Tipperary
But my heart's right there."

They sang the song twice more. Vera placed Elizabeth Rose in Jack's arms and asked, "Who'd like a nice cup of tea and a bite to eat?" She paused with her left foot on the cellar step and added, "Hey . . . have you all turned your ovens off? We could be stuck down here for hours . . . your joints'll all be ruined."

"Yes . . . we've all seen to our ovens," Florence answered for them all.

"Come on then," Bert waved his arms about, "who knows 'If you were the only girl in the world?"

Florence and Danny held hands and sang out loudly, the others joined in.

"If you were the only girl in the world
And I were the only boy.
Nothing else would matter in the world today
We could go on loving in the same old way.
A garden of roses just meant for two
With nothing to mar our joy.
I would say such wonderful things to you
There would be such wonderful things to do.
If you were the only girl in the world
And I were the only boy."

The elderly couple from next door smiled at each other and sang in old people voices — melodic but quivering and wearing out.

"A garden of roses just meant for two
With nothing to mar our joy."

Bert and Annie sang out the loudest.

"I would say such wonderful things to you
There would be such wonderful things to do."

Now they all gave it everything they could, their voices reverberating round the whitewashed cellar walls. Three more times they sang the song and their voices grew strong and defiant.

"Tea up," Vera balanced a tray, "I've made some sandwiches and there's a roast tater each. Don't feel like having a proper dinner today . . . and anyway, It's our Alex's birthday party later on . . . there's loads to eat isn't there, Jack."

"Come on everybody, get stuck in," Jack nodded at the food, "it'll put lead in yer pencils."

"Ooh, don't put ideas in their heads, Jack," Florence pressed up close to Danny, "I have enough trouble as it is."

"Take the sugar-bowl round to everybody, Alex," Vera nodded to Alex then opened a packet of Lincoln cream biscuits and piled them onto a plate, "and hand these round."

Jack looked round at his neighbours. He felt amused and yet, paradoxically, very proud. Here they all were, tucking into beef sandwiches and dunking Lincoln creams into their tea like they were at a vicar's tea-party. Any why this strange phenomenon? Because they were at war with lousy Germany and they had to show the world that they would not give in no matter what happened. Nothing and nobody was going to floor them.

11

Throw poverty through the doors, Jack thought, push hunger and unemployment down the chimneys; threaten them with Germans, gas-bombs and destruction and what did the people of Radford do? They had a sing-song, mashed tea and made a party out of the whole bloody show.

"Ey . . . let's have a picture-quiz." Jack handed Elizabeth Rose to Vera and stood up again. "Right then . . . who said, I never drink water because fish make love in it?"

"Jack!" Vera shook her finger at him and nodded towards Alex. "Little pigs have big ears, mind what you're saying."

"W C Fields," shouted Danny. "Oh, I love going to the pictures."

"Who said . . . come up and see me some time?" Danny grinned at Florence.

"Mae West . . . Mae West," everybody shouted at once.

Laughter replaced fear as they played the quiz-game then suddenly, the all-clear siren screeched its jarring monotone all over the city.

"Ooh dear, they've gone," Bert announced to everyone, "they've gone and never called me mother," he pretended to wipe tears from his eyes.

"You daft thing, Bert," Annie smiled at him, "you never take anything seriously." Her smile held warmth, like a mother for her child.

Jack thought about how Bert had rushed home to be with Annie when the siren had first sounded and imagined her flippant remark was hiding behind a veneer of deep understanding between the two of them.

"Come on everybody . . . we're safe now." Jack held out his arm for the elderly neighbour to take hold of as she struggled from the deckchair.

"What about putting our gas masks on?" Florence fussed.

"No . . . can't smell owt, Flo. You'd be able to smell it if they'd dropped any." Danny cuddled her and looked protective.

"Oh dear, I've dropped me ear-plugs in this pile of slack."

Mrs Tate from the fruit-shop rummaged about in the coal.

"Is the war over now, Dad?" Alex looked disappointed. "I like it down here in the cellar . . . playing games and singing. I'm having a lovely birthday, aren't I."

"Come on, Alex . . . it's time for Sunday school. Come and clean your shoes there's a good lad." Vera ushered him towards the cellar steps.

"Is the war over then?" Alex repeated, "won't the Germans come back again?"

"Ey . . . let's go and have a game of football on Brassey before you go to Sunday school," Jack looked at his wristwatch, "we've got time. Come on, put your old trousers on . . . come on, Bert . . . you can be the goalie." He winked at Bert. "Go and put yer Forest scarf on."

Jack ignored Alex's questions about the war but the answer he chose not to give set his nerves on edge once again. Terrifying words echoed inside his head as he thought of the reply.

No — the war was not over — it had only just begun.

Vera lifted the jelly moulds from the landing at the top of the cellar steps. The jellies wobbled, reminding Vera of fat ladies' chins. One strawberry flavour and the other raspberry — Alex's favourites.

She set the jellies down in between the sponge-cake with the nine candles stuck in the pink icing and the cut-glass bowl full of tinned peaches.

"A table fit for a king," Vera spoke to her reflection in the mirror above the fireplace and tried to think herself into a party mood. But the gloom which had descended upon Radford earlier — after Chamberlain's war announcement and the air raid warning — could not be spirited away with birthday parties.

Vera glanced at the clock, just time for a quick wash and a change of frock before everybody arrived.

"Jack!" Vera opened the door at the bottom of the stairs. "Come on, Jack . . . they'll be here soon. I've put your clean shirt out."

She turned to Alex who had just got the right-hand corner of his cowboys and indians jigsaw sorted out. "Put your best Fair-Isle pullover on, duck." She smiled at him and no smile had ever portrayed more love.

"Will Betty be able to eat some jelly, Mam?" Alex turned from his jigsaw, "I'll bet she'd like some raspberry flavour."

"Not yet, she can't" Vera slid the coat hanger out of her new Marks and Spencer's frock. Navy background smothered in big pale blue flowers — a present from Jack yesterday with a new navy hat to match — the frock was a bit tight fitting but Vera knew she would have lost a bit of weight in time to wear the frock at the christening. A good strong corset from Hilda Sharman's on Alfreton Road would squeeze everything back into shape again, she thought, and turned sideways and looked at herself in the mirror.

As she turned away from the mirror her glance rested on three small boxes in the corner at the bottom of the stairs. Vera shuddered and remembered what it had felt like — her face encased in the thick rubber gas mask. She and Jack had tried to make a joke of it, when they had taken Alex to the Forest Road school to try on their gas masks. The most horrible object, to Vera, was the special-type gas mask for all the babies. The grotesque contraption with the concertina thing at the side that you had to pump up-and-down to get pure air into the baby. The obscenities of war! Vera shuddered and in a gesture of defiance, placed her hat on Rupert the cat's head, and said, "Just let the Germans show their ugly mugs on Independent Street. We'll bash their brains in, the lot of 'em."

Alex fitted another piece of jigsaw into place and asked, "Will we all have guns, Mam?"

The cat, rheumaticky and well past the normal span of nine lives, closed his eyes and settled down underneath Vera's new hat. Vera smiled at Alex.

"No need for guns, duck," she comforted him, "the Germans won't dare come here. They can't anyway . . . we're surrounded by water. They'd be blasted out of the sea if they tried to land in this country." She took her hat off Rupert's head and added, "Now then . . . go and put yer best Fair Isle pullover on, there's a good lad. We're all going to have a lovely party . . . your pals'll be here any minute . . . wait till they see yer football."

The John West salmon sandwiches were the first to disappear off the plates and then the ham-off-the bone from Sanderson's pork shop went next.

Vera to'd and fro'd with the teapot refilling the 'best' tea-service cups as soon as they were sipped empty.

Jelly covered in custard wobbled gently down throats, closely followed by tinned peaches soaked in evaporated milk.

"Time to light the candles," Vera nodded at Jack, "come on, Alex . . . breathe in . . . get ready to blow them all out."

"Pheeeewwwwwww . . . I've done it . . . I've done it." Alex in clean white shirt and best Fair Isle pullover, sat up straight, aiming himself at manhood — nine years was a long time to a boy.

Nine years. Alex day-dreaming about the time when he would be clocking on at some factory or helping his dad on the stall down Sneinton Market. Alex thrust the bread-knife into the pink icing on his cake.

Nine years. Jack so proud of his young son and thinking about his own childhood — no candles on fancy cakes for Jack. He sat back and savoured the occasion.

Nine years. Vera wishing that time could be slowed down. Another nine years and she would probably have lost him — to a girl — or a war. She put a smile on her lips and tried to ignore the hollow feeling inside her stomach.

"Happy birthday to you . . . happy birthday to you . . . happy birthday dear Alex . . . happy birthday to you." Everybody singing and smiling.

"Wooowwwwwww!" Elizabeth Rose joined in the celebrations.

All eyes now focussed on the pram — watched little hands with fingers opening and shutting — reaching out for the comfort and warmth of Vera's life giving breasts.

Vera reached inside the pram, scooped up the squawking bundle and hurried into the kitchen to give Elizabeth Rose her feed.

Alex looked round the table at his birthday guests. Grandad Alf and Grandma who lived in Chesil Avenue; old Mrs Cohen, the Jewish lady from Connaught Street who had given his dad some money so that he could hire a stall on Sneinton Market to sell his pots from; Bert and Annie who lived three doors away: and three of his best pals from school.

"Can I go and kick me ball about a bit, Dad?" Alex stood up.

"Ah . . . go on then and don't make too much noise." Jack also stood up and handed cigarettes out to the grown-ups. "We'll listen to the six o'clock news . . . see what they've got to say about the war. I should think they'll put the bleddy wind up us again."

"What do you reckon they'll do about the Market, Jack?" Bert tapped his Woodbine on the back of his hand. "Do you reckon they'll close it down?"

Alex and his pals left the room in a noisy jostling hustle.

"Not too much noise remember," Vera called after them. Shrill boyish laughter got fainter and fainter on its way to Brassey.

Jack helped himself to another piece of birthday cake and said, "Don't think they'll close the Market, Bert. We'll just carry on as normal."

"Nowt'll ever be normal again." Grandad Alf puffed on his pipe and started to chuckle.

"Come on . . . what's tickling you then?" Maisie his wife poked him gently in the ribs.

"Just imagining Jack . . . trying to sell his pots down the Market . . . with his gas-mask on," Alf chuckling louder.

"Oh yeah . . . very funny, Alf," Jack joined in the fun, "and how are you going to

14

drink your pints of Shippo's when you've got yourn on . . . through a straw? By the·
way, I've got some home-brewed . . . from The Phoenix."

"And what about the schools closing down?" Maisie licked cake crumbs from her
lips. "They're going to hold classes in people's front rooms. The kids'll never learn
owt like that . . . they'll mess about too much. It won't be like proper schooling.
They'll never learn owt, you'll see."

"Gerroff . . . it'll be better," Alf disagreed, "it'll be better. Posh folks prefer to
educate their kids at home. They pay out good money to them posh governesses. That
way their kids get better attention."

Vera entered the room with Elizabeth Rose tilted over her left shoulder and
encouraged her to burp her wind away by a gentle stroking of back.

Jack walked through to the kitchen to fetch the wireless. He placed it on the
sideboard and fiddled about with the knobs once more.

The six o'clock pips heralded the news and again Chamberlain's sobering, terrifying
message was relayed into almost every home in England.

"Everything I have worked for . . . everything I have hoped for in public life has
crashed into ruins this morning." On and on the words pouring out from the speaker,
the obscene message stifling the country underneath a blanket of terror.

When the news ended no-one spoke. Instead they shuffled about on the chairs and
cleared their throats but no words were uttered.

Jack looked round the room at everyone and thought, this must have been how it
was in caveman times — before they knew how to communicate.

But there was always touch, he thought, and reaching over to her gave Vera a
squeeze.

"It'll be all over inside a week . . . you'll see. When we've helped the Poles out . . .
when Hitler sees we mean business . . . he'll back down like wildfire, you'll see."

He tickled Elizabeth Rose underneath her chin then stood up again and addressed
the men, "What do you all say to a game of football? Come on, men . . . let's go and
show 'em how it's done. I've kicked more goals through the goal-posts than you've
had hot dinners. Come on . . . we'll work up a thirst for our drink of ale later. Let's go
and give our Alex a birthday he'll remember."

"Yer big soft kids."

"Men . . . they never grow up."

"Alf still plays with his train-set."

"That's nowt . . . Bert still plays with his soldiers."

They struggled to break the evil mood that Hitler had oozed into their hearts and
succeeded with true English grit and humour.

TWO

Jack found the silence which had descended on Nottingham since the announcement of war ominous and unsettling. He missed the noise the children from the Mission Ragged Town School usually made at playtime. Now that the government had ordered the closure of all schools the Mission Ragged, which stood shoulder-to-shoulder with the swimming baths, crouched silent beneath a shimmer of autumn sunlight, reminding Jack of a mausoleum.

"Not much doing this morning, Jack." Bert perched himself on the corner of the stall and poked inside his left ear with a matchstick. "People've got war on the brain. That's all they can think about. Not going to come buying pots, are they."

"We'll push the fruit tommorrow," Jack answered him, "that'll bring in a few bob. You can work on Long Row in the morning . . . while I'm over at Stoke. Then we'll try that pitch down near the Walter Fountain in the afternoon. We always do well down there, Bert . . . or Parliament Street."

Jack packed unsold pots into cardboard nests of straw and old newspapers. A tune the schoolchildren sang during their playtime buzzed into his brain — the words echoed inside his head.

"The big ship sails on the Alley-alley-oo
The Alley-alley-oo
The Alley-alley-oo
The big ship sails on the alley-alley-oo
On the first day of September."

He wrapped a pot alsation inside a page from the *Daily Mirror* and thought about the children. Poor kids from poverty stricken homes — wearing clothes from the Welfare on their thin bodies and wearing suspicious looks on their thin faces.

What a world, Jack thought sadly, as he remembered his own childhood. All he had ever wanted from life was enough food, some decent clothes and a bit of affection from his mam and dad. That was all these kids needed but they were not having much luck. No shoes on their feet some of them.

All that misery to contend with and now some barmy bogger called Hitler wanted to drop bombs on them. What a bleddy crazy world.

Jack lit a Woodbine and offered the packet to Bert.

"Right then, Bert . . . we'll get this lot on the lorry and go and try a pint. No use hanging on any longer."

Bert stopped poking his ear with the matchstick and instead rubbed the head of the match across the sole of his shoe and lit his cigarette.

"Ah . . . now you're talking, Jack. Let's go and feast our eyes on Gloria. Oh, if only I were twenty years younger."

Jack coughed and spluttered and answered, "You still wouldn't be able to handle her. Oh dear, these bleddy coffin nails'll be the death of me."

"I'd like Gloria Goodliffe to be the death of me, Jack," Bert grinned and added, "a slow lingering death."

"Oh, what a way to go . . . come on then, pass those pudding-dishes up . . . then I'll have the tea-sets next."

16

Ten minutes later Jack and Bert were in the lorry and heading down Alfreton Road towards Brassey.

"Ey up, me ducks," Gloria squeezed the beer-pumps and thrust out her breasts, "two pints of mild, is it?"

Jack's mind became crammed full with erotic, sinful images of Gloria in various stages of undress. Then the tune of the children's song waltzed into his head and everything became mixed up — Gloria's thighs white against black suspenders and images of ships sailing away into the morning mists.

"You're not listening are you, Jack? I said wasn't it exciting when the sirens went off yesterday?" Gloria smiled, straight white teeth showing up nicely against deep crimson lipstick.

"Didn't you hear them this morning, Gloria?" Jack drank deeply of the pint of mild and smacked his lips. "I'd just got off to sleep again, after our baby'd woke us for her feed. I nearly jumped out me skin."

"We heard, but our dad said it was a false alarm," Gloria looked at her reflection in the mirror behind the bar and patted at her blonde curls, "so we all stayed in bed." She smiled and nodded to Clara who was waiting to be served.

"Blimey . . . ," Bert grinned at her, "you'd have been all right if they'd dropped a bomb down yer chimney."

"We all got up for a cup of tea when the all-clear sounded," Gloria opened a bottle of stout for Clara, "I didn't hear it mind you . . . I'd got me ear-plugs in. Our mam woke me up . . . she gets ever so excited our mam does. She won't go in the shelters though. Can't get her in a shelter."

"Your mam sounds like me," Clara sipped the froth from her glass of stout, "she must have claustrophobia."

"You must be a heavy sleeper, Gloria," Jack downed the last of his pint and placed his glass on the bar counter ready for a refill.

"I am . . . I sleep like a baby . . . 'specially after I've had a few gin-and-tonics."

Jack took the hint and said, "Better have another one then . . . then you can have a nice little nap this afternoon. Come on, Bert . . . sup up . . . it's my shout. I'm just having one more and then I'm going home for me dinner. I'm that hungry I could eat a horse."

"You might have to, Jack . . . if the war goes on long enough." Bert passed his empty glass to Gloria. "We could all starve to death, if they can't get food into the country."

"We'd never starve," Gloria clinked money into the till, "our dad's got tons of food growing down his allotment. And he knows where to get all the rabbits."

"Talking of rabbits, Gloria . . . Cyril England's paying two shillings for a good rabbit skin, and there's a bloke down Hyson Green buying 'em an' all . . . to make gloves out of for Christmas." Bert passed on the information.

"If things get bad and there's a shortage of food, people'll raid your allotment," Clara joined in, "everybody goes mad when there's a war on. You just wait till you've got to manage on the rations. We'll all have scurvy and rickets and scabies."

"I thought you only got scabies if you were dirty?" Gloria patted at a stray curl which had escaped from behind her right ear.

"We will be dirty an' all," Clara tried to look miserable but the enjoyment showed

17

on her face, "we won't be able to get soap . . . and they'll need all the water for putting the fires out."

"What fires, Clara?" Bert egged her on a bit.

"When they start dropping their bombs on us. I lived through the Great War, I did . . . I've seen what happens."

Bert answered, "As long as they don't drop any on the brewery we'll be all right, Clara. Leave us plenty of Shippo's to drink and we're laughing."

Jack finished his drink and said to Bert, "I'm nipping round to take Mrs Cohen her money when I've had me dinner, Bert. Poor owd duck likes to have a natter, and I want to make sure somebody sees to her when the sirens go off. Right then, cheerio everybody." He winked at Gloria and touched the brim of his trilby in a polite gesture of farewell. "Behave yerself, gorgeous . . . keep them ear-plugs handy."

Jack walked along Dennison Street whistling 'Keep young and beautiful' and with images of Gloria clad in a clinging satin nightdress in his mind.

Reality chased away fantasy as Vera greeted him with curlers in her hair and a clinging purple flowered pinafore wrapped around her body. Jack chuckled as he leaned forward to kiss Vera on her cheek.

"What's so funny then?" Vera asked, "let's all share the joke."

"Now't . . . nothing really."

"Huh . . . been at the Shippo's again, have yer?"

"Just a couple, love."

"That's enough."

"Baby in every pint." Jack put his arms around her shoulders and pressed up close.

"You mean Guinness . . . that's what they say about Guinness . . . baby in every bottle." Vera playfully tugged at his left ear.

"I'll get some in then . . . before they're rationed . . . like some other things round here I could mention."

"They've closed all the picture houses, Jack." Vera tried to steer him away from talking about lovemaking. "I was looking forward to seeing Sonja Henie and Don Ameche in 'One in a Million'. She's a lovely little skater."

"They'll soon open them again." Jack put his hat on top of the sideboard and hung his jacket on a peg near the top of the cellar-steps. "War won't last all that long. Things'll soon be back to normal." He sat down at the table and pulled his chair up close. Good job I'm a bleddy convincing liar, he thought, as he shook Daddies Sauce all over his dinner.

Mrs Cohen was sitting in her usual place, on a chair just inside the doorway which opened out onto Connaught Street. Black dress, black shoes and stockings — even the ear-rings dangling from her pierced ears were of shiny jet.

"Hello, Mrs Cohen . . . get the kettle on, love," Jack touched the side of his hat in a salute of greeting.

Her smile, on seeing Jack standing there, shone out from her black attire like a silver moon in a storm threatened sky. She stood up and said over and over, "Come on in, Jack . . . come on in . . . come on through . . . come on, Jack . . . the kettle's singing on the hob." She led the way into the kitchen and gestured towards an armchair. "Sit down then, Jack . . . I've got some of your favourite wafer biscuits in."

It seemed to Jack that the appearance of someone to talk to had made her change from a lifeless figure into an animated quick moving puppet—the difference was quite moving and Jack felt slightly uncomfortable knowing that he was the cause.

"What do yer reckon about the latest fiasco then, Mrs Cohen?" Jack sat down in the armchair and placed his hat on a plant-stand, which crouched beneath a huge hand painted pot that held an aspidistra.

"We all knew the war would come," Mrs Cohen poured boiling water into a teapot which was shaped like a country cottage, "that's all the Germans think about . . . wars and killing people."

Jack nodded at the firegrate and said, "Didn't think you'd have a fire, not on a nice warm day like this, duck."

"I feel the cold, Jack. My bones seem chilled all the time."

"You don't eat enough to keep a fly alive. That's why you're always cold. You want to cook yerself some nice hot dinners. How about a rabbit stew? I can get you a lovely rabbit from the barmaid at the Oak."

"Not got much of an appetite . . . not since my Sammy died . . . in that German camp." She clasped her arms over her breasts and rocked gently from side-to-side in the gesture that Jack now knew so well.

"Our lads'll soon give the Germans a dose of their own medicine, love . . . you just wait and see." Jack felt inside his jacket pocket for cigarettes. "Oh and by the way . . . you must get across to the shelter when you hear the sirens. You haven't got far to go . . . just across the road on Mitchell Street."

"Won't catch me leaving my home in the middle of the night, Jack. If my number's on a bomb it'll get me no matter where I am." Mrs Cohen opened a packet of pink wafer biscuits.

"You mustn't talk like that, love." Jack leaned forward and added, "Do you mind if I smoke?"

"You know I don't Jack. I told you . . . it reminds me of my Sammy. Room was always filled with cigar smoke when Sammy was here."

Jack took two pound notes from his wallet and placed them on the pot stand.

"Here's your two pounds, duck. Bit slow down the Market at the moment, but we're doing all right with the barrer."

Mrs. Cohen poured milk into the teacups.

"You know I don't need the money, Jack. When I offered you the three hundred pounds for your pot stall it was a gift not a loan. The money was given as a gift for you and Vera."

"I know it was," Jack stirred two sugar lumps round-and-round in his teacup, "but I like to give you summat out of the profits. I owe you so much . . . you'll never know what it meant to me . . . to escape from being cooped-up inside a factory all day. I feel like a millionaire now. Thanks to you I've got my own lorry . . . and my own stall down the Market . . . and a barrer an' all, with a look-out man to help me. I tell yer, duck . . . you've changed me life . . . I'll never be able to repay you enough."

"Oh, go on with you . . . You're a good worker." Mrs Cohen looked pleased.

Jack sipped his tea and helped himself to another wafer biscuit.

"I'm going to make summat out of my life, it won't stop there, you'll see. I want my own shop eventually. Nice little hardware shop . . . they're the ones that make all the money. Sell everything under the sun from a nail to a dolly-tub. You can make as much from a hardware shop as they do in a pawnshop. People are always needing nails and scrubbing brushes and bits of wood for making shelves."

Mrs Cohen sat down in the armchair facing him. She folded her arms across her breasts once again and rocked gently.

"You'll get there, Jack. You're the kind of man who'll always get on."

She placed one foot on top of the other and Jack noticed how dainty her tiny feet were. And, although her ankles were disguised by thick black lisle stockings, he could see that they were still quite trim.

"Life's what you make it, me duck."

"Yes . . . doing what makes you happy is all that matters," she answered kindly. "I'm an old woman now, but I can still remember what it felt like . . . being very, very happy."

Jack flicked cigarette-ash at the fire and then looked — really looked at the wrinkled face of his benefactress. He tried to imagine what she would have looked like forty years ago but the image eluded him. Her hair must have been black — yes, all black and shiny, the sign of good health. Her eyes were dark brown — eyes that had once sparkled with mischief and laughter — a real Jewish beauty. Now, her eyes looked sad all the time. Her husband had died and her only son had deserted her — giving up his ghost somewhere many hundreds of miles away inside a German camp. She was like an unlit lamp, housing only memories and unable to give out warmth.

"You ought to have a cat, love," Jack said for the sake of saying something, "nice ginger-tom . . . out on the tiles all night and sleeping in front of the fire all day."

"Ooh," she laughed at last, "sounds like one-or-two men I used to know."

Jack stood up, ready to go home and said, "Right then, me duck . . . I'll be off now." He reached for his hat. "And don't forget . . . when them there sirens go off . . . you get across the road into a shelter. Or go down the cellar . . . but don't you get staying in bed."

He reached the front door and added, "War'll be over by Christmas. Hitler'll get his moustache scorched sooner than he thinks."

Jack walked up Mitchell Street and reminded himself to get a cat for Mrs Cohen. Something soft to rock in those empty arms of hers. He thought about how strange it was — as soon as you got to know someone — got to know them quite well — they suddenly became another responsibility. People reached out with unseen tentacles and sometimes it was impossible to escape them.

A cat would satisfy his conscience, he decided, a big daft floppy cat like Rupert, who Mrs Cohen could talk to and spoil.

THREE

Jack felt as though he were the only man in the world as he walked along Dennison Street towards 'Brassey' where his lorry was parked. The blakey- studs in the heels of his shoes echoed in the quietness of early morning.

Jack climbed into the lorry and soon he was easing her into Ilkeston Road. He gathered speed past Wollaton Park gates and headed out towards Trowell and Derby.

The fields on either side of the road were dampened down in stillness. Cows turned their heads in slow motion as the chug-chugging of the lorry's engine disturbed their first early morning chewing on grass garnished with dew.

It was the kind of morning that made you feel glad to be alive, Jack thought, despite the war and all the terrors it could bring.

The early morning autumn mist started to waltz away to hide in technicoloured leafy woods — disappeared into ferns which now seemed to Jack to be on fire as the multitude of sparkling beams from the rising sun held them in a spotlight of sunshine.

Jack tried not to think about the war — instead he filled his mind with snatches of poetry. He was especially fond of Wordsworth and tried to recall a poem about early morning or autumn.

He remembered a poem called 'Summer Vacation'. His forehead creased into thought wrinkles as he struggled for the first line of the poem.

"Magnificent." It was something to do with magnificent he recalled. "The morning rose, in memorable pomp, glorious as e'er I had behold." Suddenly, the poem flooded into his head together with memories of his boyhood.

"The morning rose, in memorable pomp
Glorious as e'er I had behold.
And in the meadows and the lower grounds
Was all the sweetness of a common dawn.
Dews, vapours, and the melody of birds
And labourers going forth to till the fields.
Ah . . . need I say, dear Friend, that to the brim my heart was full."

Jack's mind pulled shutters down over the memories of his childhood — he could not continue with the poem. The lump inside his throat felt as big as a conker as he tried to extinguish the memory of walking across a field with his mother — and his mother reciting that same poem to him and the contact of love she had transmitted through the hand which had held his.

He cleared his throat and started to sing, the words of his favourite hymn poured out.

"We plough the fields and scatter the good seed on the land." Like father like son — his thoughts prompted a tingling feeling to flow through his body. The hymn was Alex's favourite too. He thought about his son — the extension of himself and luckily, a healthy good natured little lad with just the right amount of Vera's gentleness.

Jack thrust the engine into second gear as a steep hill challenged the lorry's performance. He looked around him — English countryside at its most beauteous. A morning sky unfolding into pale blue and white — the fields bursting with golden corn — blowing in one direction in a collective shrug against the wind.

21

Jack said out aloud, "By God . . . no bleddy German's going to take this away from us. Over my dead body they will."

Stoke-on-Trent houses and factory chimneys spread out before him in panoramic splendour. Smoke from the factory chimneys was already being ejaculated skywards.

Jack changed gear once again and helter-skeltered down the other side of the hill.

The man at the factory shook his head from side-to-side in a knowall movement and mumbled, "There'll be a shortage soon, mate. There's a rumour going round that all the big firms'll be switching to war work. I've 'eard that Andersons'll be making uniforms. You'll have a job on . . . getting pots now the war's started."

"I'll take extra today then." Jack checked to see how much money he had inside his wallet. "You'll see me right won't you, Harry? I've been a bleddy good customer. If it weren't for blokes like me, you'd be left with all yer rejects."

"I'll do me best, mate . . . you know that. But with the war," he looked furtive and lowered his voice, "it might cost yer a few bob."

"You can rely on me for a good back-hander," Jack winked at him, "as long as it don't go too far back, if you get my meaning."

The two men shook hands and then Harry led the way to the rejects room.

Lorry laden with tea-sets, pudding dishes, art-deco statuettes, chamber-pots and coffee-pots, Jack climbed into the lorry once more, reversed out of the factory yard and headed back for Nottingham.

Pheasants ran bow-legged out of the ditches as the sound of the lorry's engine once again shattered the quiet — wings flapping they took flight and glided along on streams of air. The exquisite colours decorating the cock birds reminded Jack of a painting he had once admired in the Art Gallery up at Nottingham Castle. The painting had been of retriever dogs and pheasants — the dogs sitting on a tiled kitchen floor — the beautiful bodies of the dead birds obscenely draped on the top of a wooden table. Jack recalled how sad the painting had made him feel but, nevertheless, he had been able to appreciate the talent of the artist.

Jack lit a cigarette, did the usual amount of coughing and spluttering as he inhaled smoke. He pulled the lorry window down, rested his elbow on the frame and breathed in the pungent smell of the English autumn.

Labourers moved slowly in the fields — like scarecrows come to life they toiled for wages which would ensure that they had a place to live. A meagre dwelling where they could sleep, eat and make love; a place where they could escape to unless they became too ill to work and then it was back to the dole queues and Salvation Army handouts.

The lorry reached the main road which led into Borrowash. The road sliced through farmland which spread out on either side with its fields of gold, green and brown.

Two horses pulled a plough over rich looking reddish brown earth and the morning sunshine, seemed to Jack, to highlight the splendour and dignity of the scene.

The animals, patient and gentle with the strength of giants — the farm worker walking behind them, up-and-down where they would all continue until dusk.

Jack wondered if the man felt trapped — as Jack had done when he had forfeited his freedom in exchange for a wage from the cigarette factory. Probably not, Jack mused, there was something very different about working outdoors even though you weren't your own master.

Jack experienced another feeling of elation as he thought about his own work. Free to come-and-go as he pleased; his own man: a free spirit. He decided to take the barrow along Parliament Street when he got back. If Bert had got rid of all the fruit on Long Row they could try and sell some silk stockings. Tell the women there would be a shortage now there was a war on and that would soon shift a few pairs. Nothing like a shortage to cause panic buying.

The lorry rumbled homewards — crockery safely ensconced inside paper and cardboard. Once again Jack entered Trowell, the charming village which decorated the outskirts of the City.

More farmland and also an abundance of posh houses. Many of the houses stood in a quarter of an acre — some more. A secret wish, locked away in Jack's heart, was one day to own a house at Trowell.

As a lad, Jack had walked through Wollaton into Trowell, where he had delighted in climbing trees, pinched apples and swum naked in a pond which had belonged to a kind farmer who turned a blind eye to the scruffy ragamuffins who trespassed on his land.

Two more horses almost identical to the others pulled a plough over troughs of rich earth. Blackbirds, gulls and magpies competed for food as the earth yielded up her secrets.

"Bleddy, sodding Germans," Jack shouted out aloud, "bleddy murdering swine. We just can't let them take all this away from us without putting up a fight."

Jack's imagination made him see terrible things. Germans, guns at the ready, shuffling across the rich brown earth. The scum of humanity, cruel and mindless, sweeping the fields bare of livestock and the men who toiled there. Jack imagined he could hear the obscene explosions as shells destroyed farmland, animals and majestic trees.

We can't let it happen, Jack thought gravely, they've done it to the Poles but if they try to do it over here they'll soon find out they've picked on the wrong 'uns. This is our land, our birthright and our children's birthright.

"Bleddy, sodding Germans," he shouted aloud and then decided at that very moment to enlist. "You'll look good in a uniform, old son," he still spoke aloud, "a real hot-shot." His mind raced along with the excitement caused by his decision. Bert could look after the stall down the market and he could take the barrow out as well. The war would be over by Christmas if they got stuck into the Jerries. Jack knew he was being over optimistic but the more he thought about enlisting the better he liked the idea.

He started to sing once more and did not stop until the lorry's engine sighed to a standstill on Brassey. He jumped down from the lorry and checked to see if the ropes straddling the tarpaulin were secure and then walked briskly in the direction of Independent Street.

The sun shone down from a blue sky swept free of clouds. Jack felt hungry and decided to have a nice thick sandwich filled with fried bacon and tinned tomatoes, washed down with steaming hot tea.

I'll tell Vera about my decision to join up after I've had me food, he thought, else she'll give me indigestion when she starts moaning.

23

Jack pushed open the back door and called, "Ey up, me duck . . . get that kettle on . . . I'm starving . . . do us a bacon and tomato sandwich."

"Everything all right, Jack?" Vera stood behind the kitchen table with a flat-iron in her hand — freshly ironed clothes draped over the clothes-horse.

"Yes . . . got stocked up with extra pots. Going to be a shortage soon . . . and I won't be able to get petrol for the lorry. Still, not to worry . . . I can sell other things besides pots."

Vera stood the flat-iron on its end and went through to the scullery.

"Like some fried bread, Jack?

"You're a mind reader, you are."

"Wish I was."

"That'd be fun."

Jack picked up the *Daily Mirror* and thought how awful it would be if people could read each other's minds. I'd be in hot-water most of the time, he thought, then sighed as he read the headlines. More bombings, deaths and injuries — the German madmen — ruthlessly killing and maiming innocent people.

I'll enlist next month, when I've got everything organised with Bert about the stall and the barrow, Jack planned ahead, and I don't think I will tell Vera this morning . . . I'll tell her when I've decided properly.

Jack bit into the sandwich and wiped tomato juice from his chin with the back of his hand.

FOUR

"What do yer reckon to this then?" Jack held out a letter to Vera. "It's from our Jenny. She's packing her job in, leaving the Conway Hotel and coming back to Nottingham."

"Can't blame her for that. I wouldn't stay in London not if yer paid me ten quid a week." Vera read the contents of the letter and added, "It's going to be very dangerous living in London. It'll be one of the first places the Jerries'll bomb."

"Um . . . you're right there. I read the other day that over three million people have been evacuated. Three million women, children and cripples . . . and half of that lot came from London. Soon be nobody left there at all. The Jerries'll be wasting their bombs if they drop them on London."

"By the looks of this letter, it looks as though Jenny wants to come and lodge with us. She could sleep in the attic . . . we could get a secondhand bed for her."

"She might be expecting to come here but I don't think it'd be a good idea. She's an untidy devil and she likes to come-and-go just when she pleases. That's why she went to London in the first place."

Jack undid a carton and took out packs of razor-blades. "Taking the barrow out this morning . . . try and shift some of these razor-blades. I'll get rid of the apples and plums an' all." He looked sheepish. "And then, this afternoon, I'm going to join-up."

"Oh, Jack . . . no . . . you musn't," Vera was horrified at the news, "you gave me your word you wouldn't join up. Let the young men go, you said, those without a job . . . the men without wives and families to keep. You promised me, Jack . . . you promised faithfully."

"I know I did, duck. But I've been awake nearly all night thinking about the war. I've been thinking and thinking."

"Thinking about what?" Vera picked up Elizabeth Rose and held her out to Jack. "We don't want you to go . . . don't leave us, Jack."

Jack took hold of Elizabeth Rose and swayed gently backwards-and-forwards.

"Nearly all night I lay awake thinking about the last war. All those men who were killed by the Germans. The Somme . . . where thousands of our men were slaughtered in just a few hours."

"Look how you said how much you despised the men in government," Vera struggled for opposition ammunition, "the stupid men who work out all the battles. It's all right for them, you said, sitting on their arses working out all those hare-brain schemes, while it's the men in the trenches who get killed."

"I know all about that, Vera . . . and I admit I still do think that. But do you know something, love? I've never met a German in me life . . . but I've developed a deep hatred for them . . . all of them. I won't be happy till I've helped to put a stop to them once and for all."

"I couldn't carry on if you got killed, Jack." Vera folded her arms across her breasts, her body was stiff and upright signalling her distress. "You know what happened to me when . . . when our boys drowned." The muscles in her face twitched as she struggled to continue. "Don't put me back in Mapperley, Jack . . . don't leave me."

"I'm not going to get killed, you silly gel. And I keep telling yer . . . the war won't last very long this time. It'll be all over by Christmas. What date is it now? October the sixth. Another eleven weeks and I'll be back, pushing me barrow up Long Row."

"Or pushing yer daisies up at Bulwell cemetery."

They both laughed at this remark but the tension between them hovered around then seeped into Jack's mind and clung tenaciously.

"Well, if you've decided then, your Jenny might as well come here to live." Vera tried another ploy. "I'll be glad of the company if you're going to be away."

Jack appeared not to be listening and answered, "I tell you what she could do . . . she could go and lodge in Mrs Cohen's house. Be company for the old duck . . . our Jenny would be like a daughter to her."

"Perhaps she wouldn't want a lodger," Vera's lips pouted together in disagreement, "and if your Jenny's untidy and difficult to live with."

"I bet Mrs Cohen'd have the time of her life looking after Jenny." Jack scooped the packets of razor-blades into his arms and said, "How about a bit of love tonight? If they have me in the Army you'll be going short for a few weeks."

25

"Bogger off!" Vera gave the reply he was expecting.

Jack laughed and went out to the barrow which was parked alongside the air-raid shelter in the back garden.

Bert was leaning against the garden wall, cigarette dangling from the corner of his mouth he looked upwards through squinting eyes. Jack also looked at the sky and the mountains of drifting clouds drifting through rippling strips of pale blue reminded him of the sea. Yes, he thought, it looks like a calm sea reflected through a gigantic mirror.

"Looking for enemy planes are you then, Bert?" Jack pulled back the canvas from the top of his barrow. "Taking the razor-blades out this morning and the rest of the apples and plums. Then I want to call at Hudson's factory when we've done . . . I've heard they've got some blackout fabric going at tenpence a yard. We can sell it for one-and-threepence. We'll get Vera and your Annie to cut it up into curtaining."

Bert toyed with the braces which were dangling over his trousers and replied, "Better go and put me shirt on then. Be ready in a minute, Jack."

"Make sure you have a good shave," Jack called after him, "don't want the ladies to see no prickly chins if we're trying to sell razor-blades."

"Blimey . . . what am I now? Your blooming model?" Bert called back. "Good job we're not flogging french-letters . . . although I wouldn't mind modelling one for Gloria Goodliffe."

The lavatory door at the end of Bert's garden opened and Annie appeared.

"What's that you were saying about Gloria Goodliffe?"

"Ey up, me duck," Bert grinned at her, "dint say owt, me duck."

"I'll give yer french-letters. Huh, don't make me laugh. He'd be no good, Jack." Annie pointed a finger at Bert, "not unless you dipped it in some cement . . . all it does is hang its head in shame. All talk and no action, that's Bert."

Jack laughed and called to Bert once again, "And don't forget yer gas mask . . . talking of rubber."

Bert hurried away to get ready. His laughter spilled out of the scullery window, giving an indication as to his good nature and the steadfastness of his relationship with Annie.

Jack and Bert pushed the barrow up Independent Street calling out as they did so.

"Here you are, me duck . . . beautiful plums . . . eat them now or put them in a pie."

Two women stopped to buy.

"Will you be having any more silk stockings, Jack? I've got ladders in me others and I'm going to the Palais on Saturday."

"Oh, you don't want ladders in yer stockings, duck," Bert teased her, "you never know who might try to climb up 'em."

The scales made a clanging sound as the plums landed in the scoop.

"Here you are, love," Jack tipped the plums into a bag, "bit over there but I'm feeling generous today. How about a packet of razor-blades for yer old man? Soon won't be able to get any, all the steel'll be used for making aircraft. Here you are, girls . . . penny each or five for fourpence . . . make yer old man's chins as smooth as babies' bottoms. Close yer eyes and you'll think it's Don Ameche kissing you."

"Close yer eyes, let me come round to your house and you'll think it's Rudolph Valentino without his camel, making love to yer," Bert joined in the fun. "If we get some silk stockings, can I come round and put 'em on for yer?"

The women laughed and handed over money for plums and razor-blades. Jack knew that women like to laugh — had discovered they were more likely to part with money if he could put them in a good mood. More women cluttered round the barrow and Jack felt the old familiar thrill in his stomach as he dropped the money into his pocket.

They reached Alfreton Road and as they were passing the rag-and-bone shop the owner called to them, "Morning . . . I'll have a couple of pound of them plums." Cyril England felt inside the trouser pocket of his hand-made suit and extracted half-a crown. "How's business then, Jack?"

"Can't grumble, Cyril . . . bit slow on the pot-stall, but I'm still keeping the wolf from the door." Jack handed him the plums. "Won't matter after today though . . . I'm joining-up."

"I wouldn't bother if I were you, Jack . . . it'll all be over by Christmas." Cyril bit into a plum and the juice ran down his chin. He took a neatly folded handkerchief from his breast-pocket and dabbed at his mouth. "Take for a packet of them handkerchiefs as well, Jack." He selected a packet from the barrow and added, "Haven't you got any with my initials on?"

"Blimey, Cyril . . . what do yer want for a tanner?" Bert chuckled, "you're supposed to blow your nose on 'em . . . not put 'em in a picture-frame and admire them."

Cyril pocketed his change then smiled at a woman who was approaching him with an old pram loaded with junk. "Morning, Ada . . . what yer got for me today then?" Cyril's perfectly shaped sparkling white teeth flashed a smile at the woman and his expert eye for a bargain zoomed in on the pram.

Jack and Bert pushed the barrow up Alfreton Road shouting out the prices of their wares as they went along. When they reached Canning Circus, Bert suddenly asked, "So you've definitely decided to join-up then? What did your Vera have to say about that?"

"She weren't very pleased, but I've made me mind up. I want to have a talk to you about it, Bert. Can you come round to our house tonight? I'd like you to look after the stall down the market till I get back. And if you want to . . . you can still take the barrow out. Get yourself a good lookout man and keep things ticking over till I get back."

"I'm not sure, Jack," Bert looked serious, "I'm not a man for figure-work . . . I'm no businessman, you know that, Jack."

"Vera and Mrs Cohen'll help you with the money side. You know how to go on, buying the fruit and stuff from the market. Go to Stoke, when you can get petrol for the lorry . . . get there early for the bargains. Harry'll look after you if you give him a backhander. You like driving the lorry and you could take your Annie with you . . . she'd enjoy the ride."

"Well . . . I would like to have a go . . . seeing as I'm too old for the Army. I'd much rather be sticking me bayonet in a few Germans . . . but there you are . . . you young 'uns have all the luck." Bert nodded towards the cemetery as they passed by the gate and said, "What did the male worm say to the female worm?"

Jack grinned at him and replied, "Stop wriggling."

"No," Bert laughed and added, "I'll meet you tonight in dead Ernest . . . ha-ha-ha. There's the dead centre of town, Jack," more laughter.

Jack also laughed but it sounded forced. Bert said, "Oh, I am sorry, Jack. I'm really sorry, mate. I forgot your little lads were in there. "I mean . . . " he struggled to make amends, "I mean, I'll never forget they're in there . . . but I just forgot for the minute when I thought about that joke about the worms. I'm a bleddy idiot, aren't I . . . a right bleddy fool."

"Don't worry about it, Bert." Jack stopped pushing the barrow for a moment and took cigarettes from his pocket. "Life goes on . . . you can't live with the dead, can you." Painful memories filled his eyes with tears. "Time heals . . . or so they say."

He handed a cigarette to Bert and added, "Look what a fine lad our Alex is . . . and the baby's lovely."

They puffed on their cigarettes and stood quietly for a few moment each man divided by the privacy of his own thoughts. The pain did not leave Jack's face until he heart Bert's voice urgent and loud saying, "Coppers, Jack . . . come on get a spurt on."

They pushed the barrow down Derby Road at full speed — slipping and sliding they hurried to escape the long-arm-of-the-law.

FIVE

Jack walked down the steps of the doctor's surgery and looked across the road towards the St. Michael's church. How long was it since he had been to church? His mind sifted through the debris of events in his life. Nine years it has been — when Alex had been christened.

The October sun warmed the air but Jack felt unusually cold. He crossed the road at the top of Hartley Road and walked up the cobbled path leading to the main entrance of the church.

The stillness inside the church seemed to Jack to have a feeling of timelessness about it somehow. He imagined that time had come to a halt. Everything seemed to be compressed into a still-life painting in which he was a part and from which he could not escape.

"I know I've been bad at times, God . . . but I've never done anything really wicked . . . never done any real harm to anybody." Jack's lips moved and released whispers into the air, "Don't let me die . . . not just yet. I've such a lot of things I want to do. I don't mind not passing for the Army . . . that is . . . I do mind . . . I should have liked to have done me bit with the rest of the lads. But if it's not to be, I accept it . . . only please, God . . . don't let me die. There's Vera and the kids to look after, and I've got so much planned for the future."

28

The face of Jesus on the coloured glass window did nothing to reassure Jack. Surrounded by floating cherubs the face, impassive and inscrutable, stared down at Jack and seemed to promise nothing.

"What does he mean . . . a shadow on your lung?" Vera looked frightened and tried to read Jack's mind. "Has he given you some medicine then?" What does he mean, a shadow on your lung?" she repeated. "Does the doctor mean you've got consumption then?"

"I didn't tell yer . . . Medical Board sent me for an X-ray. I've just been to see what's what . . . they told me the results . . . nowt to worry about."

"Is it TB? . . . it is, isn't it, Jack? Tell me the truth."

"No . . . it's just a shadow that's all. But if it turns to anything else I shall have to go in Bagthorpe for a few weeks. It'll give the nurses a treat." Jack was flippant. "But if I take care of meself, make sure I don't keep getting wet through, that sort of thing, I don't see any problems. The only thing that's upset me is I won't be able to have a go at the Nazis. I should have liked to have shoved me bayonet through one or two of the swines."

"Well, that's one good thing then. I was dreading you going away to war."

"I know you were, love. So you see, everything's all right. I'll take charge of the air-raid shelters. Keep the sing-songs going."

"What brought the trouble on then . . . with your lung? Was it working at the cigarette factory? Did he say it was working there that had caused it?"

"Don't know, it could have been anything. One chill on top of another . . . summat like that I suppose." He gave her a hug. "I'm not worried at all. I feel perfectly healthy. I'll keep wrapped up well in the winter and when it rains. I'll even cut down on me fags . . . get rid of me smoker's cough."

"And what about medicine?"

"Drop of Shippo's, love . . . that's all the medicine I need." Jack fiddled with the knobs on the wireless. "How about a nice cup of tea then, duck . . . before I take the barrow out. Me and Bert's got a load of fruit we want to shift today."

Vera walked through to the scullery and put the kettle on the stove. Music filtered through the gold mesh on the front of the Murphy wireless then the gentle voice of Bobby Howes added words to the melody.

Elizabeth Rose, recently fed and quite contented, was lying on the sofa behind a propped up cushion. Jack sat down on the sofa beside her and stroked her gently on the cheek. He helped himself to biscuits and then crooned along to the song as he waited for the kettle to boil.

"She's my lovely . . . de-dah-de-dah at early morning
She's my lovely . . . de-dah-de-dah de-dah-de-dah-dah
And the loveliest thing about her you see
Is she's so lovely to me."

Jack's mind grasshoppered into the future and, as usual, latched on to a plan for making more money. I should be able to make a few extra bob, he schemed secretively and his thoughts made him smile. The war had only been going six weeks but already, people were talking about selling their clothing coupons. You just had to get a nice little racket going and the money would roll in, he decided, as he helped himself to

29

another custard cream. A contact in one of the big hotels would be ideal — somebody who could get their hands on a few pounds of butter or one or two rashers of bacon.

Vera brought the tea through to the kitchen.

"Vera . . . was it Gloria's brother who went to work at the Black Boy on Long Row?"

"Yes . . . he's worked in the kitchens since he left school. He's an apprentice . . . but I can't remember what he's training for. Why do you want to know?"

"No reason really. Don't know what made me think of it." Jack knew that Vera would disapprove. The occasional bit of pilfering Vera's mother had done, from her employer's house in the old days, had been accepted because they had all been short of money so that had seemed all right in Vera's eyes — but making money on the black market would be frowned upon.

He decided on the old saying, what the eye doesn't see the heart doesn't grieve, and stirred sugar into his tea without looking at Vera's face when he added, "I thought I saw him going in the Black Boy the other day . . . that's what made me think of it I suppose."

That deep-gut feeling he had often experienced when he had felt trapped by his work in the cigarette factory was still lingering inside him. In fact he sometimes felt that the feeling was stronger than ever. He had taken the lifeline that Mrs Cohen had thrown to him when she had offered the gift of money but he still felt as though there was more rope to scramble up — the gold at the end of the rainbow was still eluding him. War or no war, he thought, I'm going to be rich. Hitler, bombs, shadows on lungs . . . come on then, God . . . test me as much as you like . . . I'll not go down without a fight.

"Jack . . . Jack, you were miles away then." Vera touched him on the shoulder, her smile was tender. "I said, how about a bit of love tonight?"

"Oh, Vera . . . do you mean it, love? It's been such a long time."

"You'll have to use something though. Don't want to catch again . . . not for a long time anyway. 'Specially not now there's a war going on."

"I've had a packet of french-letters handy for weeks." Jack kissed Vera's neck and nuzzled his nose against her ear. "You can trust me, Vera . . . I'll be ever so careful."

"I do love you, Jack. You know that, don't you."

For quite a while they held onto each other. Kindliness and tender caresses from Vera dampened down the lustfulness that had started to awaken in Jack. He gave her a kiss on the mouth that made a smacking noise, then did likewise on the cheek of Elizabeth Rose. "Me two best gels . . . me two lovely gels." He got up from the sofa and looked at his wristwatch.

"I'd better get going. See you this afternoon then . . . when we've flogged all the fruit." Jack left the house with a grin on his face.

Bert and Jack set the barrow down near the Walter Fountain just opposite the entrance to Woolworths. Bert kept a lookout for the police whilst Jack arranged the fruit on the barrow.

"I reckon we can make a bit of money out of this war, Bert."

"I was thinking along the same lines . . . after you told me they wouldn't take you in the Army, Jack. Things are going to get bleddy scarce. Look at the last war. Talk about paying through the nose for everything."

"If we can get some good contacts we'll be well away." Jack polished apples on a piece of clean rag and put them at the front of the barrow.

"Petrol coupons should fetch a good price. You want to see what they've allowed me to go to Stoke-and-back. I told them, I did . . I said, I'm running a lorry, mate . . . not a bleddy ice-cream cart."

"What did they say then?"

"They said I could always get meself a horse-and-cart. Said that ambulances and doctors cars had priority. I kicked up a real fuss down at the offices on Long Row."

"What did they say then?"

"They told me to bogger off."

"And then what happened?" Bert lit a Woodbine and offered the packet to Jack.

"What could I do . . . I boggered off." Jack chuckled and inhaled cigarette smoke. "But I told them . . . "

"Copper, Jack . . . come on, scarper." Bert's practised eyes had spied the enemy advancing down Lister Gate.

They pushed the barrow away from the danger of a fine and as they headed for Arkwright Street lost two apples and a pear in their hurry to become invisible from the strong-arm-of-the-law, as Jack called all policemen when he was in the company of ladies. What he really called them was reserved for the ears of the other hawkers as they selected their fruit and vegetables at the back of Sneinton Market in the early hours of the morning.

SIX

"Well, well . . . look who it aint." Jack opened the front door wider and grinned at the redhaired visitor. "Come on in then . . . I suppose you're dying for a cup of tea." He called to Vera and his voice held genuine pleasure, "It's our Jenny . . . get that kettle boiling, duck."

Jenny struggled up the steps with two large suitcases and placed them just inside the door.

"Ooh . . . me feet feel like me toes have been cut off." She pulled black suede shoes from her feet and followed Jack into the kitchen on tiptoe. "I ought to have worn some old comfortable shoes but I wanted to look smart . . . give the Independent Street lot summat to gawp at."

Vera bustled about arranging cups in saucers and shyness between the two women hovered in the air.

"You're looking very smart, Jenny," Vera rubbed her fingers over the lapel of Jenny's pure wool pink coat, "it's a lovely bit of cloth . . . must have cost a pretty penny." She pointed to an armchair and added, "Take your coat off then and park yer body."

Jenny handed over her coat and flopped into the armchair. She caught sight of Elizabeth Rose and forgetting about her aching feet leapt from the armchair and knelt beside the sofa.

"So this is my little niece then. Oh, you are a little duck." She stroked Elizabeth Rose on the cheek and made a clucking noise. "When are you going to have her christened? I've got a lovely new costume I could wear. I'll show you when I unpack me things, Vera. It's a lovely shade of navy blue and I've got a hat to match . . . with a veil with navy velvet spots on . . . it makes me look like Mata Hari the female spy."

"Hang on, Jenny . . . before you start unpacking I want to talk to you." Jack sat down facing her and continued, "They've turned me down for the Army . . . turned me down flat."

"What's up with you then, Jack . . . got flat feet?" Jenny's laughter came from deep inside her throat and had an infectious affect on Vera.

"Stop laughing, Jenny." Vera poured tea and then placed buttered scones onto a plate. "It's a bit more serious than that."

"I know," Jenny helped herself to a scone, "the army doctor didn't like the way you coughed." Again the rippling, infectious laughter.

"Ey up . . . what does a young innocent girl like you know about things like that?" Jack pretended to be shocked.

"Listen here . . . when you've been a chambermaid in London you know all there is to know about everything."

"Have another scone, Jenny," Vera pointed to the scones, "I've put plenty of best butter on. Soon be a shortage they reckon. By the looks of the ration books we'll all be half starved. We won't be able to manage on the rations."

"Oh, I shouldn't worry too much about rations, Vera." Jenny drank her tea right down to the tea-leaves. You can get anything you want if you know the right people can't you, Jack?"

"Oh yes . . . I'm not worrying about rationing," Jack answered, "I've got me contacts. Anyway, while we're on the subject of managing . . . I want to talk to you about your lodgings."

"Go on then, Jack . . . what about them?"

"Well, as you know we haven't got a deal of room here. There's only the attic and it's freezing up there in the winter. So, I've fixed you up with some good lodgings."

"Where's that then, Jack . . . at Sneinton House with the tramps for company?" Jenny remained flippant. She crossed her legs which were long and slim and shown to good advantage by pure silk stockings. "Or I could sleep in a tent in your garden . . . I've always fancied the outdoor life . . . those suntanned scout-masters in their knee-length shorts."

"Shut up and listen." Jack held out his cup and saucer to Vera for a refill. "I've got you fixed up with a nice old duck called Mrs Cohen. She lives down on Connaught

Street . . . in a neat little house all by herself. I asked her if she'd like a lodger and she said she'd be glad of the company."

"She's ever so nice, Jenny," Vera looked embarrassed, "she's the old girl who helped Jack to get started with his pot-stall." Vera hurried into the scullery to refill the kettle.

"Oh, I know . . . the old Jewish lady. The one who gave you that money." Jenny licked crumbs from her lips.

"Yes, that's the one," Jack answered.

"Is she rolling in money then?"

"Don't know . . . don't care. Don't know how much she's got. One thing I do know about her though," Jack chuckled, "she's got a nice sense of humour. I got her a cat from the market last Saturday and guess what she's called it?"

"Hitler?"

"No . . . but you're getting warm."

"Er . . . oh, I don't know, tell me."

"Chamberlain."

They both laughed and the noise awakened Elizabeth Rose.

"Ey . . . ey up then, me duck." Jenny leaned closer to kiss the baby — her hair rippled down and the red-gold curls contrasted beautifully against the whiteness of the shawl. She turned to look at Jack, large greeny-grey eyes full of mischief. "Hey . . . you didn't finish telling me . . . why they didn't pass you for the Army? What's wrong with you then?"

"He's got a shadow on one of his lungs." Vera returned from the scullery.

The mischief in Jenny's eyes was replaced with concern. "Not consumption is it, Jack? What do you mean a shadow? Do you mean you've got consumption?"

"Now now," Jack smiled at her, "it's only a shadow. The doctor says if I take things easy I'll live to be a hundred."

"He must have had something wrong with his lungs some years ago . . . without him knowing it. But as far as we can gather from the doctor, it healed up by itself. The doctor says there's just a bit of scarring on his lung. But it was just enough to keep him out of the Army, thank goodness." Vera looked happy and continued, "And aren't I glad. I never wanted him to join up. I don't fancy being a war widow, not at my age."

"Things have worked out all right then." Jenny also smiled.

The back door opened and Alex appeared.

"Auntie Jenny . . . hello, Auntie Jenny," his voice held genuine pleasure, "I've just been to school. They've opened all the schools again, 'cause the Germans aren't going to bomb Radford. Have they bombed anybody in London?" He edged nearer then became shy and looked down at his feet.

"I've got something for you." Jenny opened her handbag and fumbled about amongst the contents. She took out a small package.

"A mouth-organ . . . ooh, a mouth-organ." Alex was thrilled with the gift.

"Where's me kiss then?" Jenny winked at Vera and added, "A kiss for a present, isn't that what they say."

"I'd want more than a kiss from Vera." Jack winked back at Jenny and made a loud kissing noise with pursed lips. "Are you listening, Vera?"

"Little pigs have big ears, Jack." Vera grinned at him, nodded towards Alex.

"Oh, talking about pigs . . . I won't be eating any bacon at Mrs Cohen's house, will I?" Jenny looked mischievous again.

"Shouldn't worry about that too much," Vera answered, "by the way things are going none of us'll be eating any bacon . . . we won't be able to get any."

At half-past five Jack said, "Right then, Jenny . . . I'll take you down to Mrs Cohen's house when you're ready."

"Can I take the newspaper with me, Jack? I want to have a look what jobs are going."

"Yes, help yourself. There's one from yesterday as well . . . take them both."

Jack picked up the suitcases.

"See you later, Vera."

"Thanks for the tea, Vera . . . see you tomorrow. Can I take the baby for a walk in her pram, when I come round tomorrow?"

"Yes, so long as you don't go too far. Never know when we might get an air raid."

Jenny and Jack set off down the entry on their way to Mrs Cohen's house.

Vera looked round the kitchen and thought how silent it had become now that Jenny had left the room. Something about Jenny that was different — Jenny had a way of filling a room with a 'something happening' feeling. Jenny had sat in the armchair and everyone else had focussed their attention on her — the way people stare at a glowing fire, the focal point in a room — Jenny had become an instant focal point, her charisma was undeniable.

For a few moments Vera experienced a tiny trace of envy towards her sister-in-law and then, scooping Elizabeth Rose up into her arms, concentrated on housewife thoughts and decided to clean the windows.

"So you're Jenny, are you?" Mrs Cohen led the way into the kitchen. Turning to face Jenny she looked her up and down and added, "You're a right fashion piece. Come on and sit down . . . give me your coat."

"Don't know about a fashion piece," Jenny patted her hair and pushed a stray curl back behind her left ear, "I wouldn't like to guess how many beds I had to make and how many hot-water bottles I had to fill before I'd saved enough for this outfit." She handed her coat to Mrs Cohen.

"She said, she made the beds, Mrs Cohen," Jack put the suitcases near the door at the bottom of the stairs, "she didn't say she got into them." He gave Jenny a cheeky grin and rolled his eyes.

"I expect you'll miss London." Mrs Cohen gestured towards the sofa then caught sight of Jenny's shoes. "My word . . . they're smart shoes. I used to love a nice pair of shoes when I was younger . . . I have to go more for comfort now though."

"Very wise . . . and if you don't mind," Jenny pulled off her left shoe, "I'd like to get some relief from this torture. I'll put me slippers on when I unpack me suitcases." She pulled off the other shoe. "Ooh, it's agony when the blood rushes back into yer toes."

A grey and black cat sidled into the room. Not yet fully grown but with a beautifully

34

shaped large tomcat head it hesitated for a while and then selected Jenny's lap as a possible resting place.

"Ey up . . . what's your game then," Jenny scratched his head, "keep your claws in . . . don't you dare ladder my silk stockings. What did you say his name was?"

"Chamberlain," Mrs Cohen's eyes housed merriment and Jack thought what a good idea of his it had been buying the cat for her.

"You have a good look at him," Mrs Cohen continued, "he looks just like old Chamberlain. Look at his whiskers and the expression on his face."

Everyone laughed and Chamberlain joined in with a bit of purring. Jack sat back on the sofa and spread his legs out in front of him, a gesture that indicated he was at ease and felt relaxed inside Mrs Cohen's home.

"Jenny's going down the Labour Exchange tomorrow," Jack reached for the newspapers that Jenny had placed on the sofa, "might be something in here, Jen. I'll have a look for yer."

"I don't really want to be a chambermaid again, Jack," Jenny leaned over him and looked at the newspaper, "all that fluff up me nose and what we had to put up with when we delivered early morning tea . . . well, it'd curl a vicar's collar up I can tell yer."

"A good honest job'll keep her out of mischief, Mrs Cohen." Jack continued looking at the newspaper and made a popping noise with his lips.

"There'll be a good hot meal waiting for you when you get home from work," Mrs Cohen sat down and rocked from side to side her arms folded across her breasts, "I always used to cook Sammy good meals . . . and his father of course. Keep a good table, moderation in all things and all being well, God willing, you'll have a long and healthy life."

"Oh, I'll be all right then," Jack nodded agreement, "our Vera puts a good table on . . . and she makes sure I don't get too much of anything."

Jenny and Jack laughed at this remark and Mrs Cohen interrupted with, "Do you know . . . that's the first real laughter I've heard in this house since my Sammy lived here. He loved a good laugh . . . he liked to listen to the comedians on the wireless . . . especially Tommy Handley."

"You'll be all right with our Jenny living here then . . . she's enough to make a cat laugh."

They all looked at Chamberlain who was curled up into a slow-breathing furry ball and still favouring Jenny's lap as his resting place of the moment.

"Let me have a look at the newspaper, Jack."

Jack handed the newspaper to Jenny and noticed that the atmosphere of the room had changed from quietness to super-charged gaiety. As Vera had done, Jack observed how everything seemed to revolve around Jenny. She was like a magnet — animated and fun-loving she seemed to possess magical qualities. My word, he thought with amusement, the Radford blokes won't know what's hit them, when our Jen gets going.

"I'll just take your suitcases upstairs, Jenny," Jack stood up, "and then you can unpack your things when you're ready."

"I'll nip round and tell you how I've gone on at the Labour Exchange tomorrow, Jack." Jenny cradled Chamberlain in her arms and stood up. "And thanks for getting me fixed up with Mrs Cohen. It's nice here . . . very nice."

"Do you think I could have a bath, Mrs Cohen?" Jenny asked, "the train journey's made me feel really mucky."

"Of course," Mrs Cohen answered, "there'll be plenty of hot water in the boilers. I've had the fire going all day . . . feel the cold you know. Can't seem to get my old bones warm these days . . . not even when the sun's shining."

"I'll help you with the bath," Jenny smiled at her, "where are you hiding it?"

"Outside in the yard . . . hanging on a nail just outside the back-door."

They carried the zinc bath inside and set it down in front of the fire. Mrs Cohen wiped the inside of the bath with a cloth then ladled water into it from the boilers which were set on either side of the firegrate.

Jenny went upstairs to fetch clean underclothes and when she returned Mrs Cohen looked embarrassed.

"I'll stay in the scullery while you have your bath." She went into the scullery and returned with a bucket of cold water which she poured into the bath. "You can add some more cold water . . . I'll just go and fill the bucket again."

"You needn't stay in the scullery, Mrs Cohen," Jenny called to her, "I'm not shy." Jenny started to undress. "I haven't got anything you haven't got." She slipped her skirt down over her hips and took off her blouse.

Mrs Cohen returned to the scullery for more cold water and when she entered the kitchen once more Jenny was clad only in white cotton brassiere and pale blue satin knickers.

"What was it Rudyard Kipling said, Mrs Cohen? The colonel's lady and Judy O'Grady are sisters under the skin. I'll be Judy O'Grady and you can be the colonel's lady." She laughed and dangled her left foot in the water to test the temperature. "At the hotel where I last worked, I had to share a bedroom with a waitress and two chambermaids. Honestly . . . all those posh folks staying at the hotel had no idea of the conditions we had to put up with. All crushed together in one bedroom at the top of the hotel."

"Oh dear, I am sorry," Mrs Cohen looked concerned, "how awful."

"We didn't half have some laughs though." Jenny slipped the knickers down over her thighs and stepped out of them. "One of the chambermaids had very small breasts. She used to sleep in her brassiere . . . till we found out it was stuffed with cottonwool."

"Well I never." Mrs Cohen smiled.

"She sent away for a bust improver as well. Saw the advertisement in the newspaper." Jenny lowered herself into the bath and wriggled about. "Ooh! . . . it's burning me bum."

Mrs Cohen poured more cold water into the bath. "Is that better?"

"Yes, that's lovely thank you." Jenny rubbed Palmolive soap up and down her arms and added, "Anyway . . . I was telling you about Josie . . . the girl who sent away for the bust improver."

"Oh yes, what happened? I've never heard of that before."

"Well," Jenny lathered soap all over her own breasts, which were perfectly shaped — round and firm with deep pink nipples. "She got an envelope back and guess what was inside?" Jenny started to giggle.

"What?" Mrs Cohen chuckled and sat down on the sofa with arms folded across her own ample breasts. "What was inside the envelope then?"

"A large photograph of a . . . " Jenny paused, "of a . . . a man's hand." She laughed loudly and slid down into the bath — the water rinsed away the soap lather.

Mrs Cohen also laughed and did not appear to be shocked. She walked over to the airing cupboard at the side of the firegrate and took out a large towel. "I'll wash your back if you like . . . I used to wash Mr Cohen's back . . . and Sammy's when he was a boy. But Sammy wouldn't let me see him in the bath . . . not after his barmitzvah . . . when he became a man." She sighed and looked sad. "He had a beautiful body . . . very muscular like an athlete. He was very strong and healthy you know. I can't understand how he died. I can't get to know anything else about how he died."

"What happened then?"

"They said it was pneumonia . . . that's all I could find out. He was in a German camp of some sort and caught pneumonia and died. I think about it every day . . . every night . . . all the time I think about him."

Jenny sat up straight and handed Mrs Cohen the bar of soap.

"Well one thing . . . at least he didn't get blown to pieces or gassed . . . like some of the poor devils in the last war. I've seen it at the pictures. And I've read about it in that book . . . The Grapes of Wrath." She frowned and continued, "No . . . that was about fruit pickers. Er . . . I mean, All Quiet on the Western Front. I didn't half cry when I read that book."

"I haven't read that one." Mrs Cohen gently wiped Jenny's back with a flannel and continued, "I belong to the library on the boulevard . . . near the Raleigh factory . . . I'll get you a ticket if you like reading."

"Oh, I don't think I'll have much time for reading," Jenny looked thoughtful, "there's a barmaid's job going in the paper. It's at the Exchange hotel . . . the pub next to the Flying Horse hotel on the Poultry down town. I might be able to make some tips there. I've got a nice little nest-egg saved up from some of me. tips at the hotel in London. You had to give the guests a bit of soft soap but it was worth it for a good tip."

"We only get out of this world what we put in." Mrs. Cohen answered, "The Lord will provide."

"Ey up . . . talking of soft soap . . . I've lost the Palmolive." Jenny fished about in the water until she had located the soap. She began to giggle again. "I've just thought of something."

"What?"

"I hope the sirens don't go off while I'm stuck here in the bath."

"We'd have to nip down the cellar. I'm not going in them damp smelly shelters . . . full of worms and spiders."

"Oh, that'd be all right, wouldn't it . . . down the cellar amongst the coal . . . I'd need another bath after that."

The laughter between them held gentle good humour and seemed to draw them together — a knot of friendship gradually being tied.

"We'll have fish and chips for supper," Mrs Cohen nodded and smiled, "and Chamberlain can have the batter."

"Fish and chips to grease yer lips." Jenny stood up and took the towel from Mrs Cohen.

"And you can go to bed whenever you feel like it." Mrs Cohen poked at the fire with a brightly polished brass poker. "No more crowding together in one room. You'll like Sammy's room. You can see right over Sodom . . . right over to Wollaton Hall. The room gets plenty of sun . . . you'll wake up with the sun shining into the bedroom."

"Oh . . . the sun shines on the righteous." Jenny dabbed at her breasts with the towel. "I feel lovely and clean now. Just like I was brand new . . . I love having a nice bath."

"Do you think the war'll last much longer?" Mrs Cohen was not listening, "sometimes I feel ever so frightened."

"No . . . not much longer our Jack says. Our lads'll soon blow the Jerries to smithereens."

"That's a good word . . . very descriptive . . . smithereens."

"Yes, it does sound good."

"Almost as good as, would you like a nice cup of tea?"

"Not 'alf, I wouldn't."

Mrs Cohen went into the scullery to refill the kettle and for no reason she could think of, began to hum a tune she had heard on the wireless.

Jenny leaned on the bedroom window-sill and looked out over the backyards. Blackness — a blanket of sombreness hid the terraced houses — all lights camouflaged by blackout curtaining.

A half moon struggled to give light and twinkling stars punctuated miniature pathways through the blue-black ceiling of sky.

Jenny pressed her face against the window pane and sighed. The hot bath and the supper of fish and chips had completely relaxed her body — now all she had to do was turn off the switch inside her head.

"Put that light out," a distant voice, urgent and full of authority intruded into her thoughts, "put that light out . . . don't you know there's a war on," the voice growled its command once again.

Jenny turned from the window — no offending light from her bedroom to anger air-raid wardens. She drew the blackout curtains together and fumbled her way to the bed. Sliding underneath the bedclothes she luxuriated in the comfort. Clean, lightly starched pillow-case and soft sheets with their fresh-air smell. The pungent aroma of mothballs drifted into her nose and the memories of childhood drifted into her mind as she recalled the large wooden chest in the attic, housing blankets dotted with mothballs to protect them from the moths.

Turning onto her side she hugged her breasts — she always found comfort when she did this — rolled into a ball as though still in her mother's womb and also, tonight, there was the familiar feeling of sensuousness.

She imagined herself in a lover's embrace, pretended she could feel his body pressed up close to hers. Night-dreaming was her name for the thrilling, imaginary adventures she sometimes had before falling asleep.

She uncurled her body and turned over onto her back. She felt the familiar hot feeling spreading through her body — flowing through her breasts and stomach it surged down between her thighs. For a long while she lay there night-dreaming until tiredness at last triumphed. She pulled the winceyette nightdress down over her knees and turned onto her side once more — her eyes closed and Morpheus claimed her for the rest of the night.

38

SEVEN

"Well then, Jack . . . what are we going to get me Mam for Christmas? And we'll have to buy summat for Grandad Alf. We've left it till the last minute again. Can I have some extra money?" Vera rubbed lard into flour then added a few drops of water to the mixture.

"I'll give you some extra when I've sold all the Christmas stuff," Jack answered, get a bottle of Johnnie Walkers for Alf and you could give him one of them new mugs I got from Stoke last week . . . the ones with aeroplanes on the front."

"That's a good idea . . . and I'll get Mam a nice satin blouse from Marks, and a brooch from Trippetts . . . they've got some lovely brooches there."

"I'm glad they're all coming here for Christmas. We'll have a real beano." Jack looked pleased, put his newspaper down and sat upright in his chair, arms folded across his chest in his 'I've got a secret' stance.

"I'll have to buy lots of extra food." Vera slid a tray of jam-tarts into the gas oven then untied her pinafore, lifted up her jumper and offered a milk-laden breast to Elizabeth Rose. "There'll be nine of us now there's your Jenny and Mrs Cohen. And Alex eats enough for two."

"He's a growing lad. He's going to be tall like me. Not be long before he's in long trousers."

"Don't say that, Jack . . . long trousers'll mean he's nearly a man . . . nearly old enough for the Army. I pray to God he never has to fight in a war." Vera's body seemed to shrink and she hugged Elizabeth Rose to her breast in a possessive manner.

"War'll be over anytime now," Jack comforted her, "not be long now."

Vera was not listening.

"It nearly killed me when our Dougie and Frankie drowned in the Trent. I don't know how we survived that horrible time do you, Jack? The nightmares I have about it seem so real . . . just as though it only happened last week." Her eyes stared at him, frightened and filled with sadness.

Jack went to sit beside her on the sofa and put an arm around her shoulder.

"You just listen to me, duck . . . the war'll soon be over and it'll be the last. This one is the last war the Germans will ever want to fight in. This time they'll realise they can't beat the British no matter how they try."

"Ah . . . over by Christmas you said," Vera mocked him, "well they'd better hurry up then, because it's the twentieth today . . . they've only got five days left to kill each other in."

"I've managed to get a turkey," Jack changed the subject, "a bleddy beauty . . . off Hettie Needham. It's an eighteen pounder from her farm. Enough meat on it to feed all Independent Street . . . she's bringing it round on Sat'day."

"Ey . . . I haven't got a meat-tin big enough for a turkey that size. I'll only just get it in the oven." Vera looked pleased.

"I'll get you a tin from one of the shops down Hyson Green." Jack still had his arm around her shoulder. "If I can't get a tin big enough I'll shove a skewer through the turkey and roast it over the coal fire. Like they did in old Henry the Eighth's court. We'll eat the meat with our fingers and toss the bones all over the floor."

"Your imagination, Jack," Vera laughed, "you're always full of daft ideas."

"Ey . . . you'll not say that when I get you upstairs tonight. Wait till I get you to bed . . . then complain about me imagination."

"I might want to get off straight to sleep," Vera teased him.

"Oh, Vera . . . I'm feeling ever so romantic . . . now it's Christmas."

"Not yet it isn't."

"I feel full of Christmas spirit."

"Huh, tell me something new. You're always full of some kind of spirit . . . and the doctor said you were to take things easy . . . look after your bad chest."

"He didn't tell me to take things easy with me wedding tackle. I might as well go and jump off Castle-Rock if I can't have me bit of love."

"Go and make some money then, so's I can have some extra, and I'll see how I feel tonight."

"Oh, you little gold-digger . . . charging me now, are you?"

Jack looked at the clock on the sideboard and stood up. "Right then . . . I'll go and flog the Christmas wrapping paper and the boxes of crackers. I'm going to load the barrow with mistletoe and holly tomorrer . . . and I should be able to shift all those boxes of dates and the rest of the oranges. I'll bring them up from the cellar when I get back." He grinned at her and added, "It looks like a Persian market down our cellar . . . we only need a few palm trees."

Vera listened as the wheels of the barrow clattered over uneven cobbles in the entry. Her thoughts helter-skeltered all over the place and she smiled when she heard Jack's voice in the distance calling to someone, "Come on then, me ducks . . . come and get it . . . I'm feeling generous today." And Bert's voice quipping back, "He don't mind who he feels, love . . . you'd better watch him."

Vera had always had mixed feelings about Jack selling things from a barrow. She knew that some of the neighbours looked down on her and Jack. Being constantly hounded by policemen gave a criminal flavour to the name of barrow-boy.

But on the other hand she knew that the neighbours were jealous of the lorry. Then there was the pot stall down the market. Pride straightened her back when she thought of the stall and the lorry. Jack climbing into the driver's seat — her Jack driving down Independent Street in his own lorry.

Elizabeth Rose had fallen asleep. Vera gently eased her nipple from the rosebud mouth then patted the tiny back to coax up wind. She looked round the kitchen and her eyes drifted over furniture and knick knacks. Her smile held satisfaction.

If Jack's happier working from a barrow and selling his pots down the market that's good enough for me, she decided. He had been very unhappy working at the cigarette factory she knew that much and never before had she been able to buy such nice things without worrying too much about money. Why, she kissed the baby's forehead and smiled happily, Jack dresses me like a film-star. And no more worrying whether she was expecting again at the end of each month. If I do get caught again it won't matter too much, at least we'll be able to feed and clothe it properly.

She placed Elizabeth Rose on the sofa and arranged cushions in front of her so that she could not roll onto the floor. A wanted baby, that was Elizabeth Rose, not many people on Independent Street could say that about any of their children.

Vera smiled and looked at herself in the sideboard mirror. "Mind you," she said aloud, "I don't think I want another one, not yet . . . not while the war's on."She pulled her jumper tightly to her and breathed in deeply.

She thrust out her breasts and continued, "I'm just getting me figure back again."

What was it the midwife had said? Oh yes, she remembered the conversation. Breast feeding was good for getting the figure back into shape — and it was thought as long as you were breast feeding it was difficult to catch for another baby.

I'm a very lucky woman, she thought, and if it weren't for the war my life would be perfect. But the peculiar churning inside her stomach always seemed to start up whenever she thought about the war. Somehow, she could not believe that things would stay the same as they were — she was certain the Germans were planning something terrible — war did not just mean blackouts and gas masks — war meant death and destruction — war meant terror and heartache. Vera had the feeling that very soon the people of Radford would be fighting for survival. And by God we'll fight an' all, she decided, with everything we've got.

"Yoo-hoo . . . Vera . . . it's me-eee," a happy sounding voice rescued Vera from her solemn thoughts. "It's me-eee . . . Shanghai Lil."

The back-door opened and Jenny's smiling face heralded good news.

"I've got the job at the Exchange pub. The landlord said I was just what he wanted to brighten up the place. It's only part-time but it'll do to be going on with."

Vera gasped when she saw how Jenny was dressed. Navy blue, bouclé coat with a huge fox-fur collar, which she discarded together with her gas mask case onto the back of the sofa. Underneath the coat she was wearing a navy blue costume and a white satin blouse with a frill at the neck. A small navy hat sat perkily on the top of her head and a veil dotted with velvet spots covered her face. Navy shoes with a brass buckle at the side and navy soft kid gloves completed her ensemble.

"Ooh . . . let's try your hat on," Vera held out her hand, "I must get a hat with a veil . . . you look like a film-star."

"That's what living in London does for you. All the latest fashions there, Vera. Trouble is, it costs a fortune keeping up with it all." Jenny handed the hat to Vera and continued, "Most of me wages went on paying the weekly clothes Diddle-ums."

Vera put the hat on and adjusted the veil.

"I don't think it suits me, do you? Makes me face look too fat."

"You look lovely. You can borrow it if you like. Keep it over Christmas. I won't be needing it . . . the landlord at the Exchange wants me to start work straight away, says they'll be busy over Christmas."

"You're lucky to get fixed up with a job so soon, Jenny. I'll bet it's because you're glamorous. Men like a bit of glamour serving their drinks."

"I showed the landlord me references but he didn't seem bothered. He was more interested in me legs." Her infectious laughter spilled out once again. "I'll have to get another job though . . . part-time work won't be enough to pay me board."

"What's that lovely smell, Jenny? You smell ever so nice. Is it Evening-in-Paris?"

"No . . . it's Phul-nana scent. Or, ripe banana as Jack calls it."

Jenny opened her handbag and took out a scent bottle which had a picture of a belly dancer on the front label.

"Have a dab, Vera . . . put some behind your ears."

"Oh, thank you . . . but it's a waste really, I'm not going anywhere." Vera removed the tiny rubber stopper and tipped the bottle upside down onto the back of her hand.

"I'll just have a little dab then."

"It'll make you feel good, Vera. A nice perm on your hair, a new frock and a dab of scent . . . makes you feel like Ginger Rogers."

Vera handed back the scent bottle and said, "Kettle's on the boil . . . I'll mash some tea. I've made some jam tarts for our Alex. He's got to take something to the school Christmas party. We'll pinch a couple, I've made plenty."

Vera went into the scullery still wearing Jenny's hat. When she returned she looked at herself in the sideboard mirror and asked, "Are you sure it don't make me face look too fat?"

"I'm perfectly sure. You look really elegant."

"I'll get a hat to match me red coat . . . the one Jack bought for me birthday last Spring. I'll get a navy one like this . . . navy'll go well with red."

"The landlord at the Exchange says he gets a lot of rich businessmen in the gentlemen-only bar. I'll be able to earn a few tips. When they ask me to have a drink I'll keep the money instead."

"How can you do that, they'll be watching you?"

"Easy when you know how. When they say have a drink me dear . . . I'll pour a bottle of Stout into a glass or a gin with water added to it. Then I'll keep on using the same glass each time. Every time I have a drink bought for me I'll just keep lifting the glass, from behind the bar, into the air and say bottoms-up or chin-chin and each customer'll think he's bought the drink. In the hotel trade the bar-staff do that all the time."

"So that way you can't get tiddly."

"Well, you can if you get the chance to help yourself to a few gins when the landlord's not looking." Jenny's face was alive with mischief.

"I don't think Gloria Goodliffe does that. The landlord's always in and out of the bar. She wouldn't dare pinch any drinks." Vera poured tea for them both.

"Don't be so sure. You have a good look the next time you go in the Oak for a drink. I'll bet Gloria makes a nice bit on the side from tips and you can be sure she helps herself to a gin now and then."

"Oh, you live in another world, Jenny. I've led a very sheltered life by the sounds of things. Stuck here in the house with the kids, I don't know what it's like to lead an exciting life. I've never been any further than Skeggy . . . or down the Trent since . . . since . . . er . . . ,"her voice faded into a whisper.

Sadness wove silence into their friendly chatter, the tick-tocking of the clock on the sideboard became accentuated.

"I'm ever so sorry about Dougie and Frankie." Jenny stared at the fireplace. "When our Jack wrote and told me they'd been drowned I sobbed me heart out. I'd have come to the funeral but Jack didn't write till after they'd been buried. I expect you both had so much on your minds . . . I er . . . " She did not continue but instead busied herself with pouring more tea into the cups.

"It was terrible. I didn't know what was happening to me." Vera fiddled with the veil on the hat then decided to remove the hat from her head. "Just before I went into

42

Mapperley hospital I . . . well I couldn't cope with anything. I couldn't concentrate on cooking or cleaning and when I went to the shops I didn't know what to get to eat. I even forgot to wash myself and you know that's not me. I'm ever so particular about keeping the house clean and things like that."

"Oh dear, what a terrible time for you both," Jenny's voice was soft and laden with sympathy, "it must be the worst thing that can happen to a woman . . . to lose her children."

"I seemed to be floating about on air instead of walking," Vera continued, "I couldn't think of anything at all except about my little lads drowning in the Trent. If I'd been there . . . seen them fall into the water perhaps it would have been different. But they were with me Mam and Grandad Alf. Up at the hospital they said my mind wouldn't accept my boys were dead. I couldn't let go of them . . . let go of the past . . . and I couldn't face the future. I wanted to die, Jenny. Just go to bed and not wake up . . . ever again."

"Oh, I can understand that, love."

"I don't know how our Mam survived when all me brothers and our Dad got killed in the last war. Thank goodness she met Alf later on . . . he's been a jewel you know . . . a really good husband to our Mam. Yes, I just wanted to lay down and die when I lost me lads."

"I've felt like that, Vera."

"Oh you couldn't have, not someone like you."

"Yes, someone like me, Vera. My life hasn't been a bed of roses, so don't think it has." Jenny stared at the fireplace and sighed. "And you might be sure it was over a man. Served me right though. He was married of course and said he was going to divorce his wife and marry me. Load of old twaddle he gave me. You know how men can give you the flannel. Well, I took it all in like a fool and didn't find out till later that it was all lies."

"Ah . . . men can be rotten devils sometimes," Vera was grateful for the diversification from her own troubles and added, "Jack's got his faults but I've never had any trouble in that department. I don't think I could forgive him if he went with another woman."

"Oh dear, we're getting morbid," Jenny leaned over to have a look at Elizabeth Rose, "look at that little cherub. She's a good baby, isn't she. I'll bet that's because you breast feed. I'm going to buy Christmas presents this afternoon . . . draw some of me savings out. What does the baby need? And what can I get for Alex? A football to ruin his shoes on . . . summat like that?"

"He had a football for his birthday and some football boots."

"Blimey, talk about posh. Our Jack used to kick a pig's bladder about instead of a ball. And as for football boots . . . he was lucky to have shoes on his feet at all. Half the time they were somebody else's cast-offs."

"I know, that's why I'm thankful he's doing so well with his pot stall and the barrow. Jack's a real hard grafter and deserves to get on. He was talking about buying a car, but the war's put the kybosh on that now. He's always wanted a Wolseley," she grinned, "I'd feel like Lady Muck sitting in a Wolseley. The neighbours'd be ever so jealous, wouldn't they."

"War won't last forever, Vera. You'll get your car and I'll get a rich husband. I'll marry an old bloke and grease the stairs . . . after he's made his Will."

They laughed together and the former shyness between them melted gently away — like snowflakes on a brazier.

"I'm off now then, to tell Mrs Cohen about me new job."

"See you 'safternoon then if you still want to take Elizabeth Rose for a walk."

"Ooh, I do. I think I'll buy her a teddy-bear for Christmas. I've still got mine. Blooming old scruffy thing he is, but I wouldn't part."

"See you later then, duck. I'd better start getting the dinner ready. Jack and Alex'll be home soon and they're like raging wolves when they're hungry."

"Right then . . . I'll let you get on." On went the bouclé coat and the perky hat. "Ooh, I nearly forgot me gas mask. Don't want gassing before I start me new job and find meself a rich old bloke."

Vera peeled potatoes and prepared brussel sprouts ready for the saucepan. She selected a duster and took out a tin of Mansion polish. The sideboard and three piece suite were given a polish and she then decided to put an extra shine on the lino. She turned on the wireless and twiddled about with the knobs. A man's voice crooned the words to 'Making Whoopee'. Down on her knees Vera rubbed at the lino and joined in with the singing although she did not know all the words.

'Another bride another groom, another sunny honeymoon
De-dah it's thrilling, that he's so willing, to make whoopee.
De-dah de-dah . . . de-dah de-dah
The groom looks nervous, he answers twice
De-dah de-dah dah . . . de-dah de-dah-dah . . . to make whoopee'.

The crooner faded away to a whisper and another voice said, "Well everyone . . . are you ready for Christmas? Don't let Hitler spoil those festivities. Light those Christmas trees and hang those paper garlands from the ceilings. Let's all make this a Christmas our families will remember forever."

Music started up in the background and children's voices sang out their joyous message. Vera joined in and polished the lino with enthusiasm.

"We three kings from Orient are
Bearing gifts we traverse afar
Field and fountain, moor and mountain
Following yonder star . . . oh, oh . . .
Star of wonder, star of light
Star of royal beauty bright
Westward leading still proceeding
Guide us to thy perfect light."

Vera felt so full of joy she was lightheaded. War or no war, she decided, this Christmas was going to be a good one. After all, it might be their last.

She could almost smell that eighteen pound turkey — frizzling away inside the oven surrounded by sage and onion stuffing and roast potatoes and sweet, juicy onions. Life was good, she thought, and once again dabbed at the polish with her duster and smiled to herself.

EIGHT

"Mam . . . Dad . . . !" Jack and Vera were awakened by the sound of Alex's excited voice. "Look what Santa's bought me."

Jack struggled to open his eyes — peering out into the darkness he smiled then realised it was wasted in a bedroom cloaked beneath blackout curtains. "Just a minute, Alex . . . let me put the light on."

The bedroom blinked into soft light and revealed Alex — arms laden with packages beneath a face laden with happiness.

Vera sat up, propped against pillows she patted the bedspread and said, "Let's have a look then . . . open your presents, duck. Come on inside the bedclothes else you'll catch yer death o' cold."

"Ohhhh," a low moan escaped Jack's throat, "do you know what time it is? It's only ten to six."

"Santa must have had Alex at the top of his list." Vera tousled Alex's hair and kissed him loudly on the cheek. "Open that big one first . . . I wonder what it can be?"

Impatient fingers tore at Christmas wrapping-paper. Lead cowboys and Indians tumbled over the bedspread followed by wagons pulled by lead horses.

"Oh look . . . oh look . . . cowbugs and Indians," Alex held the figures in the air.

"Yes . . . just what you wanted." Jack forced his eyes open and tried to look interested.

Alex turned his attention to a long thin package. "Wowwww . . . look here!" He held a toy telescope against his right eye and aimed the viewer at Jack.

"I see no ships," Jack winked at Vera, "only hardships."

Alex reached for a bulging woollen sock crammed full with mysterious shapes. Out came a paint-box, orange, sugar-pig, rolled up colouring book, bar of chocolate, some crayons and a mixture of nuts.

"My word . . . Santa has been generous." Vera rubbed her eyes and yawned.

"Now go back to bed there's a good boy and have a little sleep before yer breakfast."

Jack turned onto his side and put his arm across Vera's waist — his fingers gently caressed the softness of her winceyette nightgown. "How'd you fancy a nice cup of tea?"

"Ah . . . and I suppose I'm the one who's going to make it." Vera slid down underneath the bedclothes.

"You're wrong there . . . seeing as it's Christmas I'm going to mash the tea." Jack got out of bed and scooped some of the presents from the bedspread. "Come on, Alex . . . back to bed, me lad. Would you like a drink of tea?"

"No thanks, Dad . . . I'm going to eat me sugar-pig."

"Oh no you're not," Vera's voice was firm, "you save that till later."

"Can't I just eat its head?" Alex pleaded as he was led back to his own bedroom by Jack.

"Nibble a bit off its tail," Jack whispered, "yer Mam won't notice that."

Jack put the kettle on the gas stove then hugging his dressing gown tightly around his body hurried across the garden to the lavatory.

45

Morning dew, fossilised by frost, decorated the shrubs and moss-covered garden path.

"Ohhh . . . ohhhh," Jack murmured and shivered as he sped back to the house, "it's bleddy freezing." His breath sent out tiny smoke signals into the cold air and so did the kettle, its lid lifted by water on the boil. Jack placed the tea things onto a tray and undid a packet of Lincoln-creams.

"Blimey, Jack . . . your feet are freezing." Vera curled herself into a ball. "Get your feet away from me."

"I've got something here that'll warm you up," Jack snuggled closer and added, "what do I get then for mashing the tea?"

"Sssshh . . . Alex'll hear you."

"No he won't, I've shut his door."

"You'll wake Elizabeth Rose," Vera played games with him, "stop it."

"She'll sleep till her next feed." Jack put his arm around her waist then stroking her hair, nuzzled and kissed her neck.

"We'd better drink us teas before they get cold." Vera reached for the tray. "Oh, biscuits as well, you are spoiling me."

They drank their teas, leaned back against propped up pillows and found contentment in simple domesticity.

"It'll be a good Christmas, Vera, "Jack dipped a biscuit into his tea, "we've got a lot to be thankful for."

"The war's spoilt everything . . . can't get the war off me mind."

"We'll be all right, love. Jerries won't come over here."

"Can't help thinking all the same." Vera sipped tea and looked serious. "Look what's happened to the Poles."

They finished the tea and wriggled down into the bedclothes. Jack wished that Vera would reach out to him first — but she never did — it was always Jack who sent out the first signals. It felt natural to him to want to make love on Christmas morning. The excitement he had always experienced as a boy, even though the presents had only been meagre, the thrill of searching inside a sock was stamped indelibly onto his heart and he wanted to crown that feeling with the joy of lovemaking.

"Your hair smells lovely, Vera." Jack snuggled closer and gently caressed her breasts. "I won't hurt your breasts, love . . . I know they're still tender . . . but I do love to touch them."

"I'm dying to open my presents aren't you, Jack? I've always loved Christmas morning." Vera smiled at him and Jack noticed that her smile was of a friendly nature — not the kind of smile he would have liked to see at that moment. He wanted desire and lust in her smile — the kind of look that could drive a man crazy. Eyes dreamy and shining, giving him the 'come-on'.

"Can I take your nightie off, Vera?" His voice was gentle, coaxing her to react to his passion.

"Oh, I'm not taking me nightgown off, Jack . . . I'll catch me death o' cold. I'll pull it up a bit . . . there you are."

Jack fumbled underneath the bolster for a french-letter. He hated using them but knew he had no choice. Vera catching for another baby would not be a good idea, not so soon after Elizabeth Rose's arrival.

"That's nice, Jack," Vera whispered, "oh, that's lovely. I feel as though you're really a part of me now."

Jack did not answer because his mind was filled with images of Gloria Goodliffe. Tempting lips inviting Jack to kiss her. No nightgown hid the sensuous contours of Gloria's body but instead, her nakedness was exposed in all its beauty. Moans of ecstasy assaulted his ears as she writhed about beneath him.

Jack imagined Gloria doing things to him that men only dreamed about in their most secret thoughts. Lustful images full of passion captured Jack's brain — he could not think of anything else — it became of utmost importance that he had to release everything into his fantasy woman. Faster and faster until, at last, everything gone from him he once again became Jack, that ordinary bloke married to gentle, ordinary Vera. The only woman he had made love to, although he had come close to being unfaithful with Iris the girl from the cigarette factory — the redhead he had gone around with when Vera had been in hospital with a nervous breakdown because of the deaths of their two little boys.

Jack switched off the bedside light and stared towards the blackout curtaining. He marvelled at the way his mind worked. After all those thoughts of lust and debauchery no feelings of guilt swamped his mind — only a great tiredness. He pulled the bedclothes over his shoulders and surrendered to the sleep of contentment.

Something tickled Jack's nose. Softness clinging to his nose like a cobweb, his fingers closed around Vera's hairnet which had escaped from the hair-grips which usually anchored it to her mane of thick dark brown hair.

Jack turned onto his back and stared at the blackout curtains — the sombreness made him feel gloomy. He reached for Vera but she was not there. A clatter of crockery from downstairs told him that breakfast was being prepared.

Jack got out of bed and pulled the chord on the blackout curtains — daylight spattered the bedroom with cheerfulness. He glanced at the alarm clock — nearly half-past eight. "Christmas Day nineteen thirty nine." Jack said aloud. "Christmas and war or no war it's going to be a bleddy good 'un."

Breakfast eaten and enjoyed Jack decided to light a fire in the front room. The Christmas dinner would be eaten in there and a cheerful fire would add a finishing touch, Jack thought, as he piled sticks and coal on top of newspaper.

The fire danced to life and transformed coldness to warmth. Alex struggled into the front room arms laden with toys.

"We'll have a game of cowbugs and Indians," Jack knelt on the carpet, "you can be the cowboys and I'll be the Indians. And you'd better watch out . . . I'm a dab-hand with me bow and arrow."

Vera pushed open the door and asked, "What time shall I put the turkey in the oven, Jack? We're going to eat about three . . . give your Jenny time to get back from the Exchange. Shall I put it in now?"

"Yes . . . that'll be about right." Jack stood an Indian behind a bush and added, "Do plenty of stuffing . . . then we can have some on our sandwiches tonight."

"You don't half love your belly."

"I love yours more."

"Jack, behave yerself," Vera nodded towards Alex, "Little pigs have big ears."

"Not if Alex gets hold of them," Jack laughed, "he eats their ears, don't you, son." Jack rolled onto the carpet and cried out, "Oh . . . a cowboy's just shot me. Quick . . . fetch the medicine-man . . . tell him to bring his magic bones."

Alex laughed excitedly and pointed another cowboy at Jack's curled up body.

"You're dead . . . you're dead! Drop your bow and arrow . . . I'm going to set fire to your wigwam." Jack rolled onto his side obligingly and asked, "Will you have time to nip across to the Oak for a sherry, Vera?"

"No . . . I want everything to be nice . . . don't want to risk spoiling the dinner, Jack. I'll pour meself a sherry while the dinner's on."

"I shan't stay long, duck. Just have a couple of pints with the lads and Bert. You're a good gel, Vera . . . don't nag me much, do yer."

"You're a good husband, if it weren't for you we wouldn't be having such a lovely Christmas. All that hard grafting you do taking the barrow out in all weathers and standing freezing to death down the market."

"Better than being on the dole, duck. Owt's better than that."

Vera knelt down beside Jack and putting her arms around his neck gave him a kiss on the cheek.

"Ey up . . . look at yer Mam being all sloppy, Alex," Jack looked pleased, "she's getting round me again."

Alex glanced at them but was not interested. "I'm going to kill another Injun," he shouted, "watch out."

Jack grabbed hold of Vera and pulled her down beside him.

"Oh . . . oh . . . you've killed another Indian . . . and his squaw."

"How," Vera giggled, "how."

"Me know how . . . me show you tonight." Jack tickled her stomach.

"Gerroff . . . gerroff." Vera struggled free and stood up. "I'll make us a nice cup of Camp coffee." She went over to the scullery.

"Oh, little town of Bethlehem, how still we see thee lie." Melodious voices blending with the magnificent sounds of brass instruments sent thrills up and down Jack's spine.

"It's the Salvation Army. Open the door, Alex. We'll sit on the step and have a listen to them." Jack stood up.

"Put your coats on and wrap yer scarves round yer necks." Vera called to them from the scullery. "And keep the door shut, Jack . . . don't let the cold air in, it's freezing outside."

"How silently, how silently, this wondrous gift is given." The voices of the singers grew louder.

Jack sat on the door-step and fumbled inside his trouser pocket for cigarettes. He felt so emotional he wanted to cry — the feeling swelled up inside him and he coughed to clear the lump from his throat.

Children appeared from nowhere — trickling slowly down the street towards the music they shouted excitedly to each other.

"Salvation Army, they've all gone barmy
Except the Captain, he's gone nuts."

Alex joined in with the chanting, mouth hidden behind his red and white Forest scarf, "Salvation Army, they've all gone barmy."

"Ey . . . you can just shut up." Jack pushed him playfully then fumbled inside his

48

jacket pocket and handed him a sixpence. "Here you are, me lad. When they come round with the tin pop this tanner in. Salvation Army do a lot of good work. You ask your grandma what they brought her for Christmas when she was a little gel, when Santa forgot to take her anything," he added quickly. "Wouldn't have had nowt if the Salvation Army hadn't took her anything."

More children poured on to Independent Street. Arms cradling dolls, teddybears, spinning-tops and skipping-ropes they showed off presents to each other their faces decorated with smiles.

You'd never know there was a war on, Jack thought, and suddenly felt very frightened. Flies never know there's a spider waiting to eat them — not till they get caught. 'Oh come all ye faithful, joyful and triumphant.' Once again the beautiful music enveloped him in its magic.

"Come on everybody . . . sit down and we'll open our presents before we have us dinners." Jack found a seat for everyone. Presents were handed round and the excitement they generated filled the room.

"Oh, look 'ere . . . what a lovely brooch."

"Ey . . . look at this, Bert . . . look what Jack and Vera's bought us."

"Thank you, Annie . . . I've wanted one of these for ages."

"Blimey . . . they'll think I'm a toff when I walk down the street in this hat."

"Ey up . . . I'll look like a film-star in this blouse."

"Look at this, Alf . . . look here . .. wait till they see me wearing this in Sodom."

"Ooh, lovely . . . me favourite scent . . . Evening-in-Paris . . . and some powder to match. I'll smell lovely, like a blooming bunch of roses."

"Wowwwww . . . this must have cost a fortune. Look here everybody . . . a real fox-fur off, Jack. All Independent Street'll be jealous when I wear this."

"Just what I needed . . . nice wool scarf and some gloves to match. Real hand knitted an' all."

Hands tearing at paper and string. Eyes searching contents of boxes, mouths smiling at moments of discovery.

"It looks like a bomb's dropped on the room," Jack nodded at the piles of Christmas wrapping-paper.

"Oh shut up, Jack," Jenny tried on a pair of pearl ear-rings in front of the sideboard mirror, "don't mention bombs, they talk about nothing else in the Exchange. It's enough to drive you to drink."

Everyone laughed and Jack said, "Good idea, Jenny. Right then, who'd fancy a nice sherry? A little apéritif before we commence dining . . . old beans," he emulated a toff.

"I should think you men have had enough to drink already," Vera winked at the women, "I don't know what you'd do if the Germans dropped a bomb on the Oak."

"We'd go to the Farmhouse," answered Bert, "you can't keep a good man from his ale."

"We haven't told you our good news," Grandad Alf folded his arms across his chest and looked smug, "we've got real good news."

"Go on then . . . tell them, Alf," Maisie prompted him, "you've been bursting since last Wednesday to tell them."

"Me and Maisie have both got new jobs." Grandad Alf paused, made them wait for the best bit. "We've got fixed up at the Raleigh. Both working together now. I've got a job sweeping up and Maisie's going to work in the canteen."

"Oh, you dark horse . . . you kept that quiet, Mam." Vera grinned at Maisie.

"You'll be able to get yer hands on some extra food, Maisie," Jack grinned at her, "you'll be all right there."

"It'll fit in nicely," Maisie replied, "us both working the same hours. We can come home together an' all . . . and both sleep at the same time . . . better than Alf being on nights all the time."

"Curl up like two little dormouses," added Grandad Alf, "and we'll not be short of a bob or two . . . things are looking up for us at last."

"Best Christmas present you could have," Vera walked towards the scullery, "now I think it's about time we had us dinners."

"That's right everybody . . . come and sit at the table." Jack moved chairs and bustled about.

"I'll sit with me back to the fire." Jenny sat down. "It's blooming freezing today, I feel chilled right through to me bones."

"I'll fetch the wireless," Jack said, "then we can listen to the King broadcast his speech."

"Bet he'll say summat about the war." Grandad Alf poured sherry into glasses which were coloured red and decorated with gold leaves. "I knew it wouldn't be over by Christmas. Them Jerries'll take some beating. We should've been ready for another war. We should've learned summat from the last one. We ought to have been building tanks and planes years ago."

"You're right there, Alf," Jack took hold of a carving-knife and brandished it like a sword, "blood and guts . . . that's the only language the Jerries understand. The only good German's a dead 'un."

Vera entered the room carrying the turkey which was on a willow-patterned plate and surrounded with stuffing, onions, roast potatoes and carrots. "Get carving, Jack, and give everybody plenty." Vera placed the huge dish in the middle of the table.

"Ooooohhhhh, "everyone said at once, "oooooohhhhh."

"My word," Mrs Cohen said admiringly, "what a beauty."

"It's bigger than the one the landlady at the Exchange's cooking," added Jenny.

"The lady I clean for hasn't bought one as big as that," Maisie was impressed.

"I'll bet it's the biggest in Independent Street," grinned Bert.

"Oh . . . that's what all the ladies say . . . intit, duck," Jack winked at Vera.

Everyone laughed and drank sherry — Grandad Alf refilled glasses and Alex was allowed a small sherry, to toast the King and Queen after the speech.

Plates were piled high with turkey, mashed potatoes, roast potatoes, onions, brussel sprouts, carrots, stuffing and thick rich brown gravy flavoured with the juice from the turkey.

"Put the King on, Jack," Grandad Alf pointed at the wireless with his fork, "I'll bet he hasn't had a better Christmas dinner than us lot here."

"No," they all agreed, "no."

"You're a good cook, Vera . . . the best there is," Jack smiled at her.

"Takes after her Mam, Jack," boasted Maisie," you've got me to thank for that."

"Yes," agreed Grandad Alf, "the minute I tasted one of Maisie's dumplings I knew she was the gel for me."

The laughter that followed was louder than usual, Jack noticed and was pleased, laughter spurred on by alcohol and the communal feeling of comradeship.

The announcer heralded the King's speech. Everyone was silent. Only the scraping of cutlery against plates could be heard as the words tumbled from the wireless. Words of encouragement and words of deep sadness.

"I said to the man who stood at the gate of the year,

'Give me a light that I may tread safely into the unknown.'

And he replied, 'Go out into the darkness and put your hand into the Hand of God. That shall be to you better than light and safer than a known way.'

May that Almighty Hand guide and uphold us all."

"He's a good bloke." Grandad Alf nodded his head and wiped up the remainder of his gravy with a roast potato. "I didn't fancy his brother . . . not after all that messing about with that American tart."

"It's a real love-match, that is," Maisie sighed, "he gave up the throne for the woman he loved."

"She's a divorced woman," Grandad Alf continued, "and we don't want no divorced tart for our Queen. The Queen we've got now's a good 'un. And she's nice looking. That other one looks like she could do with a few of your dumplings, Maisie . . . she's like a bean-pole."

"Who's got room for some Christmas-pud?" Vera gathered plates.

"I've got room, Mam," Alex looked eager, "I want to find a tanner."

Crack . . . crack . . . crack. Paper hats and pieces of coloured paper with jokes written on them tumbled out of the crackers.

'How do you make a Maltese cross? Steal his money.'

'Waiter, there's a fly in my chicken soup. Don't worry, Sir . . . it only likes tomato.'

'Kindness in women, not their beauteous looks, shall win my love. (William Shakespeare)'

'What's the briefest, maiden's prayer? A man: Amen.'

'Have more than thou showest, speak less than thou knowest, lend less than thou owest. (William Shakespeare)'

Vera handed out dishes filled with steaming hot Christmas-pudding and custard.

"Mind yer false teeth, Alf, "Maisie fussed, "don't bite too hard in case you get a tanner."

"I've got one," called out Jenny, "I've found one."

Alex sucked hard on his pudding and his efforts were rewarded.

"I've got one . . . I've got one." He licked the sixpence clean.

Laughter and happy conversation ricocheted round the tiny front room — cigar and pipe smoke swirled in opulent clouds. Suddenly, as though they had all been hypnotised, eyes closed and voices became stilled.

"I'll find some dance-music." Jack fiddled with the knobs on the wireless. "She's my lovely . . . de-dah de-dah de-dah dah-dah-dah." he hummed softly to himself.

"See if you can find some carols, Jack." Maisie put her arm through Alf's arm and added, "Me and Alf love to hear a nice carol."

51

"Hark the herald angels si . . . ing
Glory to the New-born King."

"Aaaahhh," they whispered collectively in contented whispers, "aaaaahhh."

Jack looked out of the window — late afternoon unloaded darkness onto the mist-laden street. The gas-lamp opposite offered no comfort as it stood empty of light for the duration of the war.

Neither use nor ornament, thought Jack, everywhere blacked out. He tried not to feel depressed, today was Christmas, a time for rejoicing.

Stars twinkled to life and one star outshone the others like an expensive tinsel star on top of a Christmas tree.

Blimey look at that, Jack thought how large the star seemed, the blooming star of Bethlehem, here right on time as you might say.

Arms folded across chest Jack settled down for a snooze and murmured to himself, "I'd like to see the bloody Jerries put that light out."

At half past five Jack opened his eyes. "Who wants a game of dominoes?"

"I'll have a game," Bert pulled his chair nearer the table.

"And I will." Grandad Alf poked tobacco into his pipe and lit a match.

"Are you playing, Jenny?" Jack shuffled dominoes and nodded at her.

"No . . . we're going to have our fortunes told. You men play."

"I'll mash some tea and make a few sandwiches." Vera handed Elizabeth Rose to Maisie. "Here y'are, Mam . . . look after her while I put the kettle on."

"Do the tea-leaves, Maisie." Jenny looked excited. "Ooh, they ought to call you Gipsy Rose Tea."

Everyone changed positions. The men and Alex positioned themselves round the table, setting up dominoes into rows. The women settled comfortable on sofa and armchairs, shoes left in the kitchen they spread out legs and wriggled stockinged feet.

Vera returned to the front room and handed round cups of tea and more food. "Come on . . . get stuck in . . . there's plenty more."

"Ooh . . . I didn't think I could eat anything else today." Mrs Cohen helped herself to another mince-pie. "But I may as well spoil myself . . . seeing as it's Christmas. And anyway, this time next year we might all be starving."

"No, we'll be all right," Maisie kissed Elizabeth Rose on the cheek and continued, "we're growing our own vegetables aren't we, Alf. We've got an allotment down near Radford railway station."

"I'll have to come and look at yer marrow then, Alf." Jenny laughed suggestively.

"Ey up, our Jenny . . . stop distracting his attention." Jack winked at her. "There's a serious game going on here."

Jenny drank the remainder of her tea and said, "Will you tell my fortune first? I've got to get ready for work soon."

Maisie peered into the teacup then held it out in front of her.

"Ey up . . . there's some fun and games going on 'ere. A dark-haired man and a fair-haired bloke. There's some water an' all." She paused and then continued, "There's a birth an' all so you'd better watch out, me gel."

"Go on . . . go on," Jenny leaned forward eagerly, "what else?"

"I've never 'eard owt so daft in all me life," Grandad Alf chuckled, "you're like a load of owd washerwomen . . . believe owt you do."

Maisie tipped the cup sideways and looked mysterious. "I can see a large building with rows and rows of big tubs or summat like that. And there's going to be a wedding . . . 'cause I can see a steeple."

"Ah . . . I know what that means." Jenny grinned at her. "The large building with the tubs is a brewery. I'm going to marry a rich man who owns a brewery. I'll keep you all in free Shippo's for the rest of your lives."

Everyone laughed and looked pleased at the idea.

Jenny dabbed at her face with powder and applied two layers of orange lipstick to her lips. She snuggled into her grey tweed coat and pulled the beaver-lamb collar close to her neck. "Right then . . . I'll go and make some tips. The customers should be feeling generous tonight."

"Come back here when you've finished, Jen." Jack looked up from his dominoes. "Mrs Cohen's going to stay and have a Christmas drink. So you can come back here . . . we'll save you a nice drop of something."

"Right you are then." Jenny put on grey leather gloves and slipped her feet into grey suede shoes. "Merry Christmas everybody."

"Merry Christmas, Jenny," friendly voices chorused their reply.

Later on that evening Jack and Vera stood in the scullery.

"We've got loads of food left over, Jack. I've never had such a lovely Christmas. We bought too much food though."

"Well, as Mrs Cohen said, make the best of it, duck. We might all be starving next Christmas."

"I'll bet we've had the best Christmas of anybody on Independent Street. The Wilkinsons have only had sausage for their Christmas dinner."

"Yer what? . . . that family who live on Bovill Street with all them kids?"

"Yes. Ten kids counting the new baby. Doris said she was going to cook sausages and stuffing so's it'd be like having a turkey."

"Find me a carrier-bag, Vera . . . and some greaseproof paper."

"What yer going to do?"

"Play Santa Claus, that's what I'm going to do."

Slices of turkey, half a pork-pie, mince-pies, slices of Christmas cake, apples, oranges, pork and stuffing sandwiches found their way into the carrier-bag.

"Get a bottle of Sandemans port from the front room, Vera. We've got plenty of booze to last us into the New Year."

Jack put a packet of Woodbines into the carrier-bag then called out, "Alex . . . come here a minute, Alex."

Alex appeared holding two lead Indians.

"What do you want me for, Dad?"

"How about giving the Wilko kids some of your old comics?"

"Oh, I like to read them again . . . I like to save them, Dad."

"Santa Claus ent bin to the Wilkos this year. Remember what I told you about the Salvation Army this morning?"

"Yes . . . about Grandma when she was a little gel."

"Wouldn't you like to give something to the poor then? You've had a lot of presents. You're a very lucky lad."

"All right then, Dad. And they can have me old puzzles and those adventure books . . . I've read 'em loads of times. Do you think they'd like me tiddley-winks game? I'm a bit old for that now, Dad."

"Go and get them then . . . and get yer coat on."

"What for?"

"You can come with me."

Jack and Alex walked towards Bovill Street — hunched up against the chill wind, arms laden with food, drink and comics, they screwed up their eyes as protection against the frosty air.

Rat-tat-tat. The door opened and a smell of boiled cabbage and dampness swirled out of the Wilkinson's front room.

"Ey up, me duck," Jack put on a breezy air, "how yer doing."

"Oh, er . . . 'ello." Mrs Wilkinson stared at Jack and Alex.

"Hope you won't be offended," Jack continued, "but we've got tons of food left over and the missis said it'd be a shame to throw it away . . . 'specially now there's a war on . . . and seeing as your mester's still on the dole . . . I thought . . . ," his voice trailed away.

"Come on in," Mrs Wilkinson opened the door wider and beckoned them inside, "it's freezing out there int it."

Faces filled with questioning turned to look at Jack and Alex. A fire did its best to look cheerful but instead, only heightened the poverty of the surroundings. Little girls clad in the uniform of the poor — cotton dresses and cardigans with buttons missing. The boys wore jumpers with holes at the elbows and ill-fitting short trousers.

"Ey up, Jack." Mr Wilkinson, unshaven and with the haunted look of a man who had lost his pride, got up from his chair. "How's the barrer trade then? Making a few bob, are yer?" He fidgeted with his braces and looked embarrassed.

"Keeping the wolf from the door, mate." Jack grinned and winked at Mrs Wilkinson. "What's he bought yer for Christmas then, duck? Diamond necklace was it, or a musquash coat?"

They laughed together and then Jack repeated, "I hope you won't be offended . . . but I know what it's like being short of a few bob." He placed the carrier-bag on the table and nodded to Alex to do likewise with his gifts.

"Have to get going now," Jack turned to go, "there's an important dominoes match about to start at our 'ouse. I've got to show the owd boggers how to play."

Jack noticed that the children had neither moved nor spoken. Must be shy of strangers, he thought, and felt sad at their lack of communication due he felt, to feelings of inferiority because of their poverty.

"Merry Christmas then, everybody." Jack and Alex stepped into the street once more.

"Merry Christmas . . . and . . . and we'll not forget," Mrs Wilkinson struggled to thank them.

"No . . . we not," echoed Mr Wilkinson, "we not."

Tears smarted Jack's eyes and he blew his nose loudly.

"Are yer crying, Dad?" Alex looked up at him.

"Me! . . . no! . . . big lads and men don't cry. It's this cold wind . . . makes yer eyes water. Ey, me lad . . . don't you ever forget tonight. There's a lot of people needing help in this world. Your turn might come one day and then you'll know how it feels. Don't hurt yer to lend a hand to them that needs it."

"Didn't their house smell funny, Dad. I wouldn't like to live there."

"It must have been the damp. It gets damp if you can't afford to buy coal."

They reached their own home and as Jack opened the door a different smell wafted out into the cold December air. The aroma of roast turkey and stuffing still lingered, all mixed up with furniture polish, cigar smoke, pipe tobacco and Phul-nana perfume.

A nice smell of cleanliness and a good table, Jack thought happily, as he stepped inside the front room and closed the door on poverty, hunger and war for the time being.

The front door opened and Jenny stepped inside the room. Her face was whipped red by the icy wind and her hair billowed in unruly auburn fluffiness.

"Oooohh," she took off her gloves and held out her hands in front of the fire, "it's freezing out there. Too cold to snow, but the skies are full of it. I'll bet we'll be snowed under tomorrer."

Jack poured whisky into a glass and handed it to Jenny. He then refilled the other glasses and proposed a toast, "To the King and Queen . . . God bless 'em."

"To the King and Queen," they raised their glasses.

"And an end to the war."

"An end to the war."

I wonder what Gloria Goodliffe's doing at the moment, Jack thought and smiled to himself. He decided to slip Gloria a couple of pairs of silk stockings. Since the war had started they had become very scarce but Jack had his sources — a few words in the right places and stockings appeared out of thin air.

Vera fed Elizabeth Rose before settling her down for the night, then bustled Alex off to bed. Jack followed her upstairs and after tucking Alex into bed he took hold of Vera's hand and led her to their own bedroom.

"I feel ever so loving tonight, Vera." Jack kissed Vera on the lips and gently rubbed his hands up and down her back.

"Behave yourself, Jack," she shrugged away from him and added, "better get back downstairs."

"No . . . I didn't mean . . . I just wanted to tell you," Jack murmured unfamiliar love-talk, the words he was certain other men would have considered cissy. "I love you very much, Vera . . . you are my life . . . you and the kids . . . just let me hold you, love."

"Yoo-hoo! . . . Jack! . . . Vera! . . . we're going home now," Maisie's voice eradicated the magical moments from their brief, loving communication, they went back downstairs.

"I've had a lovely day . . . thank you both very much." Mrs Cohen hugged Vera and beamed a smile at Jack.

"It'll be the aspirin bottle for 'im," Annie nodded at Bert, "he'll have a right bad head in the morning."

"See you tomorrer . . . I'll take Alex on the Forest if it's been snowing," Jenny shrugged into her coat, "it's years since I sledged down that path at the side of Cleopatra's Needle."

One by one they spilled out into the street. Jack shivered and said, "Blimey . . . I'll bet it's below freezing point out there. I'll need another whisky to hot me up again."

"Give 'im a big one," Maisie winked at Vera, "he'll go out like a light."

"Ah . . . or it'll put a flame in his torch," chipped in Bert.

"Sssshh . . . mind the step."

"Merry Christmas."

"Merry Christmas, duck."

"Silent night . . . holy night . . . all is calm . . . all is quiet," Bert sang out as he put his arm around Annie's waist.

"Blimey . . . it was till he started singing," laughed Jack, as he closed the door once and for all on Christmas nineteen thirty nine.

NINE

For most of January, Radford hid beneath a caparison of sparkling snow. Wellington boots on red chillblained feet tramped the streets — slithering, sliding, keeping to the paths covered with cinders, the people endured hardship and continued with everyday living.

Jack and Bert struggled to make a profit from the pot-stall and barrow but after a while Jack discovered the best profits came from the sale of blackmarket goods — magicianed from underneath the stall or from out of sight beneath the barrow sackcloth.

"I ask you, Bert," Jack banged his feet up-and-down on the snow packed pavement outside the County hotel, "how can yer manage on two ounces of tea and butter?"

"Not me and our Annie," Bert agreed, eyes swivelling to left and right on the lookout for policemen, "and a man needs plenty of 'ot dinners inside 'im this weather."

"You're right . . . plenty of stews . . . mind you, I've seen plenty of times we couldn't afford to buy meat for stews."

"Oh . . . I wish it were spring . . . I'm bleddy freezing, Jack." Bert opened a packet of Woodbines and offered the packet to Jack. "Funny thing about life."

"What do you mean?" Jack inhaled smoke and began to cough. "What's so funny about life then?"

"Well, when you can't afford meat and whatnot, there's plenty of it about. But, when you can afford it, you can't get yer hands on enough."

"Got some rabbits on order for Friday. Gloria's dad promised me half a dozen. We can sell the furs to make gloves out on."

"I could do with a rabbit fur down me trousers . . . to cover up me meat and two veg. The wind isn't half whistling up me trousers."

A young woman stopped to buy flowers, she picked up a bunch of chrysanthemums and gently stroked the cluster of gold.

"Just going up to Bulwell cemetery . . . I'll have this bunch. How much are they, duck?"

"Here you are, duck . . . blooming lovely aren't they. Ha-ha-ha . . . do yer get it, duck . . . blooming?" Jack began flirting with the woman. "Don't look so fed-up . . . lovely young lady like you." he leaned closer and whispered, "How'd you fancy a nice pair of silk stockings to go on those lovely legs of yours?"

She was wearing Wellington boots and thick woollen red socks.

"How do you know what me legs look like?" she was interested in the stockings. "They haven't got ladders in, have they?"

Jack conjured up a pair of stockings from the inside of his overcoat. "If yer find a ladder in these, duck, I'll give you a free pair next time you see me."

"Coppers, Jack . . . coppers coming!" Bert started to push the barrow towards Wollaton Street.

Jack thrust change into the woman's hand and told her, "If you fancy a rabbit for yer dinner come down Sneinton Market next Sat'day. You'll find me on the pot-stall."

"You lady-killer, Jack," said Bert as they hurried away from the policemen, "all the tarts give you the eye."

"I'm all talk, Bert . . . it's good for business . . . keeps the money rolling in."

"I used to be a ladies man years ago," Bert grinned at him, "but me engine's running out of steam now."

"You mean your Annie keeps her eye on yer," Jack grinned back at him. "How about a bag of chips each? I've had enough of this lot, Bert. Let's bogger off home."

"Right then . . . fancy a fritter with yer chips?" Bert let go of the barrow, "they might have some left."

They ate hungrily — making a sucking noise as the hot chips burnt their tongues — batter on fritters soaked in vinegar making a delicious crunching sound.

The journey back up to Canning Circus made them out of breath. Snow and ice slowed them down as the wheels of the barrow slithered a zig-zag pathway on the road. They reached the top of Brassey and Bert asked, "Coming for a pint, Jack?"

"Not this dinner, Bert. Got some drink left over from New Year's Eve. I'll go straight home and pour meself a large whisky. If I don't thaw out soon summat might drop off."

They laughed — mouths wide open — and at that moment snowflakes began to fall once again, fluttering into the laughing mouths of the two friends. Faster and faster, imitating a deluge of goose feathers until Jack and Bert looked like figures in the middle of a snowstorm paperweight. They parted company outside the Oak.

Jack quickly emptied the barrow of fruit and flowers. Shutting the back door behind him at last he shook snow from his overcoat and removed his hat.

The warmth and comfort of the kitchen reached out to him. He sat in his armchair, stretched his feet towards the fire and wriggled his toes to coax back circulation.

After a while Jack switched on the wireless — dance music played a fox-trot. He turned down the sound a little so as not to awaken Elizabeth Rose who was afternoon napping inside her pram.

"Is that you, Jack?" Vera called from upstairs.

"No . . . it's the insurance man . . . I've come to give you a premium."

Vera opened the door at the bottom of the stairs. "I'm glad you've come home, love. The skies have opened up haven't they . . . it's snowing heavens hard out there now. I'll mash some nice hot tea."

"Right you are, duck . . . and I'll have some whisky in mine." Jack patted her behind. "All me bits and pieces are frozen solid."

"Better behave yourself then," Vera looked mischievous, "or summat might drop off."

"That's what I said to Bert not long ago. I bet I've got frost bite in me vitals. I need hotting up a bit, duck. How about a bit of love when we've drank us teas?"

"Oh, it's freezing upstairs," Vera called from the scullery as she busied about preparing tea."

"Who mentioned the bedroom?" Jack took a whisky bottle from the sideboard cupboard. "It's nice and cosy in here. Lock the back door, Vera . . . we'll pretend we aren't in if anybody knocks."

Always me who has to make the first move, Jack thought, as he removed the top from the whisky bottle. If Vera would only show a bit more affection towards him. Oh, she tousled his hair sometimes and kissed him on the cheek, but she never caressed him down below or did anything suggestive. Lift her skirt up perhaps and let him have a look at that bare bit of thigh between her stockings and suspenders — that never failed to arouse him. But she was still a prude after all this time, Jack sighed, there were lots of things they could do that would really excite him but Vera would never agree. Oh, for a night with a hot-blooded woman, a woman who could let herself go.

"Do you want something to eat now? . . . I can do you a bacon and egg sandwich to keep you going till tea-time." Vera carried the teapot into the kitchen.

"No thanks . . . I'll just have the tea and whisky . . . me and Bert's had some fritters and chips. Come and sit on me knee . . . you can cuddle up and get me warm. I still can't feel me feet."

Vera sat on his knee and put her arms around his neck. Jack squeezed her to him then placed his hand on her knee. Very gently he lifted her skirt and his fingers made contact with the soft flesh of her thighs. Her knickers were satin and when Jack stroked the smoothness the erotic feeling he experienced made him breathless.

Once again Vera moved away from him. "One of the neighbours might come round . . . or your Jenny."

Jack heard her words but they only made tiny stabbing impressions upon his mind. He was once again journeying into his fantasy world — the place where Vera had not yet entered.

"Vera," he moved so that he could see her face, look into her eyes, "will you take your skirt off and lie down on the rug? Show me your legs and tempt me a bit. Pretend you're one of them tarts who pick men up down on Long Row. The door's locked . . . nobody'll come in."

"Oh, Jack . . . I'm not doing that . . . I'd feel silly. And you know I'm shy . . . I don't like you looking at me, not like that. You know I'm self-conscious about my figure when I've just had a baby. My stomach's still flabby . . . I don't want you looking at me stomach."

"You've no need to be shy," Jack lifted up the jumper of her twin-set and gently caressed her breasts, "you've got a lovely rounded, womanly figure. I love looking at you, Vera . . . you've got lovely legs and beautiful soft breasts. Come on," he pulled her down onto the rug, "take your skirt off then and let me look at your suspenders and knickers."

Vera removed her skirt and then slowly lifted her underskirt up over her thighs revealing soft white flesh and pink suspenders peeping out from below deep-pink satin knickers.

Jack knelt down on the floor beside her and for a while just looked at her. The familiar pounding inside his head began to start and he breathed heavily through his mouth.

"Take your jumpers off . . .here, let me help you." Excitement made him fumble as he removed the twin-set. He knelt closer and reached for the straps on her brassiere.

"No . . . don't do that, Jack . . . leave that on. My breasts are still ever so tender." Vera covered her breasts with her arms.

"All right, all right then," Jack whispered coaxingly, "just let me kiss you there then . . . I'll be ever so gentle." He caressed her breasts with the tips of his fingers then gently kissed her nipples. Reaching down he removed her knickers and then his fingers began to explore her body with more urgency.

Jack eased himself up so that he covered Vera's body with his own. Vera put the palms of her hands against his shoulders and pushed him away.

"Jack . . . you'll have to put something on. We'll have to be careful again now."

"Damn!" Jack got to his feet and then, naked and rampant, ran up the stairs to fetch the french-letter to the accompaniment of the sound of Vera's laughter.

Jack returned to the room, still aroused, he knelt on the floor and with trembling fingers put on the sheath.

He tried to make his lovemaking last a long time — keep the thrilling ecstatic feelings going for much longer than he normally did. But, because of the excitement of making love downstairs — a rare occurrence — Jack found it impossible to hold back for long. The explosion of passion when it did occur seemed to Jack the best he had experienced.

They lay quietly together — Jack still inside her — joining them together with physical love. Arms wrapped around each other they closed their eyes — guarded secret thoughts.

After a few moments Vera felt the gasps of breath on her neck which told her that Jack had plunged into a deep sleep. She turned gently to look at him and then glanced over to the pram where Elizabeth Rose was also fast asleep.

Vera smiled and then thought that it had seemed so very long ago, the time when she had been young. For years now, she never felt like anything but a mother. If only I could turn the clock back, she sighed, what fun I'd have.

Jack murmured incomprehensible words and snuggled closer to her. Ah well, she thought, as long as Jack's happy. He *is* the man of the house, the bread-winner. She sighed softly so that Jack would not hear the dissatisfaction in the sound and wished that just once she could experience something like the ecstasy that Jack seemed to feel whenever they made love. She stroked a stray wave of hair back from Jack's forehead and allowed herself another sad sigh then decided to let Jack take her nightdress off when the weather turned a bit warmer. She fell asleep worrying about her flabby stomach and the stretch marks on her thighs.

TEN

Jenny turned the key in the lock of Mrs Cohen's front door and called, "Yoo-hoo . . . it's me, Mrs Cohen." Chamberlain the cat opened one eye and stretched to full length on the sofa. Mrs Cohen appeared from the scullery, wiped her hands down the front of her pinafore and asked, "How did you get on then? Did you get the job?"

"Start in a week's time, after I've served my notice at the pub. I'll be sorry to leave but I can't manage on part-time money. I should be able to earn some good tips at the Black Boy."

"It's a lovely hotel, Jenny . . . I used to meet Mrs Leivers there for afternoon tea . . . before she died . . . they used to do lovely teas."

Jenny hung her coat up and exchanged shoes for the comfort of slippers. She sat down next to Chamberlain and continued, "I think they were impressed because I've worked at a posh London hotel. Mind you . . . I told them a few fibs . . . said I'd worked as a waitress as well as a chambermaid."

"What if they check your references?" Mrs Cohen looked serious. "Honesty is the best policy my husband always used to say."

"Not when you're in need of a job and money it isn't," Jenny nodded her head in disagreement, "and anyway, a kid could balance a tray with a few drinks on it. All I've got to do is serve snacks, beers, shorts and coffees in the lounge. I'm going to get every Sunday off and Friday half-day. I'll get a free dinner as well and a snack in the evenings." She laughed and added, "I'll look like Desperate Dan in the Dandy before I've finished."

"You won't be wanting a meal here then?" Mrs Cohen placed a thick slice of bread on the end of a toasting-fork and held it in front of the fire. "I'll reduce your board."

"Don't worry about that, Mrs. Cohen . . . we'll see how things work out before you do anything daft. I'm very comfortable here and anyway, I'll be having my Sunday meals as usual. I tell you what I'll do with you. I'll drink more tea and dip more biscuits in me tea if that'll keep you happy."

Mrs Cohen buttered the toast and handed it to Jenny. She tousled Jenny's hair and said affectionately, "You're a good gel . . . it will help now we're on rations."

Jenny poured tea and munched on the toast then she rubbed her forefinger along the toast and let Chamberlain lick butter from her finger. The cat did not shift from his stretched out position but stuck out his tongue and licked her finger slowly.

"Lazy boy," Mrs Cohen nodded at him, "been out all night courting again."

"Who's the lucky girl then?" Jenny tickled his head.

"Tansy . . . the tabby cat that belongs to the Gleadalls next door but two. Pretty little thing . . . likes to sit on the lavatory roof in the sun all day."

"Does more than sit on the roof by the looks of Chamberlain." Jenny continued tickling his head and Chamberlain closed his eyes and gave out purrs of ecstasy which vibrated through his body. "By the way, Mrs. Cohen," Jenny placed one foot on top of the other and looked down at her feet, "talking of courting . . . I've got a young man interested in me. Been coming to the pub a lot and buying me drinks."

Mrs Cohen showed great interest. "How long has this been going on then? What's his name? . . . does he live round here?"

"Ah-ha . . . that's got you thinking," Jenny chuckled, "like to have a look at him, would you?"

"Yes I would . . . I'll give him the once over for you . . . I'm good at judging characters."

"Well, his name's Reginald . . . but everybody calls him Reggie. He lives down the Meadows with his grandma and grandad and he supports Nottingham Forest. Oh," she chuckled again, "and he's mad about redheads."

"What does he do for a living?"

"A fitter I think he said."

"Don't get too serious, Jenny . . . he could get called up at anytime."

"I'm not serious . . . and I'm certainly not looking too far ahead. Anyway, our Jack reckons the war won't last much longer."

"Don't be too sure about that. They said that about the Great War and look how long that lasted."

"Oh, never mind about the war, Mrs Cohen . . . me and Reggie are going to enjoy ourselves while we can. I'm meeting him tomorrow afternoon outside the Castle. Then we're going for a stroll through The Park . . . look at all the posh houses. We're going to go to Croshaws after we've been for our walk . . . have some of their lovely Welsh-rarebit."

"Oh . . . I used to go there with Mrs Leivers . . . lovely rarebit."

"Can I have a bath, Mrs Cohen? . . . is there any hot water ready?"

"Off gallivanting this evening as well, are you?" Mrs Cohen helped Jenny to lift the bath from the nail on the outside wall and manoeuvred it into the kitchen.

"Yes," Jenny nodded, "I'm meeting Florence Wilkins . . . the widow who lives near our Jack. Her milkman's joined the Army and she gets a bit lonely. We're going to go in Yates's first for some of their jungle-juice and then we're going down the Palais."

"My Sammy loved to go to the Palais," Mrs Cohen lifted the lid on the fire-range and ladled boiling water into the bath. "The girls loved to dance with him . . . especially the tango, he used to tell me. He always wore a flower in his button-hole and polished his shoes till you could see your face in them." Mrs Cohen carried on ladling water and remembered the son who would never dance again. Her Sammy, with the flower in his button-hole and nimble feet that danced the tango.

Jenny noticed the sadness in Mrs Cohen's eyes — the worry lines that puckered the flesh of her upper lip. In a moment of impetuosity Jenny put her arm around Mrs Cohen's shoulders and kissed her on the cheek. "N'mind, duck," she said softly, "n'mind then."

Mrs Cohen smiled and they both understood.

The weather was typical of April. Like a fickle lover — first warm then changing suddenly to goose-bump chillness. Buds were to be seen everywhere — nature gathered her glorious army of beauty together and waited patiently for the final invitation from the sun — the warmth that would make everything burst from the earth in an uprising of magnificence.

Jenny walked up Friar Lane and before she reached the top could see Reggie leaning on the wall near the entrance to Nottingham Castle. The beautiful grounds, denied to the public for the duration of the war, stood secretively behind ornate iron gates.

Reggie caught sight of Jenny and straightened up in expectation. A smile broadened into a wider smile and he raised his hat in greeting.

"Lovely afternoon."

"Yes, isn't it."

"Quite warm for April . . . almost like June."

"Yes . . . just like June . . . been waiting long?"

"No . . . not too long."

They strolled through the entrance to The Park Estate and before they had reached the end of the narrow road leading into the estate Reggie had taken hold of Jenny's hand and entwined his fingers around hers.

Splendid houses were everywhere — spreading out before them inviting admiration. Tree-lined roads gave a majestic appearance to the scene and brick walls of red and grey, built high to protect the privacy of the rich, reflected rays of sunlight giving the appearance of enamelled glass. Foliage, draped over the walls, reminded Jenny of bedding hanging out to dry. She was intrigued by the quietness of their surroundings. Houses such as these must surely accommodate large families, with cooks and cleaning staff in attendance. She relayed her thoughts to Reggie, "I wonder where everybody is today?"

"Search me. I suppose a lot of the men have joined up. They'd get some good officer material out of these houses."

"I'd like to live in one of these houses, wouldn't you?"

"Not bothered, duck. The way things are going I'll be happy just to live." He laughed sardonically and added, "Don't bring happiness . . . being rich."

"No . . . but you can be miserable in comfort," Jenny teased him, "I'd sooner cry in me gin than sob in me tea."

They strolled along in quiet companionship and at last came to a steep flight of steps.

"Let's go up there," Jenny nodded towards the steps, "it leads up to the General Hospital. You can see all over Nottingham from up there."

They reached the top of the steps, stood near the wall at the side of the entrance to the hospital and regained their breath. After a while Reggie put his arms around Jenny's waist and lifted her onto the top of the wall, then he climbed up beside her.

The wind tugged at Jenny's hair but she did not worry at the disarray. The panoramic view was breathtaking — she wanted to spread out her arms and fly — towards the river Trent as it flowed right through the heart of Nottingham — veins of water surging through the countryside, tentacles of movement reaching out for the sea.

Boats bobbed gently along down the winding canal, laden with cargo. Trolley-buses lumbered along the highways, laden with people.

"You wouldn't believe there was a war on, would you?" Jenny turned to look at Reggie. "Everything looks so normal."

"There's a war on all right," Reggie held onto his trilby hat as a gust of wind tried to claim it, "I've got to go for my medical next week . . . joining the Army if they'll have me."

"Shan't be seeing much of you then." Jenny watched a pigeon land on a roof below and envied the bird its freedom.

"Don't expect you will," Reggie paused and looked shy, "but perhaps you'd like to write to me? And I'll get leave . . . I could see you when I get leave. I'd like to see you . . . very much."

"Let's make a pact." Jenny felt like doing something reckless.

"All right then," Reggie looked amused, "what shall we do?"

"Let's meet here after the war ends. No matter what happens to us . . . let's meet again and stand right here." She tapped on the top of the wall with her left foot.

Reggie took a pen-knife from his pocket and jumped down from the wall. He clicked out the blade of the pen-knife and said, "I'll put our initials here and we'll know the exact spot. What's your surname by the way . . . I don't know your surname."

"Denbey . . . Jennifer Denbey . . . what's yours?"

"Bailey . . . Reggie Bailey." He scraped the blade along the brick.

"J D and R B". Jenny laughed and the wind carried the sound up and away until it died into silence somewhere over the top of the majestic roof-tops.

ELEVEN

Jack unloaded crockery onto his stall and called to Bert, "Well you can't be right all the time . . . I blame the government. If we'd have been prepared for war like the Germans were it would have all been over by Christmas like I said. We beat the Jerries last time . . . and we'll beat 'em this time. It'll just take a bit longer that's all."

"Not longer than last time I hope," Bert answered. "But any road, they're doing a good job at Dunkirk. If they get all our lads back from Dunkirk that'll be summat to shout about." Bert peered at a carton that Jack had placed underneath the stall. "What's in there, Jack? . . . more stockings?"

"Our new line, Bert," Jack grinned at him, "it'll shift like hot-cakes."

"What is it then? . . . let's have a dekko."

Jack took a small jar from the carton and undid the lid. "Here, have a sniff at this." He held the jar underneath Bert's nose.

Bert sniffed and said, "Blimey . . . that's a bit of all right. What is it then? . . . smells like Evening-in-Sneinton."

"Brylcreem. Real, home-made Brylcreem. Made it last night in our Vera's big saucepan. I reckon we'll be able to charge half-a-crown a jar." Jack sniffed in the jar then replaced the lid.

"Yer can't call it Brylcreem, Jack . . . not if it's home-made."

"I know that . . . I've called it Brilliantshine."

"Sounds like summat you clean saucepans with."

"Blokes'll buy owt to put on their hair now there's a shortage. They don't like going around looking like fuzzy-wuzzies."

"What have you put in it, Jack? Won't send the customers bald, will it?"

"Ey up . . . there's an idea. We'll tell them it's got hair restorer in it as well. I tell you, Bert, we're on a winner when the word gets round. We'll have a queue a mile long."

"What's in it then, tell me," Bert looked cautious.

"Beeswax and borax . . . and liquid paraffin."

"Ugh! . . . not liquid paraffin."

"And oil of violets from Woolworths to cover up the pong." Jack wrote, 'as used by film-stars' underneath the word Brilliantshine. Two young women approached the stall. They picked up plates then put them down again. Next, they examined cups which they also replaced on the stall.

"Morning, me darlings." Jack bustled about with cardboard boxes behind the stall. "What can I do yer for? How about a nice tea-set? Look lovely and posh when you're having tea on the back lawn."

The two women giggled and linked arms.

"I can think of better things to do on their back lawns," Bert winked and edged nearer the women, "I'm like a good cup of tea, gels . . . strong and sweet . . . and red-hot."

"How about these then, ladies?" Jack held two packets of stockings out in front of him, "last two pairs but you can have them for half-a-crown a pair, seeing as you're good looking."

"Last you a lifetime, gels . . . if you keep away from men with rough fingernails," Bert added.

The two women giggled again and held out their money.

"Will you be having any more?," one of the women asked.

"All depends on the silkworms, duck," Jack winked at her, "try next Sat'day . . . might have some more then."

The women tucked their precious packages into handbags and strolled away, whispering and giggling.

After a while three servicemen stood in front of the stall — two in Army uniform, the other a sailor.

"Now then, lads," Jack spoke softly and bending forward added conspiratorially, "got just the thing for you blokes."

He showed them a jar of Brilliantshine and added, "You won't be able to get this for love-nor-money soon. I usually charge three bob . . . but seeing as you're doing your bit for yer country . . . I'll let you have a jar for half a crown. Not many jars left so get yer money out, lads."

"Got hair restorer in," Bert added, "it's where that saying comes from 'keep your hair on' and it'll do the trick all right."

One of the soldiers undid the lid of the hair-cream and sniffed the contents. "Blimey . . . what a pong," he held it underneath the other soldier's nose, "make yer smell like a bleddy Pansy bloke."

"No . . . it's a real woman trapper," Bert chimed in. "Wear that on a moonlit night and the women'll go crazy for yer." He addressed the sailor, "You'll have more than one gel in every port when they smell that on yer hair."

One of the soldiers looked interested and said, "Can't afford half a crown . . . not on a soldier's pay." He fumbled for money inside his tunic pocket.

"Now that's where you're wrong, mate," Jack replaced the lid on the jar. "Buy a jar and take it back to the barracks. When the other blokes see you using it, they'll want some. You can charge them sixpence a dab. Five dabs and you've got yer money back. Ten dabs and you're on hundred per cent profit."

The three men walked away, each carrying two jars of Brilliantshine. Jack held out one of the half-crowns to Bert and told him, "Time for one of Nellie's bacon sandwiches and some strong hot tea, Bert. I've got a feeling we're going to do well today."

"So have I, Jack . . . so have I." Bert tossed the coin into the air and hurried towards the café whistling the tune of "Keep Young and Beautiful.'

Jack perched himself on an empty orange box and casually observed the people before him. They strolled past the stalls just as they had always done. You wouldn't think there was a war on, Jack thought, then remembered the thousands of men who were, at that very moment, escaping with their lives across the English Channel.

Bert approached the stall, arms laden with refreshments. "Nellie put fried bread in the sandwiches, Jack. And I've put some sauce on for yer."

Jack bit into his bacon and fried bread sandwich and said, "I wish I could've joined up, Bert. Kill a few bleddy Jerries . . . do my bit for the country."

"Can't all join up, Jack. And anyway, we've joined the A.R.P. . . . somebody's got to look after things here." Bert sipped tea noisily and added, "If it gets nasty here we'll come in handy. I feel as though I'm doing my bit, now I'm an air-raid warden. Women and kids'll need looking after if there's an air-raid. Hey, did you know they've brought in the death penalty, for anybody they catch burglarin' during an air-raid?" Bert shook his mug and tea-leaves showered down onto the dusty ground, looking like stationary ants.

Jack wiped grease from the side of his mouth with the back of his hand. "I'd shoot the boggers on sight."

"I'm with you there, Jack."

More people milled round the front of the stall and Jack saw his chance to make money. "Just had a load of hair-cream in, lads."

He bent nearer and lowered his voice. "Nobody here's a copper, are they? Or a German spy? If Hitler gets to know about the secret formula in my hair-cream he'll want some for his moustache."

The crowd laughed and waited expectantly.

"Show 'em then, Jack," Bert played his part, "hair-cream as used by George Raft and Clark Gable. Only a few jars left. Straight off the black market, so keep it under your hats."

"If it's hair-cream, that's where it will be," chipped in a wag, "how much yer doin' us for then?" He pushed forward. "Let's have a dekko."

Jack held out a jar and said, "Half a crown and that includes the jar." The crowd laughed and edged nearer the stall. Jack lifted the jar higher. "It's got hair restorer in as well. You'll grow hair just like Doctor Jekyll if you rub some of this on yer heads."

"I'll have a jar," called a man with a moustache, "it'll keep me moustache from drooping in me soup."

"Blimey . . . I'm surprised you've been able to grow a moustache under that big konk," Bert grinned at him, "it's a bit shady under there, mate."

"You know what they say about men with big noses," the man quipped back, "and it's true an' all."

"No," Bert answered him, "that's men with big feet."

"Ey . . . your missis must get frustrated, mate," said the man with the big nose to Bert, "you've only got a button for a nose."

"It's not what you've got, it's what you do with it," Bert kept the banter going for the enjoyment of the crowd.

"Blimey . . . you've got a good memory, mate," the man with the moustache looked round at the crowd and grinned. "He can remember right back to nineteen twenty." More laughter from the crowd.

"Right, you lot," Jack butted in, "who wants a jar then? Come on, gels . . . you'd better hurry up, I haven't got many jars left. Treat the lads to this luxurious hair-cream. You'll think you've got Rudolph Valentino in bed at side of you if your bloke plonks this on his head . . . back from the dead to do his tango, gels."

"I'll have a jar."

"Can I have one for me dad? He's got a lovely 'ead of 'air."

"I'll have one for me old man. He put lard on his head last week and kept slipping off the piller."

"Give us a jar, duck . . . I love George Raft."

66

"I'll have one . . . my mester's got a load of hair that sticks up all over the place when he's washed it."

"Saps your strength," the wag joined in again. "Too much hair takes all the strength away from somewhere else."

"Samson had plenty," Bert stepped forward, "past his shoulders it was and all curly."

"Ah . . . and looked what happened to him." The wag rolled his eyes and looked round at the crowd. "Delilah made a monkey out of him."

"That's because he didn't have none of this hair-cream to rub on his head." Jack wrapped another jar in a sheet of newspaper and popped more money into his pocket. "No more left. That's it now. Come back next week and I might have some more then."

People still hovered in front of the stall — women bought plates, pudding-basins, and chamber-pots with pretty cottages painted on the inside.

There was a brief respite in trading. Jack lit a Woodbine and handed the packet to Bert. They leaned against the stall and puffed quietly on their cigarettes. Jack thought once again about how unreal everything seemed. People acting out the part of normality and pretending everything was the same as it had always been; the sun showering them with warmth: the same sun that was shining down into the boats in the English Channel, warming the hearts of brave men who would now live to fight another day. Jack forced a smile and said, "It's a grand day, Bert . . . marvellous what a bit of sunshine can do."

"Yeah . . . sun's quite hot on me neck, Jack. If I get sunburnt, our Annie'll think I've been to Skeggy for the day instead of working."

"We'll take the barrow out this afternoon, Bert. Shift all that fruit we've got left. If we pitch near the Walter Fountain we should do well. Get all the Woollies crowd."

They planned their business manoeuvres like two tycoons. Jack's spirits lifted as a fat woman offered money for a tea-service and two pudding basins. Not a bad life, he thought, as he tucked a ten-shilling note into his wallet.

TWELVE

"I'm just nipping across to the Oak, Vera." Jack tied his shoe-laces. "Then I'm going to Radford Baths for a game of cards. Bert's on A.R.P. duty tonight. He'll be glad of some company."

"You and your cards," Vera nursed Elizabeth Rose, "don't you go and lose all your money."

"Why don't you nip across to the Oak for a drop of port later on?" Jack put on his trilby and tilted it at a jaunty angle.

"Not tonight, Jack. Elizabeth Rose seems a bit off-colour. Look at her cheeks, how flushed they are."

"You know kids, duck. Up one minute and down the next. But, if you'd rather stay with her." Jack kissed Vera on the cheek and walked towards the door. "Just keep the bed warm, duck, and don't worry about me. If I see any Germans, I'll hit them with me stirrup-pump." He laughed and closed the door behind him.

Jack pushed open the door of the Oak and was immediately encircled with warmth and friendliness.

"Put that light out," Jack called out, "don't you know there's a war on." Laughter reached out to him and the voluptuous shape of Gloria Goodliffe drew him nearer the bar — reminding Jack of an actress on the centre stage — the lights behind the bar framing her youthful beauty and sensuality.

"Usual is it, Jack?" Gloria asked with smiling red mouth. Jack edged nearer and replied, "Yes please, duck." He tried not to stare at the perfectly rounded breasts thrusting out beneath the canary-yellow jumper and instead, concentrated on the rope of pearls which swayed away from her chest each time she bent over the beer pumps.

"You're looking lovely tonight as usual, Gloria." Jack reached for his wallet. "Better have a drink on me . . . keep that bright light burning in yer eyes."

"Better have a good look then, Jack . . . won't be here for much longer." Gloria scooped change from the till and closed the drawer with a flourish. "I'm joing the Land Army."

A few men cheered and held their glasses in the air. Jack drank deeply from his tankard and said, "Ooh, you'll look lovely in a pair of overalls, Gloria. And I can just imagine you rolling about in them there haystacks."

"Rolling who with then, Jack?" Gloria stared straight into Jack's eyes, taunting him with her roguishness, safely ensconced behind the bar. Jack knew she felt safe to flirt and tempt without any fear of commitment to her admirers.

"You want to watch him, Gloria," an old man joined in the fun, "keep an eye on his stirrup-pump. It's his secret weapon."

"That's right, dad," Jack responded to the frivolity. "I can hit my target from twenty feet." More laughter as the men understood his meaning.

The evening, full of generous camaraderie, seemed to Jack to head for closing time with the speed of an express train.

Three soldiers and four airmen, all local lads, had somehow given Jack a feeling of urgency. The realities of war seemed much closer, Jack thought, when servicemen stood drinking at the bar beside you. They too seemed to be experiencing similar feelings — downing pints of Shippos as fast as they could — laughing loudly and flirting with the girls as though it was the last chance they would get to have a good night out.

At closing time Jack edged nearer the bar and beckoned to Gloria. "Got something for you, Gloria . . . can't give it you now . . . I'll wait on Brassey for you. Don't be long, duck. I'll be near the air raid shelter."

Gloria nodded and smiled. "Right you are, Jack." She bustled about washing glasses and emptying ashtrays and flirting with the young servicemen — breasts jutting proudly she played her part well and did her bit for her country.

Jack stepped forward and took hold of Gloria's arm. "Let's nip in here . . . got a key now I'm warden," he steered her towards the air raid shelter, "got benches in . . . we can sit down for a few minutes. Then I'll see you get home safely. Don't want no Jerries taking you prisoner."

They fumbled their way into the shelter and Jack switched on his torch-light.

"Oooh, put that light out," Gloria giggled, her sense of humour heightened by the amount of gin she had consumed earlier.

Jack placed the torch at the end of the bench and sat down. Beer consumed in the Oak had made him light-headed and light-hearted.

"What do you think to these then?" He produced two packets of stockings from his inside jacket pocket and held them in the torchlight's beam.

"Oh, Jack . . . you shouldn't," Gloria sat down beside him and reached out for the stockings, "you do spoil me." The stockings disappeared into her handbag.

Jack moved nearer — alcohol induced bravado made him daring. He placed an arm on her shoulder and edged nearer still. Perfume on her hair and neck made him feel doubly intoxicated. He removed his hat and placed it on the bench together with his gas mask. "I'll miss you when you go in the Land Army, Gloria. I'll miss seeing your smiling face behind the bar." He sighed. "All the best things seem to go from our lives when there's a war on."

"Everything'll soon be back to normal, Jack." She turned to face him and her eyes, half hidden in shadow, held a look of tenderness.

Jack's heart seemed to somersault right over, he could feel it pulsating against his chest. The froth of blond curls and waves made her face look vulnerable and childlike. "You're too beautiful to have to slave in some farm-yard, Gloria. You're like a film-star."

"Ooh, hark at you . . . just like a poet, you are." Gloria giggled and started to sing, 'You ought to be in pictures . . . de dah de dah de dah.' Hey, I wouldn't mind being in pictures. I'd like to do a love scene with Charles Boyer."

"How about doing a love scene with me?" Her body responding to his in the semi-darkness made Jack feel reckless. Like those men he admired so much on the Wall of Death down at the fair. Revving up for that final whirl towards the perimeter — dicing with death and loving every second. Blokes who knew how to get a thrill out of their lives, men who knew how to really live their lives.

Jack kissed Gloria on the lips and she responded eagerly — arms encircling his neck, fingers tugging at the hair in the nape of his neck, she pressed her breasts against his chest and moaned softly.

Jack took a chance and gently explored her breasts with his left hand. The feel of her breasts, warm and yielding, made him want to cry out. A fierce need inside him drove away all feelings of guilt or caution. Everything in his mind now concentrated on one thought — to enter Gloria's wonderful body — experience the ultimate in ecstasy — make his fantasies come alive at last.

Very gently he coaxed her to lie down. Lips seeking her neck he kissed the soft perfumed skin. Never before could Jack remember experiencing such magnetism. His

69

caresses became more urgent, mouth seeking her mouth and his hands no longer gentle, he held her down with the full weight of his body. His hands sought out the warmth of her thighs and the soft wispiness of her knickers.

"Jack! . . . Jack! . . . " Her voice seemed to call to him from far away. Husky and with a trace of fear she repeated his name, "Jack . . . are you listening?"

Jack turned to face her and the quickness of her breathing as she placed her mouth to his ear made him crazy with longing to possess her completely.

"Jack, you'll be careful, won't you?" Her legs moved closer together in a movement of cautiousness. "I don't want to catch for a baby."

Her words filtered through the labyrinth of passionate thoughts and Jack fumbled in his pocket for a packet of french-letters. Momentarily, he felt angry at the intrusion into their love-making but he knew he had to take precautions.

Gloria, once Jack had put on the french-letter, behaved like a wild-cat. Writhing beneath him, she clawed at his neck, pulling him nearer and nearer until he could give her no more. Gasping and moaning, she urged him on-and-on until Jack felt as though his heart would burst.

"Jack . . . oh, Jack . . . it's never been like this before. Never . . . oh, never." She thrust her body upwards to meet his and Jack could hold out no longer. He seemed to be giving up his very life — the emptiness inside him was so intense as his lust flowed out of him into the eager body beneath him.

The night enfolded Jack in its dark quietness. He longed for morning with its clanging milk bottles, barking dogs, clip-clopping horses and laughing, shouting children.

Physical and mental exhaustion gave a heaviness to his footsteps. Shoulders hunched, Jack walked in dreamlike slow motion towards Bentinck Road and only looked up when he had reached St. Michael and All Angels. Sitting down on a wooden form at the side of the church's tiny graveyard he lit a Woodbine then flicked the spent match onto a gravelled path.

He tried to analyse his feelings of profound guilt. What had taken place between Gloria and himself had seemed to pulverise his conscience. Wondering if other men experienced such feelings Jack tried to wash the thoughts from his mind. It's not important, he told himself, since the old bible times men had behaved as he had just done. What harm could possibly come of it! Vera would never find out. He was certain that Gloria would never let on to anyone about their love-making. Why, he smiled to himself, poor old Gloria was probably feeling guiltier than he was, right this minute.

But the churning inside his stomach did not stop, the guilt had taken hold of his guts, like a bulldog with its jaws locked onto somebody's leg.

Jack tried to imagine what Alex would think if he found out what sort of things his dad got up to on the quiet. Jack wanted his lad to be proud of him — an example of how a man should conduct himself — a good provider and someone to respect.

Jack took a last draw on the Woodbine and threw the remainder onto the gravel. He realised how cold the night air had become. Leaving the church behind, he strode towards Dennison Street and, as he did so, promised God that he would never be unfaithful to Vera ever again. It just wasn't worth all the guilt he was feeling. The anguish that rode in on the aftermath of deceit and lustful activities just did not balance the enjoyment, he decided, and thanked his lucky stars that he had taken precautions.

Jack walked up Independent Street still weighed down with his guilty conscience. Avoiding life was sometimes trickier than avoiding death, he mused, as he put the key in the lock of his back-door and thought how nice a cup of tea would taste at that very moment.

THIRTEEN

"I'm getting married, Vera." Jenny's face, radiant with excitement made her look like a schoolgirl, thought Vera. She smiled and listened to the news with wide open eyes then answered, "Married! . . . blimey, Jenny, you don't waste much time . . . not having a baby, are you?"

"Not likely. I'm not that daft," Jenny laughed, "plenty of time for babies after the war's finished."

"Why the rush then? You've only known Reggie since April."

"He's being sent to Portsmouth with his unit at the end of next week. We won't be able to see each other for ages. Reggie says he wants to make sure nobody else gets me while he's away." She looked pleased with herself. "He thinks he could get sent abroad as well . . . with him being attached to the Gordon Highlanders."

"Not much use being married then," Vera looked doubtful, "if he's abroad and you're left here."

"That's partly the reason we decided to get married. If anything happened to him . . . God forbid . . . I'd get a pension."

"Seems a funny reason to get married, for a pension. Are you sure you're not having a baby? You can tell me, I won't be shocked."

"I'm positive, Vera. Mind you, I'm not saying we haven't had a bit of love." Jenny giggled. "If Mrs Cohen knew what went on in her front room after she'd gone to bed she'd have a fit."

"You're a devil, you are." Vera opened a packet of Lincoln-creams and put some on a plate. "It'll be at Shakespeare Street then, the wedding? What are you getting married in? You can have your do here if you like. Invite as many as you want. You won't get a honeymoon . . . not with Reggie being in the Army. May as well have a good do instead."

"We've already had the honeymoon." Jenny bit into a biscuit. "Don't be shocked, Vera. Men like it so much don't they . . . it's the least we can do to keep them happy." She laughed and added, "It's my war effort. I'd make a damn good spy, I would. It's surprising what men tell you when they're trying to get you to give in to them."

71

"Don't you like it very much then, Jenny?" Vera asked shyly, "you know . . . that side of marriage? If you were married?"

"It's all right I suppose. But it all seems to be over so quickly. It's a lot of fuss about nothing if you ask me."

"Yes," Vera nodded agreement, "I suppose you're right."

"Older blokes are best so they say." Jenny's eyes crinkled up with mischief. "Last all night an old bloke can. But who'd fancy an old bloke, not me."

"Nor me, Jenny. Get it over with so's you can get off to sleep."

"I'd rather have a good hot dinner." Jenny stirred sugar into her tea. "A nice plate of steak and kidney and some chips from the chip shop."

"Or some nice sausages from Sandersons and a big dollup of mashed potatoes."

They laughed together — drawn closer by shared secrets.

"Ey up . . . what's going on then?" Jack walked into the kitchen. "Sounds like you two are having a party."

"Soon will be, Jack." Vera nodded towards Jenny. "Your sister's got something to tell you. Go on, Jenny, tell him your news."

"I'm getting married, Jack. Me and Reggie have decided."

"Well I'll be blowed." Jack looked pleased. "A wartime romance right under me very nose."

"We're having the do here, if that's all right, Jack." Vera fetched the kettle from the scullery and added more water to the teapot. "We could do with cheering up. A lively party."

Jack put on his slippers and sat in his armchair. "You're right there, me duck. I've been reading about the war this morning. Bleddy Italians've declared war on us now. No wonder owd Chamberlain resigned. Churchill wants to get cracking and sort this lot out else the war'll go on forever."

Vera handed him a cup of tea and said, "I'll need a new frock, Jack. I've nothing suitable for a wedding."

"Blimey . . . not another one." Jack winked at Jenny. "Thinks I'm made of money you know."

"And I've seen a lovely hat in Trippetts." Vera ignored him. "Only ten shillings and it looks like a model."

"Ten bob for a hat!" Jack pretended to choke on his tea. "I have to sell a lot of fruit off me barrow to earn that much profit. Work like a Trojan, I do . . . so's me missis can look like a film-star."

"Best dressed woman on Independent Street your Vera is, Jack." Jenny egged him on. "Like a peacock you are, when Vera's walking up the street on your arm."

"Women . . . you've always got an answer. I'd better get some extra Shippo's in then. We'll have a real good beano. Take our minds off Herman the German for a bit. Ey up . . . you're not? . . . you haven't got to get married have you?"

"Oh blimey, not another one. No, I'm not having a baby. You've got a one track mind, our Jack. You think everybody's a rum 'un like you."

Jack lit a Woodbine and replied, "If you get a bloke like me you'll get a good 'un. Won't she, Vera? You tell her, duck."

"Yes, he's right. Always been a good provider. And no womanising, not like some of them I could mention." Vera smiled at Jack.

72

Jack grinned and hoped that Vera could not see the guilt behind the grin. "Better let Maisie and Alf know about the wedding." He changed the subject. "And you can treat yourself to that new hat." He picked up Elizabeth Rose and hid his face in her neck. "I'm hen-pecked, I am."

"Happy the bride the sun shines on." Grandad Alf emptied a packet of confetti over Reggie and Jenny. "Here comes the bride . . . dah-dah de-dah," he sang loudly. "You lucky beggar, Reg . . . she's as pretty as a picture." He moved nearer and whispered in Reggie's ear, "I wouldn't mind swapping places with you tonight."

"I heard that." Maisie handed a rolling-pin decorated .with pink satin ribbon to Jenny. "It's all in his mind, love. Like a ship without a sail, Alf is."

"Get off with yer." Grandad Alf chuckled and added, "My rudder's in good working order."

"It might be," Maisie continued, "but it's always anchored down if you ask me."

"Keep still please. Let's have a nice big smile." The photographer bossed them. "Show us yer pearly whites."

"Go and stand across the road." Bert nodded towards the University College which stood in magnificent ancient splendour immediately opposite the Registry office. "Your wedding photos'll look posh if you get the university in the background."

The guests followed Jenny and Reggie across the road — adjusting ties and hats they jostled each other and stood in a friendly line-up waiting to be included on the wedding photographs.

Reggie leaned closer to Jenny and kissed her on the cheek. The look that passed between them held intimate tenderness. Jenny's smile, thought Jack, slightly enviously, came right from inside her somewhere; never before could he remember ever seeing such a genuine expression of love on anyone's face. Oh yes, he smiled to himself now, it was there when Vera smiled at Alex and Elizabeth Rose. But he had never received such a gift from Vera.

"I'm ready for a drop of Shippo's aren't you, Jack?" Bert talked of more real things. "You need a drink after watching another bloke give up his freedom."

Jack wondered what it would be like, married to Gloria Goodliffe. Passion every night and lots of laughs. He began to fantasise about Gloria — her perfumed skin and beautiful breasts.

"Hark at him, Jack." Annie hugged her handbag close to her chest and looked indignant. "It's me that has a life of drudgery. I could have married Albert Simms . . . been a rich woman by now. It's me that gave up the freedom."

Jack forgot about Gloria and joined in the friendly banter. "He's good looking though, Annie. You can't have it all roads."

"Right you are," the photographer lifted his camera from the tripod and began to pack the equipment away, "I'm sure you'll be happy with the results."

Jenny and Reggie led the way back into the city centre, their guests straggled behind them. Carnations proudly displayed in button-holes, hair decorated with confetti, they brightened up the day for all onlookers. Smiles appeared on the faces of passersby and spread with the swiftness of a bushfire.

"Love makes the world go round." Jack took hold of Vera's arm.

"Ah . . . and I'm getting more than my fair share." Vera spoke teasingly from underneath the veil of her new pink satin hat.

"Serves you right for looking like a film-star." Jack looked at her appreciatively. He noticed that the new frock she was wearing showed up the womanly curves of her body. Full breasts cradled in pleated crepe-de-chine and the material hugging the outline of her hips which were plump and rounded — a childbearing legacy.

"I hope they'll be happy," Vera whispered, "they look well suited don't they."

"If they turn out happy as us they'll be all right. I'm happy enough I suppose. Health and strength . . . me own boss and a few bob in me pocket." Jack tried to remember the old days. He wondered if he had felt any happier then. Perhaps he had never been really happy — not completely satisfied with life. He pushed the thoughts away and said loudly, "Look at that blue sky. It's going to be a scorcher. You were right, Vera . . . we'll be able to sit outside."

The wedding party walked down Independent Street singing "There was I waiting at the Church". Jenny and Reggie walked in front, faces happy and smiling, arms locked together in loving intimacy.

"Hitler can go and take a running jump at hisself," Jack said as he walked up the entry. "Nobody can put a damper on our Jenny's wedding-day."

"You're right there, Jack," Bert agreed, "we're the bulldog breed, we are. We're not frightened of that little squirt."

"Nice display, Jack," Grandad Alf nodded towards the garden. Roses, snapdragons and marigolds tilted their faces towards the sun and contributed to the happiness of the occasion with their show of beauty.

"I'm going to grow more vegetables at the bottom there," Jack pointed to the garden, "what we don't eat I can sell on the barrow."

The wedding guests stood in the backyard. Sunshine warmed them on the outside — port warmed them on the inside.

"Hope you've got the bridal suite ready, Mrs Cohen."

"Stitched the sheets up have you, Mrs Cohen?"

"Hope you haven't got woodworm in the bedroom floor, duck . . . they'll fall right through if you have."

"Or the bed-posts. They have to be strong, bed-posts do."

"Need any help tonight, Reggie?"

"Ignore them, Reggie. Fancy a nice ham sandwich, duck?"

"I know what he does fancy and it isn't a ham sandwich."

"I've gotta joke for yer." Grandad Alf held his glass out for a refill and continued, "There was this bloke yer see and he was talking to his neighbour. This bloke said, my wife won't let me have a bit of love. She says she's gone off it and we've only been married a year."

"Oooh," everyone shouted at once, "the poor bloke."

"Well now," Grandad Alf continued, "I'll tell you what to do with her then. Buy her a big box of chocolates, one with a ribbon on. Get her to have a bath in some nice bath crystals. Then pat her all over with talcum powder and get her to wear a nightgown that's all silky, and whatnot." Grandad Alf paused and had another drink. "Then put some nice dance music on the wireless. And then. . . and then. What, what said the bloke, what shall I do then? Grandad Alf paused once again and then said, "Then . . . send for me."

Everyone laughed with Grandad Alf laughing the loudest. Glasses were held up for refills and Vera and Maisie handed round sausages-on-sticks, ham sandwiches and slices of pork-pie.

It was going to be a good day from beginning to end, Jack observed happily. One of those 'extra specials' that you store away in the back of your mind — unwrap and examine until it fades away forever like a cobweb disintegrating or a snowman melting. Jack bit into a piece of pork-pie then drank deeply from his tankard of Shippo's mild. He felt swamped with good sensations. The way he felt whenever he looked at Gloria Goodliffe.

"Jack . . . Jack . . . you were miles away." Vera put her hand on his shoulder. "Penny for your thoughts."

"Just thinking about Jenny and Reggie," he lied. "Shame there's a war on."

"Not even a war can stop people falling in love, Jack."

"Who'd like to hear a song?" Bert undid the buttons on his jacket and breathed in deeply. "How about this one?" He tilted his head and looked at the sky.

"There'll always be an England, while there's a country lane."

Bert sang the song through once and then everyone joined in. Their voices soared into the air and into the hearts of anyone who could hear.

"Good health and happiness, Jenny and Reg."

"God bless you both."

"Good luck and plenty of laughs."

"May all your troubles have dummies in their mouths."

The wedding guests crowded around the smiling couple — they reached out as though wanting to touch the happiness — take away some of the magic with them — share the joy as though it was their right to have a piece.

People always want a part of you, thought Jack, as he leaned against the backyard gate and watched. 'No man is an island' he recalled the poetry of John Donne, 'Don't ask for whom the bell tolls — it tolls for thee.' Only this time it's wedding bells. Jack finished his drink and walked over to the table for a refill. Only this time it would have been, if there hadn't been a bleddy war on.

"My turn to sing a song." Jack stood with feet apart and head held high.

"Land of hope and glory . . . mother of the free."

Everyone joined in the song. Linking arms they swayed from side-to-side and sang out loudly. People who had been passing by the entry drifted slowly towards the frivolity, curiosity moving their feet nearer to the singing.

"Land of hope and glory . . . mother of the free."

Jack conducted the singing with a tablespoon, arms waving frantically he led them towards a magnificent crescendo.

"God who made thee mighty . . . make thee mightier still."

One by one people departed, like actors in a play, leaving the centre stage to the two main players — Jenny and Reggie standing together in the spotlight.

Evening embraced the setting sun, a whispering breeze made curtains wave from half-open windows and old ladies sitting on doorsteps in Independent Street wrapped flowered pinafores up over their arms and tried to stay awake.

"It's been a lovely day, Jack. Just how a wedding should be. Shared with family and friends." Vera pulled a hairnet over her curls and snuggled down into the bedclothes.

Jack pressed himself closer and kissed Vera's cheek. "I'm feeling ever so loving, Vera. Can I have a bit of love?"

"I'm ever so tired, Jack. I've never stopped all day. I ache all over."

"All right . . . go to sleep then, duck. I'll just hold you." They fell asleep simultaneously, bodies entwined in intimate closeness and escaped into private dreams which would divide them by miles.

FOURTEEN

Vera knew something was wrong the minute she heard the coughing. Continuous barking like a dog with a piece of bone fast in its throat the noise pierced the quiet of early morning slumbers.

Vera retraced in her mind the past few days. Alex with a temperature and off his food. Chesty cough which had persisted despite dosing him with cough-stuff.

Vera's stomach churned with anxiety. Whooping-cough! She allowed the dreaded words a space inside her mind. Alex had whooping-cough she was sure now. Her mother instinct took over.

Down the stairs, across to the sideboard, sorting through insurance books, old comics and cookery books. Vera thumbed through the Medical Encyclopedia. 'Whooping Cough' — the germs are spread through the air. There is a severe attack of coughing which the child is unable to control; the face may become blue and finally, the breath is drawn in with a crowing sound. There is also vomiting. Ideally the child should be isolated until the cough has gone; but the most infectious period of the disease is the early stage before the "whoop" develops.'

Too late — it was too late! Vera stared at the book. Terror made the words on the page merge together. 'Ideally the child should be isolated.' Vera moaned softly to herself. Elizabeth Rose was sure to be infected. Alex had already started to 'whoop'. Perhaps there was still a chance for Elizabeth Rose! She rushed over to the cupboard at the side of the fireplace. Then she took out a pink blanket and spread it on the floor. She went into the scullery and took a bottle of Jeyes fluid from the shelf above the copper. She poured half the contents of the bottle into a bucket and added water. The mixture of Jeyes fluid and water swirled itself into a pattern of muddy white, like a pulsating opaque glass window.

Vera took hold of the bucket and bending down scooped the disinfectant up with her hands and splashed the blanket all over with the liquid until the bucket was empty.

Nails were found and a hammer. Vera hurried up the stairs arms laden with soggy blanket which she then nailed to the door of Alex's bedroom.

"What yer doing, Mam? Are you spring cleaning?" Alex called to her.

Vera sat on the bed and stroked Alex's forehead. "You're a bit poorly, my love. But you'll soon be better. You've got a nasty cough and a poorly chest. You'll have to stay in bed for a few days till you get better."

"Can't I come downstairs?"

"Not yet, duck. I'm going to send for the doctor. He'll listen to your chest and tell you when you can get up. And I want you to keep away from our Betty."

"Can I have a comic to read?"

"Course you can. I'll nip across to the paper shop when your dad gets back." Vera squeezed his hands — they felt hot — the clammy feel of sickness.

"Please God . . . don't let my baby catch it," Vera chanted her request to invisible ears. "Don't let Elizabeth Rose catch it. You've took two of my babies . . . don't take my beautiful Elizabeth Rose." Vera poured more Jeyes fluid and water into the bucket and dipping a floorcloth into the mixture she then washed door handles, doors, picture-rails, furniture and, finally, every inch of Elizabeth Rose's pram.

The doctor wrote out a prescription for medicine. "Keep him as warm as you can, Mrs Denbey. Cold air makes the coughing bouts worse. Don't let him exert himself. Just let him take things nice and easy for a while. I'll call and see him again on Friday."

"What about the baby? Do you think she'll catch it, doctor?"

"There is a possibility, I'm afraid. But so far there's no sign of temperature or coughing. We might be lucky. Keep her away from Alex . . . we might get away with it then."

"Thank you, doctor . . . see you Friday then." Vera held the prescription to her chest as though it were a magic cure that would end all her troubles.

"How's that husband of yours getting along?" The doctor smiled and put his spectacles back inside their leather case.

"Oh, he's all right thank you, doctor. Make him wrap up well, I do. Try to make him keep his chest warm. Would you like a drink of tea? It won't take a minute."

"Haven't the time I'm afraid. Got a lot more calls to make. Put a cup out for me on Friday." His kindly smile reassured her.

"Er . . . you don't think I'm daft, do you? . . . hanging the blanket up? They hang blankets up when there's scarlet-fever. I thought it might help."

"I usually find that mother knows best at times like these, Mrs Denbey. You do what you think is best."

Vera searched his face for dishonesty or cynicism and found neither. "Thank you, doctor. We'll see you on Friday then."

"Yes, Friday." He snapped his medical-bag shut and left.

Vera was pulled from sleep straight into a real life nightmare.

"Mam! . . . where are you, Mam!" Alex's voice held fear. "I can't breathe." Loud coughing followed and then came the "whooping" sound.

77

Vera fumbled her way across the landing and switched on Alex's bedroom light. Alex was sitting upright, his face flushed red caused by the strain of coughing.

"Mam . . . I . . . ," again the coughing started and this time Alex began to heave as though about to vomit.

Vera placed the chamber-pot on the bed and said, "Be sick in there if you want to, duck. There then . . . my poor lad. I'm here with you now. I'll stay here with you till you feel better."

More heaving and coughing then Alex vomited into the chamber-pot. More coughing, and again the terrible "whooping" sound. Phlegm hung from his mouth in an obscene string — he grasped at the bedclothes and fought to get air into his lungs.

Vera pulled at the phlegm — it seemed endless — a coil of disgusting germ-filled fibre slowly unwinding itself from somewhere inside Alex's heaving chest. ·

"There, there . . . get it up for your mam then." Vera stroked his hair which was wet with perspiration. She wiped his mouth with a handkerchief and held his hands. "I'll give you some more medicine." She reached for the bottle and spoon.

Jack appeared in the doorway, eyes half closed with sleep, voice trembling with agitation. "Now then, me lad . . . it'll soon be morning. Things are always better when it's light." Jack winked at him and added, "I'll fetch you one of our pillers. Then you can go to sleep propped up. And I'll get you another comic from the paper-shop when they open. We'll see what owd Desperate Dan's getting up to." Jack fetched the pillow then returned to his own bedroom but Vera would not leave Alex alone. Sitting in darkness on a chair at the side of the blackout curtained window she guarded Alex, watching and listening, afraid that he might escape from her the way his two brothers had done; her two sons who had drowned in the Trent one sunny day when she had let them out of her sight for a while. She wished that she could push Alex back inside her womb; keep him there so that *she* could bear the agony of his illness: suffer everything for him and then give birth to him again — a strong healthy lad safe from all harm.

Faint streaks of light trickled from underneath the blackout curtain. Vera pretended it was a good sign; an omen that meant Alex would soon be well again.

Sparrows twittered, working up appetites for breakfasts of grubs and worms. Far away, as though from another world, Vera could hear the faint clip-clop of horse's hooves, milk crates heralded the beginning of a brand new day.

A cup of tea, thought Vera, a nice cup of tea and then I can face anything. She was ready to come out fighting. Like a boxer spurred on by fear. She checked Alex's breathing and crept downstairs to meet the new day.

"I'm dreading tonight, Mam." Vera looked at Maisie and sighed. "He couldn't get his breath last night. It was awful to hear him fighting to get his breath."

Maisie nodded sympathetically and answered, "Try burning some sulphur. That's what I used to do. Keep the sulphur burning all night . . . it'll help him to breathe."

The back door opened and Annie appeared holding out a packet of candles. "I've bought these for you. Tallow candles for his chest. Melt them down and spread the warm wax all over his chest. A gipsy told me about them . . . they're ever so good for whooping-cough." Annie placed the candles on the table. "And Bert's sent these." She held out two sticks of barley sugar. "Give him energy, they will, bless him. Can we go up and have a look at him then?"

78

They climbed the stairs in silence and entered Alex's bedroom.

"Hello, duck."

"How are you then, me old china."

Fussing and petting they punched his pillows and tucked in sheets, filling the room with the woman and child bond that appears from nowhere whenever illness strikes.

Alex sucked on barley sugar and basked in the attention they gave him. Vera watched him, her eyes searching his face, her ears measuring his breathing. The corner still had to be turned, she knew that, and felt strong enough to guide him around a thousand corners.

The acrid smell of sulphur, mingled with the animal-fat tang of tallow, permeated through every part of the house.

"Oh, blimey," Jack grimaced, "smells like the fires of hell. Are you sure it'll do him some good?"

"Our Mam and Annie say it will. I'll try anything to help him breathe properly." Vera pressed melted wax against Alex's chest.

"They say tar's good for whooping-cough. If we can get some tar for him to have a sniff at! I'll have a look round tomorrer see if any workmen are digging the road up." Jack felt helpless and angry. He longed to help in some small way to make Alex well again. He struggled for something to say and blurted out, "The Germans have landed on Guernsey. It's not far away you know, me lad. They've only got to send the Jerries over here on some boats and they'll be all over the place. Then you'll see some real fighting. Just like at the pictures."

"Oh, Jack . . . don't frighten him," Vera scalded.

"Will we see Germans coming down Independent Street?" Alex brightened up at the idea, "with real guns and sticking their bayonets in people?"

"Not likely," Jack winked at him, "soon as they land, our blokes'll kill 'em all. Shoot 'em . . . blow 'em up . . . take 'em prisoner."

Jack gnashed his teeth and pretended to bite Vera's neck. "Nobody can beat a bulldog when he bites yer . . . like this." He buried his teeth in Vera's neck and made her fall back onto the bed. "Grrrrrrr . . . grrrrrrr."

Alex started to laugh then the laughter turned to coughing. Louder and louder until the obscene phlegm once again spurted from his gasping open mouth.

"It's all right . . . all right." Vera tried to disguise the fear in her voice. "You get it all up then, there's a good lad." Once again she pulled at the phlegm — frantically pulling at the grotesque string which threatened to choke him to death.

Soon, Alex began to breathe more steadily. The coughing subsided into a gentle crackling inside his chest.

"Not so bad that time," Vera lied, "that means you're getting better. You get some sleep now and I'll sit with you. I'll sit in this chair." She sat in the chair. "I'll be here all night if you want me. I won't budge an inch till morning."

"Shall I read this book to you?" Jack sat on the edge of the bed. "It's Treasure Island . . . you like this one. Owd Peg-leg and his parrot."

"I'd like a story about Hitler." Alex reached for his teddy-bear and then rested his head on the propped up pillows. "I like war stories, Dad."

"Right then." Jack smiled at Vera and winked. "Once-upon-a-time, there was an ugly little boy called Hitler. He lived with his Mam and Aunt Fanny Adams in a great big castle called Frankfurter Fortress. One day he decided to go out into the world and make a big nuisance of himself, so he bought a pound of sausages and some cream cheese, and wrapped them up in a red and white spotted hankie, and started walking towards a place called Hammyburger near Dustitoff."

Alex drifted into sleep with a smile on his face. Vera fussed the flannelette sheet over his chest and prepared herself for a sleepless night filled with watching and listening. "You go back to bed, Jack. I can always catch up with sleep tomorrow afternoon, when you get back from work."

"I'll keep me tabs open then." Jack kissed her forehead. "Call me if you need me. If he gets worse I'll fetch the doctor."

"He's calling in the morning. We'll try not to bother him in the middle of the night."

"Goodnight then, Vera."

"Goodnight, Jack."

Vera glanced at the clock at the side of Alex's bed and wished she could speed up the hands. She closed her eyes and despite her efforts to stay awake soon fell asleep.

Two hours later another coughing-bout 'whooped' into her dreams. Voice soothing, hands comforting, Vera concentrated on medicine, sulphur, tallow and prayers. Someone, somewhere must have heard her, she thought later, because that night Alex turned the corner and did not awaken again until dawn had broken.

Days and nights paraded a variety of happenings and soon, after three weeks had evaporated into thin air, Vera was confident that Elizabeth Rose had escaped infection. Alex returned to school and whooping cough crackled into the background.

More weeks went by and other important events gave everyone something else to worry about.

"Well, Bert . . . Hitler said he was going to bomb London off the map and it looks like he's going to keep his word." Jack polished red apples with a clean dishcloth until they shone like a farmer's cheeks.

"We'll give him some of his own medicine back though, Jack. Our pilots won't let him get away with it." Bert placed a set of scales on top of the barrow, next to a pile of brown paper-bags. "Our lads gave Berlin some hammer a fortnight ago. I still bet yer it'll all be over by Christmas."

"He'll go for the docks, Bert, you'll see. Lord Haw-Haw was on about it on the wireless last night."

Jack pushed the barrow towards Dennison Street and added, "It won't be over by Christmas, mate. Things are getting really bad. Hitler's a bleddy lunatic. He'd kill his own mother if she burnt his dinner."

Jack manoeuvred the barrow up Independent Street and called out, "Apples . . . pears . . . 'ere you are, ducks," he grinned at a group of women who were standing in a gossipy group outside the Methodist church. "Lovely pears . . . juice'll run right down to yer elbows when you take a bite out of these."

"Got owt special, Jack?"

"Any stockings, duck?"

"Got any salmon, Jack? I'd do owt to get me hands on a tin of salmon."

"Yeah . . . Doreen's craving for salmon, Jack. She's expecting again. I used to eat coal when I was having our Freddie."

"Might manage some sardines-in-tomato." Jack winked at them. "I'll be in the Oak later on tonight."

"If he can't manage to get any sardines, you can have our goldfish on a slice of bread, Doreen." Bert pretended to be serious.

"Ooh, you cruel thing," the women hugged shopping baskets to their chests and looked indignant.

"Tonight, gels . . . in the Oak," Jack told them, "might be summat good going on the owd black market."

Jack and Bert continued on their way down to the Walter Fountain. Jack looked all around him and puffed on a Woodbine. The sunshine made him feel good. It was a typical autumn afternoon with just enough breeze. A deep blue sky was adorned with clouds that looked extra white — clouds that reminded Jack of puffed up pillows.

People strolled in the sunshine and occasionally stopped at Jack's barrow to buy. Pears, apples, plums and damsons found their way into people's carrier-bags and mouths. The sunshine had put them in a spending mood.

Later that day Jack removed the tablecloth from the kitchen table and emptied the days takings onto the smooth wooden surface. He switched on the wireless. 'Pip-pip-pip-pip-pip-pip.' "Here is the six o'clock news." The announcer's voice spilled into households like lava from an erupting volcano, terrifying, real and unstoppable. Jack listened with all his concentration and the news made him gasp. Over three hundred long-range bombers, escorted by more than six hundred other planes, had spewed their bombs all over the docks in the east of London. Hitler had kept his word. Jack shook his head and looked at Vera. "Oh, bleddy hell, Vera. The poor boggers."

"There has been considerable damage," continued the newsreader, his matter-of-fact voice cloaking the emotion he must have been feeling.

"Huh . . . considerable damage. I'll bet there has." Jack looked at the assortment of pennies, sixpences, shillings and threepenny-bits which were still spread out on the table. "We'll have a celebration tonight, Vera." Jack forced a smile and winked at Vera. "Get dolled-up and I'll take you to the Oak . . . we'll have a right beano."

"What are we celebrating then, Jack?"

"That we're alive, duck. That a good enough reason for yer?" He sorted the coins into heaps, lines of worry still creasing his forehead.

He thought that whilst he had been enjoying the sunshine outside Woolworths — enjoying the bartering and friendly chit-chat with his customers — other people not all that far away had been blown to smithereens.

Jack felt such hatred for the Germans at that moment he thought his head would burst with the passion of his hatred.

"We'll celebrate being alive," he repeated, then picked up Elizabeth Rose and clasped her to his chest as hard as he dared without hurting her. Elizabeth Rose gurgled her approval and tugged at his hair.

Jack felt panic rising inside his chest — suppose the maniacs brought their bombs over here — what if they bombed Independent Street?

He felt the warmth of Elizabeth Rose's fragile body; smelt the pure perfume of her breath; the sweet scent of talcum powder and soap flakes on her clothes: and he felt as if his heart would break into a thousand pieces.

On and on, the war dragged more people into its debris of wrecked towns and cities. Time marched its army of days and weeks towards Christmas once again — Hitler marched his army of men and officers towards foreign soil.

The people of Radford worried about news bulletins, newspaper reports and food shortages, then rallied round pulling up railings and park benches, anything they could find, for use as scrap to build more aeroplanes.

Vera pricked sausages with a fork then dropped them into a dish of Yorkshire-pudding batter. "Toad-in-the-hole for your tea, Jack. And I've got some potatoes baking in the oven."

"Have you got any saucepans you don't use, duck?" Jack looked up from his *Evening Post*. "It says here the factories are desperate for more scrap for planes. They need more aluminium. Listen to this, Vera. They're asking for car mascots, name plates, hot-plate covers and bathroom fittings. They must think we all live like lords. Bathroom fittings, I ask yer! The only bathroom fitting we've got's the nail on the wall outside, that the bath's hanging on."

"There's your old watering-can, Jack . . . and I've got that old saucepan with the loose handle. We can spare a few coat hangers as well."

"Have a sort round then. Somebody once said we'd fight owd Hitler with knives and forks if we hadn't got owt else." He laughed and put down the newspaper.

"They weren't far out then, Jack." Vera opened the oven-door at the side of the firegrate and checked the baked potatoes. "We've ended up fighting him with coat-hangers and watering-cans."

"Ah . . . he forgot we're the bulldog breed, Vera. You see if I'm not right. If them there bells at Saint Michaels' aren't ringing again at Christmas, I'll eat my hat."

Jack lied about his true thoughts — well, you had to for the sake of the women. It was quite enough him worrying his guts out about the war without frightening Vera to death as well.

FIFTEEN

"Well, I honestly thought it'd all be over by Christmas, Bert." Jack pulled his red and white Forest supporter's scarf tighter around his neck and stamped his feet up and down. "Don't know where the bleddy Jerries keep getting their tanks and aeroplanes from."

"Don't forget they were prepared for war, Jack. Factories were going full blast long before nineteen thirtynine."

"Yeah, you're right. This country's too slow to carry hats. Oh, by the way . . . managed to get some petrol for the lorry last night. Want to come to Stoke with me in the morning? See what we can beg, steal or borrow from the factory."

"Right you are, Jack."

"I could do with a navigator now they've pulled all the signposts up. Don't know whether I'm coming or going. We could end up in Skeggy."

"Or Queer Street, Jack."

"Ah, I've been there already I can tell you."

The children at the Mission Ragged School shouted and shrieked announcing it was playtime. Girls skipped with skipping-ropes and pieces of clothes-line. The boys jostled each other and kicked at stones, their down-at-heel boots scraping 'blakey' studs against the concrete playground surface. The girls chanted rhymes as the skipping-ropes swished over their feet and heads.

"Eva weaver chimney sweeper
Bought a wife and couldn't keep her
Bought another, didn't love her
Up the chimney he did shove her."

"Fancy a sausage sandwich, Jack? I'm dying for a mug of tea."

"Tell Gert to put plenty of sauce on mine."

"En't yer got enough of that, Jack?

"And get me one of them tarts with the icing on."

"Want to keep away from tarts, Jack," Bert called over his shoulder, "bring yer nowt but trouble, tarts do."

"Ada apple, lemon tart
Tell me the name of your sweetheart."

Childish voices filled with exuberant innocence. Jack listened to the laughter and thought, war or no war — that's how it would always be. Life goes on — children go on — we all go on because we have no choice.

"Ada apple, lemon tart
Tell me the name of your sweetheart."

Images of Gloria Goodliffe flitted in and out of Jack's mind. He pictured her eyes sparkling with laughter and her mouth creasing into that bewitching smile — those blonde curls frothing into a golden halo around her head accentuating her womanliness. Jack could imagine what every part of her body looked like.

"Bought another, didn't love her
Up the chimney he did shove her."

A shrill whistle halted the laughter and skipping rhymes. Gloria Goodliffe faded away into yesterday. Jack straightened coffee pots with butterflies on the lids and suddenly, felt very old.

April sprinkled the earth with showers that were gentle as angels' tears. Snowdrops and crocuses pulled earth over their heads, settled down to sleep for another year and made way for daffodils. Like ubiquitous yellow wax, the beauty that had blossomed inside Wordsworth's heart once again carpeted gardens, parks and countryside of England.

Vera listened as the voice of Jack Buchanan sang 'Goodnight Vienna' from the wireless. She sighed contentedly and pearled to the end of the khaki scarf she was knitting as part of her war effort.

"Yoo-hoo . . . it's me-eee!" Jenny closed the door behind her and stood at the side of the sofa.

"Take your coat off then," Vera put down her knitting, "won't take long for the kettle to boil."

Jenny removed her coat, revealing the uniform of waitress. Black dress, white lace collar, black shoes and stockings which always gave her a sombre appearance, Vera thought.

Suddenly, Jenny started to cry, then she gulped out, "I've had a card from Reggie. He's been posted to Glasgow."

"That's not too far away," Vera tried to sound cheerful, "not by train."

"He must have handed the card to somebody at Derby Station last night. The train must have stopped at Derby. The card's got a Derby postmark." Jenny's cheeks caught the overspill of tears. Her face creased into a grimace of misery. "Reggie told me . . . if they move the men quickly, it usually means they're being sent overseas."

"You'll be able to see him soon then? He'll get leave before they send him abroad." Vera tried to comfort her.

"Can't be certain." Jenny's tears overflowed once again. "I miss him ever so much, Vera. I've got a man in a million. I don't know what I'd do if he got killed."

"That's daft talk. He won't get killed." Vera poured tea and offered Jenny a home-made jam tart. "He'll be right as rain, you'll see. How's that job of yours going?" Vera changed the subject, "earning plenty of tips, are you?" She fiddled with the knobs on the wireless. A dance band with an abundance of saxophones accompanied a crooner who sang about 'love in the moonlight'.

Jenny helped herself to another jam tart and said, "It's my night off, Vera. Thought I might go out for a drink with Florence Wilkins. Why don't you come with us? Girls only . . . out on the town for the night. Go on, Vera, I could do with a bit of company, I'm feeling ever so miserable since I got that postcard from Reggie."

"All right then," Vera agreed, "we'll go to Yates's for some of their jungle-juice.

Jack's on warden duty, but I can ask Annie to keep an eye on Alex and Elizabeth Rose. She worships them, you know. Loves them like they were her own kiddies."

"Reggie's boat could be torpedoed." Jenny was still on the track leading to misery. "He could be drowned and I wouldn't know where, or anything. Oh, why do we have to have wars, Vera? People like me and Reggie don't want to kill anybody. I've never even met a German . . . wouldn't know one if I saw one. Why do they want to blow us up and gas us?"

Vera could not think of a reply, but also felt miserable. Good idea we going out for a drink and a laugh or two, she thought, before the Jerries blow us all to smithereens.

"I'm going to wear my bright red coat tonight," she said cheerfully, "and my hat with the big brim and the red cherries on the side."

"Ooh . . . red hat no drawers," laughed Jenny, "you saucy fast cat."

Vera had never thought of herself as being saucy or fast but somehow, because of the uncertainty of the war, she did feel slightly reckless, not quite her usual self.

"I'll be back about eight then." Jenny put on her coat. "Just going to see Florence. Did you know she's been seeing a Polish officer?"

"Yes. I think she's finished with Danny the milkman since he joined up. He wrote to her from India a couple of times but she hasn't heard lately."

"Her officer's ever so handsome. He brought her in the Black Boy for some lunch the other day. He's got a gold tooth." Jenny walked towards the back door. "See you later then, Vera."

"Right, I'll be ready for eight."

Vera cut slices of bread and opened a large can of baked beans ready for teatime.

Elizabeth Rose sneezed and came drowsily out of her afternoon nap. Vera reached for a packet of Farley's rusks. War or no war, she thought, everybody still needs feeding.

Jenny, Florence and Vera walked up Independent Street like three fashion models. High-heeled shoes making a clinkety-clink sound, intermingled with laughter and snatches of conversation, a joyful sound, an ignoring the war sound, they swaggered and posed.

One or two elderly ladies, sitting on chairs in doorways enjoying the quiet and warmth of the April evening nodded, smiled and travelled in their minds on the same destination as the three young women.

"There could be an air raid tonight, gels. Mind how yer go, you lot."

"Watch out for the sailors . . . gel in every port that lot have, me duck."

"Got any Evening in Paris in your handbag, duck? Give us a dab behind me ear-'ole."

"If there's owt going on the black market get us summat, Vera. Them tins of pineapple your Jack got me were beautiful. Just like they'd fell straight off the tree into me mouth."

Jenny dabbed scent on old, hard-of-hearing ears and Vera promised, on Jack's behalf, more tinned fruit.

Up Alfreton Road, past Canning Circus, down Derby Road they reached Long Row at last. The city centre looked like a condensed Piccadilly Circus, Jenny thought, remembering her time spent in London. A continuous flow of humanity. Like wound-up clockwork toys, people young and old, civilians and armed forces, they strolled in companionship in and out of the hotels and pubs.

Vera looked up at the Council House clock. Eight-thirty said the hands on the face, but the chimes kept the time secret, hiding away inside the pulsating mechanism for the duration of the war.

They opened the door at the front of Yates's Wine Lodge and stepped inside. Smiling, flirting servicemen made way reluctantly and eyed the three women up and down appreciatively. Jenny pushed forwards towards the bar, Vera and Florence followed.

"Three schooner sherries, love." Jenny took out her purse and held a ten-shilling note out to the barmaid.

"Please . . . I would like to pay." A handsome face smiled at Jenny. "Please, I would be pleased to buy a drink for such beautiful ladies."

Jenny took a good look at the Polish airman who was so eager to buy them all a drink. Tall, lithe body and film star good looks. Jenny looked at her companions, they smiled and shrugged non-committally. The ten-shilling note found its way back into her purse.

The Polish airman selected a pound note from a wallet bulging with money. Two other airmen smiled and moved nearer.

Jenny whispered, "One each. I like the tall, fair haired one."

"Jenny!" Vera was slightly shocked. "We can't stay with them. Tell them we're married. Let them see our wedding rings."

"I'm not married." Florence smiled and flirted with the airmen. "And Poles are so gentlemanly," she lowered her voice, "and ever so passionate. The things I could tell you about my officer."

"Oh, if Jack could see me now he'd never let me come out with you two again." Vera sipped at her sherry and tried to look ladylike.

"It's only a bit of harmless fun, Vera." Jenny raised her glass to the airmen and said, "Cheerio, lads . . . here's to victory."

"Ooh . . . mind what you're saying," Florence giggled, "they might get the wrong idea if you wish them victory."

Vera looked around her. Everywhere, people talked excitedly as though everything had to be said that evening, before it was too late. Laughter ricocheted from wall to wall as men told jokes to men who needed something to laugh about.

Huge barrels holding sherry, rum, white wine and red wine, stood behind the bar like a row of fat polished skittles. Barrels holding dreams, spilled secrets, weak-willed nights of passion and mind shattering hangovers.

The upstairs balcony was also crammed full with people. From where she was standing Vera could see a large grandfather clock whose stately casement stood at the top of the stairs which led up to the balcony. The pendulum danced slowly from side-to-side, as though mocking the surrounding frivolity. Drink and be merry, thought Vera, time sneaks away with your youth and all the good times.

Music floated down from the balcony. 'Take a pair of Sparkling Eyes' harmonised violin and saxophone to the accompaniment of a piano.

"Ey up, Vera! Come back to us then." Jenny's voice was teasing and extra loud. "You were miles away. Do you want another one in here or shall we walk up to the George?"

"May we accompany you?" The airmen gathered round smiling and nodding, eyes saying we're lonely, homesick, please say yes.

"It's lovely in the George." Florence finished her drink. "Nice and old-fashioned. All the posh people go in the George Hotel."

"What are posh people?" The tall, fair haired airman moved nearer.

"People with plenty of money," Florence answered.

"Good place for us then. We have received pay. We are posh people today." He smiled showing off perfectly shaped teeth. Vera looked for gold teeth but they were all white.

"Come on then, Vera." Jenny took hold of Vera's arm and manoeuvred her towards the door. "You look after me and I'll look after you."

"And I'll look after the nice little sergeant." Florence laughed and added, "Bit of a come down from my officer, but I'm not seeing him again till Sunday."

They walked up Long Row closely followed by the Polish airmen. The evening wore an extra hour of darkness. Unlit gas-lamps hung their lanterned heads in jetless gloom and shop windows guarded the secrets of their night-filled stores.

They reached the front entrance of the George Hotel. A revolving door swizzled round and round, its windows covered with blackout curtaining. The door swirled them into the grandeur of the hotel. Again, a throng of people all behaving the same as the crowds in Yates's, Vera observed, only this time, instead of wooden floors sprinkled with sawdust, there were carpets on the floors and pictures in ornate gold frames decorated the walls. A twinkling glass chandelier hung from the ceiling and waiters dressed like undertakers balanced trays laden with drinks.

One of the waiters gestured to a table which was surrounded by empty chairs. The airmen held out chairs for Vera, Florence and Jenny and ordered drinks from the waiter.

"You are, Vera?" One of the airmen moved his chair nearer. "I am called Stefan. And this is Roman." He gestured towards the fair haired airman. "And this is my cousin, Marek. We are so lucky to be posted to the same Flying School at Hucknall."

Florence leaned towards Marek and said, "This is Jenny.·And this is Vera, my neighbour. And I'm Florence. We're all ever so pleased to meet you. Over here doing your bit . . . to protect us from the Germans." She beamed a smile at them.

"Ah, Florence . . . like the beautiful city." Marek kissed her hand. "A beautiful lady. You are all very beautiful."

"What did I tell you, girls!" Florence patted at her hair and twiddled with an ear-ring. "Very gentlemanly they all are. And ever so romantic. Don't they look handsome in those uniforms? I go weak at the knees when I see a man in a nice uniform."

"Please . . . you speak more slowly, please . . . then we can understand." Stefan looked puzzled. "Our English is er . . . not good."

"It's a lot better than our Polish." Florence giggled and crossed one leg over the other, flirting with her eyes for good measure she basked in the flattery and attention.

The waiter brought their drinks and Stefan proposed a toast. "We drink to three beautiful ladies . . . and thank you for your company."

"Three beautiful ladies," echoed Roman and Marek as they raised their glasses in tribute.

Vera smiled at the airmen and felt a warm glow all over her body. It was very flattering to have such enthusiastic admiration and despite the feelings of guilt that accompanied the warm glow she found herself being drawn towards the attentive and good looking Stefan.

Time passed pleasantly and soon it was 'last orders'. People clamoured round the bars to order drinks before 'time' was called, Roman gestured to the waiter and ordered another round of drinks. The noise grew to an alcoholic induced crescendo. Florence and Marek leaned closer and talked easily to one another — using the language of hands and eyes when communication became difficult — Jenny and Roman did likewise.

With Vera and Stefan communication proved more difficult. For some strange reason Vera felt shy of Stefan. His smiles triggered off a strange sensation deep inside her; a blood pounding warning signal as though something dangerous was about to happen.

"I am afraid we must go now." Stefan shrugged his shoulders and addressed Marek and Roman. "The transport will not wait. It is a long walk back to Hucknall, yes!"

"Where's your transport waiting then?" Florence looked at the clock behind the bar. "What time does it leave?"

"We have to be outside the Theatre Royal at ten thirty."

"We'll walk with you then. We have to go that way." Florence slipped the strap of her gas mask case over her shoulder, Vera and Jenny did likewise. They downed the remainder of their drinks and at ten-fifteen the revolving door tipped them out into the dark street once more.

Florence and Marek walked arm in arm, Jenny and Roman followed behind them with Vera and Stefan close behind.

Stefan did not attempt to hold Vera's arm but instead, left a considerable gap between them. To Vera, this felt more intimate, the shyness between them seemed to bring them much closer than touching would have done, she felt. An invisible bond had materialised between them during their brief meeting. Vera had never experienced such feelings and she felt afraid of them.

They reached the Theatre Royal and approached the waiting lorries. Other Polish airmen stood around in groups, laughing, joking and smoking cigarettes.

The dark night covered many secrets. Roman gave Jenny a quick kiss on the cheek, but Marek and Florence embraced and kissed each other on the mouth.

Motor engines on the lorries rumbled to life as airmen climbed aboard. Like animated laughing shadows the airmen piled into the dark interiors of the lorries.

Stefan turned to look at Vera and reached for her hand. He leaned forward and very gently kissed her hand then stood to attention and released her hand. "Beautiful lady . . . goodnight."

"Goodnight, Stefan."

"See how lovely the stars are tonight," he whispered.

"Yes . . . a lovely clear April night. The blackout always makes the stars look extra bright."

"You will be my April lady. Always, I will remember tonight."

"Stefan . . . come on, Stefan," voices calling from the lorries, "hey . . . we go without you . . . we leave you behind."

Another moving shadow, like a black panther, silent and stealthy, Stefan climbed aboard the covered lorry which then sped off into the darkness towards Hucknall.

Vera linked arms with Jenny and Florence and felt like a young girl again. She held onto the feeling and told herself it was a once only luxury. Never again must she put herself in the way of such temptation.

"They're coming to Nottingham again in a fortnight," Florence informed them as they passed the cemetery at Canning Circus. "They want us to meet them again in Yates's on the Friday night."

"I'm not meeting them again," Jenny answered her, "not with poor Reggie about to be sent to goodness knows where. I don't mind a bit of harmless fun . . . but you can't keep on meeting the same men. They begin to get ideas."

"Jack'd murder me," Vera said, "I hope nobody knew me in Yates's or the George. If it got back to Jack I was out with some Poles he'd murder me."

"Oh, you haven't done anything wrong, Vera," Florence giggled, "you didn't have time. Ey . . . Marek kissed me ever so passionately. I told you the Poles were passionate. They know how to treat a woman as well, don't they? They make you feel like Ginger Rogers."

They reached the top of Independent Street still arm in arm. An air raid warden stepped from the doorway of a cobbler's shop and said, "Goodnight, gels . . . mind how you go now." He shone his torch on their legs and added, "Goodnight then, duckies. Seen any Germans on your travels?"

"They wouldn't see you for dust if a Jerry appeared," Florence joked with him. "Goodnight, duck."

Vera said goodnight to Jenny and Florence but before she closed the front door she stood for a while and looked up at the sky. She had done wrong, drinking with men in pubs and worse still, the men had been strangers from a foreign country. A Polish airman, who had smiled at her in a special way, kissed her hand and awakened a desire which had been hidden deep inside her — a desire that now refused to go away.

"Had a nice time, Vera?" Annie greeted her. "Kiddies have been as good as gold. Not a peep out of them."

As good as gold, thought Vera, as she put on her nightdress and wondered what it would be like to snuggle down in bed locked inside Stefan's arms.

SIXTEEN

Jack's good mood had sat upon his shoulders all evening — a feeling of elation that had started earlier that day with the journey out to Stoke-on-Trent. A dozen tea-sets, two dozen dinner-plates, two dozen soup-dishes, three dozen pudding-basins, one dozen stew-pots, statues and numerous odds and ends that had made his trip to the factory more than worthwhile.

Jack ordered another pint of mild before 'time' was called. He sipped at the froth then had a good drink — he placed the tankard on a ledge near the door. The new barmaid, Gloria Goodliffe's replacement, shouted 'time gentlemen please' and placed teatowels over the hand-painted beer pumps.

Edna the barmaid was 'fair, fat and forty' with extra curves that bulged in all the wrong places; a kindly, willing woman who listened to troubles and made good heads on pints.

Jack lit a Woodbine and for a second, thought he could see Gloria Goodliffe standing behind the bar, smiling at him through the haze of cigarette smoke. The image disappeared, Jack reached for his tankard and downed the remainder of his drink then he stepped into the quietness of the warm May night.

The moon looked as though someone had set a million bonfires alight on its surface; a huge golden jewel hanging there against a backcloth of deep blue: stars shimmered around the moon but their beauty was inconsequential compared to the magnificent spectacle of the glowing yellow ball.

"Put that light out," an air raid warden's voice called out to an offender, making Jack laugh out aloud at so ludicrous a situation. Why, Jack thought with great amusement, if a Jerry plane came over Nottingham tonight he'd be able to drop his bombs right smack on target. The moon would light his path all the way from Germany.

Jack pushed open the door of the fish and chip shop which stood on the corner of Edinburgh Street, hiding its lights behind blackout curtains, but the delicious aroma of frying chips and fish could not be suppressed.

"Got any fritters, mate? I'll have a couple if you have and two bags of chips, please."

Jack sprinkled salt and vinegar onto his supper then popped a chip into his mouth. The salt tingled against his palate and the vinegar coaxed saliva from his taste buds.

Jack opened the back door and called, "Here you are, Vera, some nice fritters and chips to grease yer lips. Cut a slice of bread, duck." He handed her the supper wrapped in newspaper and went over to the wireless. "I'll find some dance music."

He undid the laces on his shoes and then slipped his feet inside his slippers. "You should see the moon tonight, Vera. It looks like daylight outside."

Vera cut bread and spread it liberally with margarine.

"I've seen it. It's a loonies' moon. Our mam swears something bad always happens when there's a full moon."

"It's a bombers' moon, you mean." Jack fiddled with the knobs on the wireless and dance music drifted into the room.

The good mood still lingered with Jack. A contented stomach, three pints of Shippo's and soothing music on the wireless. He closed his eyes and drifted into sleep.

Vera picked up her knitting and clicked her way to the end of the row in time to the music.

YEEEEEOOOWWWWWWWWWW! . . . YEEEEEOOOWWWWWWWWWW!!
Jack was hurled out of his slumber straight into wide-awake alertness. "Oh blimey! Here we go again. Fetch the kids down, Vera. Better safe than sorry. Don't think the Jerries'll bomb Radford though. If they bomb anything it'll be Rolls Royce at Derby."

"Shall I take them into the shelter again, Jack? Or shall we go down the cellar?" Vera hurried towards the door at the bottom of the stairs. "I think we ought to take them in the shelter. Oh dear, I wish we'd let them be evacuated. We could still let them go into the country." She rushed up the stairs and after a short while returned with Elizabeth Rose wrapped in a blanket and with a bleary eyed Alex clasping a blanket around his shoulders.

The siren stopped its yowling and was soon replaced with the sounds of people calling excitedly to each other.

Jack opened the front door and peered into the street. People scurried about getting nowhere.

"Come on, Dot, never mind about yer curlers. Put yer headscarf over them. If they drop a bomb on Independent Street that'll make your hair curl all right."

"Ooh! . . . I've forgot me gas mask, Fred. I'll have to go back for me gas mask."

"Save us a seat in the shelter, duck. I'm going back to put me knickers on. There's mice in them shelters."

"Bring some more sandbags over here, Harry. Need more sandbags near the entrance to the shelter."

"Don't forget to bring yer matches, Jim, so's we can light the spirit-lamps. I can't stand being in the dark."

"I don't know about spirit-lamps, me duck . . . I could do with some spirits. I'm going to nip back for me bottle of whisky. Bogger the Germans . . . I need a drink."

"I'm going down me cellar. I'll get pneumonia in that damp shelter. I'm not going in that damp shelter."

"You'll get covered in nutty slack, Hilda, if they drop a bomb on yer."

"Have you got your ear-plugs, Mam? You know you can't sleep without your ear-plugs in."

"What? What did you say?"

"Oh, Mam . . . take your ear-plugs out . . . the planes aren't here yet."

Jack went back inside the house and put on his tin hat, shrugged into his warden's jacket and slung his gas mask over his shoulder.

"I want you all inside the shelter." He ushered Vera and the children out of the house and led them down the entry towards the entrance of the shelter. "You'll be all right in there with Florence and Annie. Stay put till you hear the all-clear." He kissed Vera on the mouth and tousled Alex's hair. "Look after your mam, there's a good lad. I'm just going to make sure everybody's out of bed."

Jack walked back up the entry. He strained his ears, tilted his head sideways and listened for the familiar drone of aeroplanes. Silence cradled the sky. Maybe it was a false alarm! Perhaps some daft bogger had started the alarm off by mistake!

Jack pushed the gate open which led into Florence's back yard and knocked on her door.

Florence opened the door and smiled out at him. "Ey up, Jack . . . I was just coming." She was wearing a musquash coat over her nightdress. "I want to look good if there's an invasion." She clutched the fur coat tightly round her and looked up at the sky. "Perhaps they'll parachute loads of Germans down on us tonight." She grinned at Jack. "I see you've got your stirrup-pump at the ready again, Jack."

"Ah . . . and I'll squirt it up your rabbit-skin if you don't hurry up and get in that shelter."

"You're all talk, Jack," she giggled.

Jack pretended to aim the pump up her legs. Florence scurried towards the shelter, squealing and clutching her coat and handbag.

Annie hurried into the entry. Handbag underneath one arm, hot-water bottle underneath the other.

"Bert's on duty at Boden Street Baths tonight, Jack. I've got half a bottle of rum in me handbag for him. I'm just nipping up to the Baths. He's been saving the rum for an emergency."

"You go and get in that shelter," Jack took hold of her arm, "I'll take his rum for him. Give it to me."

"Can't hear any planes yet, Jack. There's plenty of time. And anyway, I want to be with Bert."

"Look here, Annie . . . your Bert'll have his hands full tonight. Can't have you getting in the way."

Ummmmmmmmmmmmm! . . . Ummmmmmmmm! . . . Ummmmmmmmmmmmmm!

Ever so faintly, an aeroplane droned its terrifying approach sound across the sky.

"Give me the rum, Annie." Jack held out his hand. Annie reluctantly handed over the bottle of rum. Jack guided her down the entry and watched until the darkness inside the entrance of the shelter had swallowed her up.

Jack turned to look at the sky and dread churned his stomach. Muffled thudding from anti-aircraft guns heralded the approach of enemy planes. Thud-thud-thud. The guns discharged their ammunition into the skies but the droning still came nearer. Louder and louder.

Ummmmmmmmm! . . . Ummmmmmmmmmm! . . . Ummmmmmmmmm!

Flares floated down from the skies — like slow-motion shooting stars. The planes were now overhead.

Jack remembered what Vera always said about making a wish whenever you saw a shooting star. "Please, God . . . please let them keep going. Don't let them bomb Nottingham."

More flares cascaded down. Jack prayed for a miracle but knew deep down that God would not hear him above all that din.

The moon lit up the way for a line of bomber planes — fearsome dragons that sounded like wasps.

Jack raced from house to house, knocking loudly on doors and shouting, "Is anybody in there? There's an air raid on."

He repeated his message and as more bombers approached his cries grew louder. His knuckles hurt as he wrapped them against unyielding doors.

The streets were emptied of civilians. Air raid wardens and young men volunteers congregated at the entrances to the street shelters and talked in loud voices as if to show they were not afraid.

"God-luv-a-duck! Hark at that lot. Are they Jerry planes? Do you think they're Jerries?"

"They're Jerry planes all right. Sounds like there's bleddy hundreds of 'em."

"Don't worry about it, me lad. They can't aim for toffee. Couldn't hit a shelter at a hundred feet."

"Blast that moon. I feel as though they can see us standing here." A young lad gestured with his fist in the air and shouted, "Come on then, yer bleddy Krauts. Let's have yer, you bastards."

"I'll bet they'll aim for the gun-factory."

"God help us if they hit it then. They'll blow the whole of Nottingham sky high if they hit that lot."

One of the bombers flew in front of the moon — a black shadow floating — leaving a silver vapour trailing across the sky.

Jack stared upwards and watched as more trails of vapour decorated the deep blue of the sky — patterns left behind by camouflaged machines bringing death.

Jack thought of the planes as vampire bats. Dark and sinister with outstretched wings and bombs that would search out blood. The human blood that would gush away amongst the rubble if the obscene bombs found their targets.

The bombers continued on their way across the city. Jack willed them to keep going then felt ashamed as he realised that he was wishing death upon people in other towns.

Incendiaries followed the flares and then the bombs hurtled down. No time for heroism yet, Jack thought, as he dodged inside the street shelter. I'll be no good to anybody with a bomb dropped on me. He looked around the shelter as his eyes grew accustomed to the dim light from the spirit-lamps — people stared back at him — huddled together in communal terror.

Nobody spoke — all their efforts were concentrating on listening to the sounds of the bombs and the planes. The light from the spirit-lamps threw shadows across their faces accentuating their terror.

Anti-aircraft guns discharged more ammunition and the earth vibrated underneath the shelter.

"I don't like it, Mam." A little girl clung to her mother — the mother's arms encircled her in a cradle of protection.

"It's like bonfire-night, Mary. It's only fireworks going off." She started to sing.

"Bonfire-night, stars are bright
Three little angels dressed in white."

The child still remained hidden in her mother's embrace. Jack thought about Vera and knew that she would be embracing Alex and Elizabeth Rose. The garden shelter would protect them all right, he comforted himself with the thought, there was plenty of earth packed down tightly and he and Bert had piled extra sandbags at the front of the shelter.

"Let's have a fag, while they mess about up there." Jack handed out Woodbines and comfort. "Then I'll go and squirt me stirrup-pump about a bit." One or two women giggled.

Jack peered hard at a woman who was sitting hunched up in a corner of the shelter. "How' do, Miss Wrigley. It is Miss Wrigley, isn't it? I didn't know you with yer hair-net on." He teased her and continued, "I heard you sing at the Sunday School anniversary. How about singing something for us now?"

Miss Wrigley did not move from her hunched up position. Jack cleared his throat and began to sing.

> "We push the damper in and we pull the damper out
> And the smoke goes up the chimney just the same.
> De-dah-de-dah-de-dah
> De-dah-de-dah-de-dah
> And the smoke goes up the chimney just the same."

A swishing, whistling sound, getting louder and louder, screeched from above. This was followed by a loud explosion that felt to Jack like an earthquake.

More whistling and swishing followed by more explosions as bombs smashed into the earth.

"Blimey," Jack said loudly, "the Jerries didn't like my singing." He bent down to Miss Wrigley and said, "Come on, Miss Wrigley . . . everybody's terrified. Do something to help. How about giving us Jerusalem? You sang that lovely at the anniversary."

Miss Wrigley stood up — a tall, skinny, past the prime of life spinster dressed in blue woollen dressing-gown and plaid slippers with red pom-poms on the front. She walked to the middle of the shelter and clasped her hands in front of her in the manner of the professional.

> "Last night I lay a' sleeping, there came a dream so fair
> I stood in old Jerusalem, beside the temple there."

Miss Wrigley's glorious contralto voice sang out the words clearly — a true 'gift from the Gods' housed in the gawky frame of the plain spinster.

The whistling and crashing still continued all around them but Miss Wrigley sang out loudly. Now everyone in the shelter joined in.

> "Jerusalem . . . Jerusalem . . . lift up your gates and sing
> Hosanna in the highest, Hosanna to your King."

Louder and louder they sang, as though confident that the singing would save them from the bombs — like a lucky charm all around them. Afraid and yet defiant, they sang out, trying to drown out the awful accompaniment of the crashing bombs.

Miss Wrigley had now taken charge. Conducting the singing, her long slender arms coaxed top notes from voices that had never been there before.

94

"Rule Britannia — Britannia rule the waves,
Britons, never never never, shall be slaves."

Miss Wrigley led them straight from one song into the next and soon, the crashing
and banging outside the shelter became less frequent, the earth beneath them trembled
less and the droning of engines began to fade into a distant hum.

"Come on, lads," Jack walked towards the entrance of the shelter, "let's get cracking
then. Stay where you are, ladies . . . we'll be back in two shakes of a donkey's tail."

Jack and his fellow wardens were not prepared for the scene outside the shelter.
Bombs and incendiaries had started fires all over Nottingham. At the top of
Independent Street three fires were blazing fiercely. Water gushed from fractured
water-pipes and thick black smoke hurled itself around.

Jack and the other wardens, along with the willing young lad volunteers, worked at
top speed throwing sand over fires — stirrup-pumps swishing furiously they sprayed
water over anything aflame no matter how small.

Independent Street had escaped the worst of the bombing, Jack observed gratefully
as he hurled sand over flames and cursed the German pilots, "Bleddy rotten swines.
There's women and kids down here. You lousy lot of bastards!"

"Do you think they'll come back tonight, Jack?" A young lad of about fourteen
handed Jack a sandbag and wiped his nose across the end of his shirt sleeve.

Jack looked at the frightened face and replied, "Not likely, me lad. They'll have a
few of our Spitfires up their arses by now. They'll be bleddy lucky to make it back to
Germany once our lads get stuck in. There'll be more dog-fights up there than at a
bleddy dog-show."

Jack pointed at the sky and stared with smoke sore eyes. He gasped and stared in
horror. It seemed as though the sky had been set alight. A red glow spreading right
across the sky now made a new backcloth for the moon. It looked to Jack as though the
whole world was being swallowed up by flames from Hell.

"I'm going to check that my missis and kids are all right." Jack touched the young
lad on the shoulder. "Keep the home fires burning till I get back." They laughed at the
shared joke.

The entry looked just the same — the shelter was still intact. Jack entered the
shelter and peered into the interior. They were all right. Vera, Alex, Elizabeth Rose,
Annie, Florence and the old couple from next door. Vera was cradling Alex in her
arms, her face close to his face. Elizabeth Rose nestled fast asleep in Florence's arms
— covered by the musquash coat only her face peeping out, she looked like a koala
bear, Jack thought, as his body became less tense, his brain less numb.

Shuffling sideways over to Vera, avoiding treading on feet in the cramped space,
Jack knelt on the ground in front of Vera and stroked her shoulders and arms. No
words would venture outside his mouth — throat dry the words stayed locked inside.
He continued to stroke her shoulders and arms. Vera also remained silent — her eyes
alone conveyed her thoughts.

YEEEEEOWWWWW! . . . YEEEEEOWWWWW! . . . YEEEEEOWWWWWW!
The all-clear siren broke the spell.

"I hope they missed Brassey." Jack addressed everyone. "My lorry's parked on
there. It's all loaded up with pots. If they've broke me pots there'll be a row."

Vera laughed out loud. Bombs had hurtled down all over Nottingham — probably blown hundreds of houses to smithereens and here was Jack worrying about a few pots.

"It'll be a miracle if they're still all right," laughed Annie.

"One miracle's good enough for me, Annie," replied Jack.

"We're still alive . . . there's a miracle for yer, duck. I must go now. See you soon, Vera. Put the kettle on."

Jack left the shelter and walked towards a fire which was leaping into the air from the direction of Dennison Street. He hurried towards the fire to see what he could do to help.

Jack was tired and yet felt strong. The strength that comes with adversity — at the hatred towards an enemy.

Suddenly, as he hurried along, Jack started to cry.

"Cry-baby, cry-baby, cry-baby cry!" The words eclipsed the reasons for his crying. Jack thought back to his schooldays; the upsets of childhood: cruelty of other children. He longed for his mam and dad. Dead for many years and yet, Jack could feel their presence quite plainly. His mam, hands covered with flour and the smell of carbolic soap on her pinafore. Dad, his face black with coal dust from the pit and the aroma of pipe tobacco on his clothes.

Jack turned the corner of Dennison Street, tears still making patterns on his smoke grimed face.

"We need more sandbags over here, mate," he shouted, then gave the fire his full concentration.

The air was heavy with the feeling of death. A grey fog spread a mourning veil over the whole of Nottingham — like a huge black winter cobweb it swirled depression into houses and minds.

The smell of burning rubble, leftovers from once raging fires, gave out its message of destruction and terror. Jack closed the back door and tried to escape from the sadness. Inescapable, the smoke and stench drifted aimlessly yet somehow permanently, a reminder that death was always just around the corner — waiting to take you by the hand into eternity. All it needed was a bomb with your name on it, thought Jack, and then bang, you became another war statistic. Male or female, young or old, bombs had no built-in-discrimination — they gobbled up human life like piranha ripping into wounded flesh.

Jack spread the *Evening Post* out on the kitchen table and sat with head bowed, shoulders hunched.

"It don't say anything about the Co-op bakery in here, Vera."

"Don't suppose they want the Germans to find out how much damage they did last night, Jack." Vera looked over his shoulder.

"All it says is 'and there was quite substantial damage over the East Midlands last night, with raiders and fighters playing hide-and-seek amongst the searchlights' . . . huh, they did a bit more than that." Jack turned the pages of the newspaper and added, "I'm telling you, Vera, there must have been hundreds killed last night. Bert's cousin said the Co-op bakery got a direct hit. The poor blokes on night shift didn't stand a bleddy chance. He reckoned there must have been over fifty people killed at the bakery alone, and there were dozens badly injured."

"What about the Lace Market?" Vera sat down on the sofa. "It went up like a tinder-box. That's what made the sky look blood red."

"Yes, I know. You mark my words, there must have been hundreds killed."

"Have you noticed that peculiar smell, Jack? It's like a mixture of smouldering rubber and wet fog."

"Yes . . . me and Bert were talking about it this morning. You can sense death everywhere you go. I've never noticed the quiet as much as I have today."

"It's like November instead of May. All that misty fog hanging about. I'm frightened, Jack. I've got a feeling of dread inside my stomach. Do you think they'll send more planes tonight? Perhaps we'll all be killed tonight." Fear clutched at clear thinking.

"Try not to think about it, duck." Jack placed his arm around her shoulders. "I tell you what we'll do. Let's invite the neighbours round later on . . . and our Jenny and Mrs Cohen. I'll nip down to Sodom as well and invite your mam and Grandad Alf. I'm not on duty till later. Don't you worry . . . the Jerries won't come back tonight. They'll be too busy trying to find Rolls Royce. We'll have a beano. Plenty of Shippo's and nice bit of Sanderson's pork-pie. And you can make plenty of ham sandwiches and roast beef sandwiches with loads of hot mustard on."

"Oh yes," Vera sighed, "and where am I going to get that lot on our rations?"

"Go and look in that cardboard box down the cellar." Jack took hold of her hands and pulled her from the sofa. "The box marked sugar." He patted her behind. "Then when I get back from warden duty you can show me how pleased you are with me."

Vera went down into the cellar and lifted the lid on the box.

"Jack! Where's this lot from? Not from the Black Boy hotel, is it? Your Jenny hasn't pinched this stuff, has she?"

Jack grinned at her as she returned to the kitchen, arms laden with slices of ham and beef, jars of pickled onions and a large pork-pie.

"They're from No-man's-land, so don't worry your head about it. Just be grateful I've got good contacts on the black market."

"You could tell me, Jack. I wouldn't let on to anybody."

"No, Vera," he grinned mischievously, "the Gestapo might capture you and torture you if they landed here. What you don't know about, you can't give away. They'd put you on the torture-rack till you screamed, stop, stop, I'll tell you where I got the pork-pie from."

"You're . . . you're an incorrigguble rogue, Jack."

"Ha-ha-ha. You can't even say it."

"Well anyway," Vera laughed, "I know what it means and that's what you are, you devil."

"And don't you love it. That's what all the women go for . . . a rogue and a devil. You're lucky, you're married to one."

They laughed together again then Jack had a shave before setting out to tell everyone about the beano.

"Put that light out." There was a knock on the kitchen window. "Can you hear me in there? I said put that light out."

Jack opened the back door to two air-raid wardens.

"Heard you were having a beano, Jack." One of the wardens grinned from underneath his tin hat. "We've just done our shift . . . finished for tonight . . . unless the barmy boggers start dropping bombs again." He held out two quart bottles of Shipstone's mild. "We've brought a bit of something."

"Come in, lads," Jack ushered them inside, "there's standing room only in the ninepennies. Squeeze 'em in, Vera . . . they've brought some Shippo's."

"Floor's good enough for me, duck." One of the men sat on the floor next to Florence's chair. "How' do, Flo. You're looking glamorous tonight. I could do you some good if you'd just say the word."

"You're all right, Flo, don't worry about him. He's left his stirrup-pump outside." His friend joined in.

"He's no use to me then," laughed Florence, "I like a man who can put me fire out."

Everyone joined in the laughter and fun.

"Watch him, Flo," Grandad Alf patted pork-pie crumbs from the front of his pullover and chuckled, "these air-raid warden blokes are like magicians. They've got eyes in the back of their 'eads and they can see in the dark."

"It's all them carrots they give us to eat at the Food Centre." The warden unscrewed the stopper on a quart bottle and poured himself a drink. "And you know what rabbits get up to . . . and they live on carrots." More laughter from everyone as they began to relax in the warm atmosphere of friendship.

"See if you can get Lord Haw-haw on the wireless, Jack." Bert opened a sandwich and spread a generous helping of Colman's mustard onto the ham. He held the end of his nose and mimicked the German broadcaster. "Hello. This is Germany calling . . . Germany calling. Attention . . . attention . . . all you English swinehunds. We are coming to take over all your breweries . . . and cigarette factories."

Jack turned from the wireless and said, "Now then, Bert, remember careless talk costs lives. There might be a German spy hiding under our table."

"Ooh . . . have a look, Jenny. He can teach me how to goose-step." Florence sipped at her port and lemon — cheeks extra pink, eyes sparkling, she sat back in her chair and enjoyed the friendly chatter.

"Shut up a minute," Jack fiddled with the knobs on the wireless, "I think I've got Ambrose and his Orchestra."

The music grew louder as air waves did their magic act and transported a tango into the midst of the laughing revellers.

"Come on 'ere, Maisie," Grandad Alf took Maisie into his arms, "let's show the young 'uns how it's done."

They danced up and down in front of the fireplace.

"Come on, Rudolph Valentino," Annie held her arms out to Bert, "my desert tent is waiting."

The air-raid wardens danced with Jenny and Florence, and Jack coaxed Mrs Cohen gently to her feet. He winked at Vera and said, "You'll have to share me, ladies. Ten cents a dance if you want the next waltz, Vera."

The old couple from next door moved slowly in time to the music. Arms draped around shoulders they nodded, smiled and held on to each other.

Vera moved chairs back and made more room for the dancers.

"My Sammy loved to tango," Mrs Cohen remembered her dead son, "always at the Palais he was . . . wore a carnation in his button-hole . . . the ladies loved to dance with him."

"Bend right back, Mrs Cohen . . . that's it. Who taught you to dance like that, duck? . . . was it George Raft?" Jack tried to make her forget about death. Exaggerating his movements, he stamped his feet, held his back straight and shrugged his shoulders up and down in time to the tango music.

YEEEEEOOOWWWWWWWWW . . . YEEEEEOOOWWWWWWWWWWWWW

"Blimey, the Jerries must have heard about our beano." Jack stopped dancing and took charge immediately. "I don't think they'll bomb us again tonight but we'd better be prepared. Vera, you'd better fetch Alex and Elizabeth Rose." The words were unnecessary, Vera was already rushing towards the bottom of the stairs.

Jack, Bert, Grandad Alf and the two wardens stood in the back yard and looked up at the sky. The moon was still as bright — hanging as though in the middle of a gigantic stage — with searchlights dancing attendance all around — waiting for the chorus of planes that would soon appear on that stage in a macabre formation dance of death and destruction.

Distant thud-thudding from anti-aircraft guns gave out a warning message as enemy planes approached.

Jack listened to the gun-fire and for some strange reason thought about tom-toms. If only it was that simple, he thought, those natives in the middle of their jungle could hide from enemies. They could nip off into the trees and wait till it was safe to go back to their villages. Or they could meet their enemies head on — stick spears into each other and all stand the same chance of living or dying. But this was a different show altogether. Bombs raining down, incendiaries by the thousands, and all you could do was sit inside a shelter and pray the bombs would land in the middle of a field — or in the Trent.

'Ginger-nut fell in the cut, frightened all the fishes
One popped up and swallowed him up
And that's the end of Ginger-nut.'

"Better go down the cellar till we see what's going to happen." Jack opened the cellar door and handed Maisie a spirit lamp. "If things hot up again . . . if they start using us for target practice, we'd better get you all across to the shelters again." Jack ushered everyone towards the cellar steps and added, "Have you all got yer gas masks?"

"Hey, do you want to hear me make a raspberry, Dad?" Alex put on his gas mask and exhaled, making a loud rasping noise through the front of his gas mask.

"That's what we all think to Hitler," laughed Grandad Alf, who then did likewise with great enthusiasm.

Jack left the cellar and went back outside.

Ummmmmmmmmm . . . Ummmmmmmmm . . . Ummmmmmmmmmmmmm. The gut-churning noise of the aeroplane engines seemed to be overhead.

"Looks like they might give us a miss tonight, Jack." One of the wardens stepped out from the side of the entry. As he did so, incendiaries came spinning down, like fire-flies but capable of destroying, in a few hours, houses and buildings which had taken months to build, thought Jack, as he pressed closer to the entry wall.

Swishing, screaming bombs again searched out targets but, unlike the previous night, they seemed to Jack fewer and far between. At last the terrifying hum from the German bombers grew fainter — as though they had flown straight through the moon and got lost somewhere on the other side.

Fires once again licked tongues of flame against sides of buildings but with less outrage and magnitude.

Searchlights still searched for the enemy planes for a while then anti-aircraft gun sights were lowered as operators lit cigarettes and poured tea from flasks.

The night settled down and held its breath in anticipation of more onslaught. One by one fires were extinguished by brave men and boys who worked at full speed with sand and water.

Smoke once again shrouded the city, as though trying to hide the destruction, it billowed up and up pawing at the sky. No amount of smoke could hide the luminosity of the huge yellow moon.

Jack lit a cigarette and leaned for a while against the back-yard gate. He remembered what Vera had said. Something bad always happens when there's a full moon. A loony's moon. A hunter's moon. A bomber's moon. It was a bomber's moon all right.

Jack inhaled cigarette smoke and coughed, the coughing was accompanied by a rattling sound in his chest. "A loony's moon," he repeated to himself aloud, "don't need a moon to tell me that. The whole bleddy world's loony." He smiled and his lips felt stiff. There was no other explanation. Hitler, Mussolini, Goering, why they were all raving loony, every single one of them.

They buried their dead and the hearts and minds of all the people in Nottingham were present at the gravesides. It seemed as though everyone knew of someone who had died.

Curtains were drawn together, blackout blinds were lowered. People blocked out the sun and shut in their grief. Neighbours showed with this simple gesture a united, profound heartache.

Laughter became a stranger in the shops and public houses, children were told not to shout or play games.

"War," Jack said the word out aloud, "such a small word. Raw . . . raw," he said the word backwards. "That's how it makes your insides feel," he looked across at Vera, "As though somebody's sawn right through your insides."

"Jack," Vera spoke softly, "let's say a prayer for all the people who are being buried today."

"All right." Jack closed his eyes and waited.

"God bless all the people from the bakery and all the other poor souls who got killed." Vera's prayers were heartfelt and whispered with sincerity.

Jack listened to the prayers and felt as though all the people who had been killed were also listening. He felt weighted down with their presence and felt guilty somehow that he was still alive.

SEVENTEEN

Jenny kicked off her shoes and sat down on the sofa. She held her hands out in front of the fire and said, "Well at least Reggie's somewhere nice and hot, Vera. It's freezing outside . . . my nose looks like W C Fields's." She held out her arms to Elizabeth Rose. "Come and give me a kiss then."

Elizabeth Rose stood on tiptoe and placed chubby arms around Jenny's neck.

"Have you had another letter then?" Vera took hold of the coal-tongs and poked about in the coal-scuttle. Placing more coal onto the fire she then used the brass poker to coax more flame.

"Yes." Jenny lifted Elizabeth Rose onto her knee. "He's still in Bombay. Not having a bad time of it as far as I can make out. I wish somebody would send me on a cruise to all those foreign lands. Plenty of nice hot sunshine would just do me fine."

Vera looked at Jenny closely and said, "You're missing Reggie very much aren't you."

"Yes, I am." Jenny hid her face in Elizabeth Rose's neck, hiding the intensity of her feelings of loneliness and unhappiness. "Oh, by the way, I've made up my mind about leaving the Black Boy. I've decided to go on munitions after all. I was talking to some girls down Dennison Street. They've got jobs in that factory on Garden Street. They're working as fitters I think they said. Doing work on cylinder blocks or summat like that. I've decided to have a bash . . . do my bit for the war effort."

"It'll be damned hard work, Jenny. A man's work I'd reckon."

"Yes, but the money's good and the factory's right on my door-step. It's shift work . . . ten or twelve hour shifts I think those girls said . . . but if the money's good I don't care. I'll be able to save more money towards new furniture for when me and Reggie get a little house of our own."

"I don't expect you'll be working there very long." Vera poured tea then conjured up some chocolate biscuits. "Surely the war can't last much longer."

"They've all been saying that for two years now." Jenny reached for a biscuit. "Ooh, lovely chocolate ones. Open wide my little duckie." She broke off a piece of biscuit and popped it into Elizabeth Rose's mouth. "Taste more delicious, don't they, when they're black market."

"Yes, I don't know how Jack manages it. People look down their noses at us because they know Jack's on the fiddle . . . but I've never known anybody refuse a pair of stockings or some extra meat."

"Take no notice. As long as you've got enough to keep going. Oh, by the way, I'm meeting one or two of the waitresses tomorrow night. A farewell drink in Yates's. Come with us, Vera. You haven't been out for ages, have you? Annie'll look after the kiddies for you. No need to worry about air raids . . . the Jerries seem to be giving us a miss now."

"All right then, I could do with a change. I'll get dressed up like a dog's dinner and I'll wash me hair. Better put me curlers in." Vera patted at her hair. "I'm having a Eugene perm the week before Christmas. I've joined a Christmas club diddlum at the hairdressers."

They sipped their tea and ate chocolate biscuits — sat quietly for a while and stared at the fire.

"I'll bet it'll seem funny to Reggie . . . having Christmas somewhere hot." Jenny broke the silence first. "There'll be no snow in Bombay," she laughed, "not even a frost or a friendly bit of fog."

"Never mind . . . next Christmas you'll be together again." Vera touched her gently on the shoulder. "In your own little house, buying lots of nice furniture and decorating the house up lovely."

"Yes, I suppose we will," Jenny replied half-heartedly, "next Christmas everything will be back to normal."

Vera saw him immediately the door opened. Standing in the middle of the room, he was leaning against a ledge and sipping whisky.

Jenny's friends were already there. Jenny introduced everyone. Vera smiled at the women but could not look away from him.

He had not seen her. Conversation with companions held his interest. Hands gesticulating he turned slightly and Vera stared at the handsome profile. Her heart catapulted blood more quickly through her body and her mouth felt dry. The room seemed to shrink in size — other people became inconsequential blurs — she could see only him.

Jenny nudged Vera's arm playfully and asked, "Hey, Vera . . . I said, aren't you with us then? Would you like a schooner of sherry or some of Yates's jungle-juice? I'm going to get large ones before the barrels run dry."

"Oh . . . er . . . ," Vera was flustered, "I'll have sherry please."

Jenny bought a round of drinks then she and Vera stood with the three waitresses in a giggling, whispering circle. Huddled together they enjoyed the attention from the servicemen — a cluster of lovely womanhood, well-groomed and smelling of Californian Poppy and Evening in Paris perfume, they drew the men towards them — the men like moths, all eager to chance getting burned on the flames of temptation.

Stefan glanced in their direction and his gaze homed in on Vera. Recognition accentuated the smile on his face, he waved and pushed his way through the crowd.

"Vera . . . you are well I hope." He approached but shyness kept a distance between them. "I have looked for you many times but," he shrugged his shoulders, "but you are never there."

"Don't get out very much, Stefan. There's the children and . . . and I am a married woman you know." She laughed and knew it sounded forced.

"Ah . . . you remembered my name." His smile grew wider.

Vera also smiled and then realised that she and Stefan were being observed with amusement by Jenny and her waitress friends.

"Oh, I'm sorry." Vera blushed and felt like she did sometimes in a dream; the one where she was naked and could not hide. "This is Stefan. He's stationed at Hucknall."

"Ssshhh," Jenny giggled, put her fingers to her lips," you know careless talk costs lives." She raised her voice and added, "Where did you say you were stationed then? Is it Sodom?"

Everyone laughed and one of the waitresses said, "That's what we all say, duck. Sod the lot of 'em."

102

"I do not think I can see any spies here in Yates's." Stefan put his hand very lightly on Vera's arm. "May I buy all lovely ladies drink? Then perhaps my companions and I could come over to talk for a while, yes?"

Vera looked round the room, everything was just the same as before, she observed, like going to the Windsor picture-house and sitting through the same film. The noise and loud conversation; that distinctive smell of beer, spirits and sawdust; the music drifting down from the balcony; the huge grandfather clock at the top of the stairs still ticking their lives away — tick-tock, enjoy yourselves — tick-tock, time is precious.

Another large sherry was thrust into Vera's hand. Because the room was tightly packed with people she could feel the pressure of Stefan's arm against her arm. A tingling, thrilling sensation circulated round her body like an electric shock.

"You are looking very beautiful, lovely lady." Stefan whispered into her ear. "I look for you every times we come to Yates's but always you are missing."

"Have you noticed," Marek addressed everyone and pointed to his arm, "we get promotion, you see. All get promotion . . . now we are important people. Fly in planes and win war . . . kill many German pilots . . . Hitler is more afraid now we take bombs to Germany."

Everyone laughed and raised their glasses in a toast.

"Here's to the Polish Air Force."

"Down with Hitler."

"Up with the planes."

"Bottoms up."

"Here's to Churchill."

Vera nodded and smiled with the rest but still could not look away from Stefan. Immaculate blue uniform, buttons sparkling as they caught the light. Blue shirt neatly pressed and cap worn at a slight angle, accentuating his aristocratic good looks.

"When do you think the war will finish?" Vera spoke slowly and distinctly so that he would understand. "Do you think it will go on much longer?"

Stefan shrugged his shoulders and took a drink of his whisky.

"Now Japanese planes have attacked Pearl Harbour . . . who can say when. Maybe now America has declared war on Japan it will help. But on the other side to look at this . . . I . . . er . . . could be much worse. Many more peoples to be killed." His eyes were pain-filled, lips drawn tightly together with sadness made him look older. "I like for war to be over . . . I like to go back to my beloved Poland. But, in this meantime . . . I fly planes and help Poland that way."

"Have you got a wife back in Poland?" Vera had to know.

"No wife, but what you say?" . . . , he pointed to his wedding-ring finger, . . . "my sweetheart who is called, Anya. With diamond ring to say we will marry one day."

'Take a Pair of Sparkling Eyes', the music drifted down from the balcony.

"Where is your husband this evening?" Stefan smiled at Vera.

"Oh, Jack's on warden duty. I think he enjoys himself on the quiet. Few bottles of beer and a game of cards with the other men." Vera blushed and added, "He did try to join the Forces but didn't pass on medical grounds."

"All war work is important," Stefan said politely, "there must be men to organise . . . to put out fires and to help women and childrens when bombs come."

Vera found his Polish accent delightful. The modulation of his voice showed breeding, she found herself trying to speak correctly when she answered him. She remembered her aitches and did not clip the ends of her words. "Jack was very brave when we had that Blitz last May . . . when all those people were killed."

"War brings out best in peoples and also the worst." Stefan finished the remainder of his drink and passed his glass to Marek for a refill.

"Will you come to this place at Christmas?" Stefan took a cigarette case out of his inside tunic pocket and offered cigarettes to everyone. Vera and Jenny declined but two of the waitresses accepted his offer. He produced a cigarette lighter and holding the blue flame out in front of him lighted their cigarettes first.

A real gentleman, thought Vera and felt flattered. Out of all the other women in the room he preferred *her* company. All his attention was for her and she could not break away from the spell of his captivating charm.

"Will you come to this place at Christmas?" Stefan repeated.

"We'll try but it might be difficult," Jenny answered him, "I'll be doing shift work so I don't know when I'll be able to get out at night."

"We will try to be here at Christmas Eve . . . we try to get pass. We will not bomb Hitler that night." He laughed and showed off his perfectly shaped teeth. "We like to come to Yates's . . . plenty peoples to see."

Everyone decided to stay in Yates's. Tempted by the warmth of temperature and companionship the women sipped at sherry and laughed easily. The Polish airmen soaked up the friendliness of the Nottingham women — relaxed and smiling they leaned against the ledges and spent their pay gladly.

The grandfather clock at the top of the stairs raced to ten o'clock. The trio ended their repertoire with a selection from 'Top Hat' and 'Shall we Dance'.

Vera listened to the music and sang the words inside her head. 'No, no, they can't take that away from me.'

People sipped at drinks and made them last — as though willing the evening to go on forever.

Jenny finished her sherry and asked, "What time have you got to get back to barracks? Time all good little boys were tucked up in bed."

Everyone laughed and one of the waitresses added, "Depends who you're tucked up with, don't it. I'll come and tuck you up anytime."

"Ooh, that's right, gels . . . get them going." A peroxide blonde joined in the conversation. "Come home with me, duck." She grinned at the Polish airmen. "I'm extra good to airmen, I am. My brother's an airman. Come and spend an hour with me, lads. I'll soon make you forget all about owd Hitler and his gang. Two quid to airmen . . . and a bacon sandwich and a nice strong cup of tea after you've done." The blonde prostitute laughed raucously and blew cigarette smoke into the air.

"Behave yourself, Rosie," Jenny answered her, "we saw them first."

"She's just having a bit of fun." The prostitute embarrassed Vera. "Take no notice, Stefan."

"Peoples in oldest profession have lot of fun." Stefan was amused. "In war . . . there is much loneliness, yes. Lots of Polish airmen in England are lonely. You can understand me, yes? Men seek much company of ladies." He shrugged his shoulders and smiled again.

"Time now please, ladies and gentlemen." A fat barman with a body the shape of the wine barrels behind him, draped teatowels over the beer pumps and then clicked open the drawer in one of the ornate brass tills and commenced scooping money into a leather bag.

The night was December chilled. Vera looked up at the sky and shivered. Like Jack Frost etchings, stars shimmered out of the ink black night. The Council House with its war silenced clock stood in ghostly splendour like a stately home that no longer wished to share its treasures with outsiders.

"Goodnight then, gels." The waitresses scurried headlong into blackout oblivion. "Might see yer at Christmas."

Marek took hold of Jenny's arm and guided her towards Market Street. Stefan looked at Vera and said, "We go to transport. Same place as before. I am pleased for you to walk with me to Theatre Royal. We must be ready for ten-thirty. I would like if you would come to transport, Vera."

"Don't go home without me, Vera," Jenny called back over her shoulder. "We'll walk back up Wollaton Street together." Jenny and Marek headed towards the waiting lorries which were once again parked outside the Theatre Royal.

Vera and Stefan followed behind and walked for a while in silence. They crossed over the road and walked past the Theatre Royal.

"This is the Empire Theatre," Vera pointed at the building, "they get ever such good turns on there. I used to go every Friday night before I was married." She pointed into the darkness and added, "The stage-door's up there. That's where we used to queue for autographs."

Stefan peered at the alley leading up to the stage-door.

"We go to look, yes? I am interested in theatre." He ushered Vera up the alley — rows of sand-filled buckets stood on either side and a huge pile of sandbags guarded the entrance to the stage-door.

Stefan stopped and leaned against the wall of the theatre. He pulled Vera towards him — gently but with some urgency.

All at once his mouth found her mouth. Soft warm lips caressing her lips. He whispered endearments, "Beautiful lady, please let me hold your beautiful body. You are so very lovely. My darling, I have thought of this moment for so long." He kissed her neck, ears, forehead and then, as he became more passionate, he kissed her on the mouth again — harder and harder, his breathing becoming more laboured.

Vera entwined her arms around his neck and found herself being carried away by the intensity of her feelings. The handsome Polish airman with his shy nature and perfect manners. Here in her arms, wanting her, needing her. A man isolated by war — away from family and friends — such a man needed friendship and kindness.

Vera knew that she had to keep a hold on her feelings but the nearness of Stefan and the knowledge of how much he needed her sent all common-sense reeling off onto a carousel of abandonment.

"I love you . . . I love you," Stefan pressed against her, "my lovely April lady of the night. My darling . . . oh, my love." He held her so tightly she could hardly breathe.

"I love you, Stefan." Vera kissed him passionately and did not push his hands away when they began to explore her body.

'Beware, beware' a warning voice whispered inside her head. Vera thought of Jack and then images of Alex and Elizabeth Rose flitted in-and-out of her mind. 'But this is wartime, nothing is quite the same', said another voice.

The nearness of Stefan, the magical mixture of the right chemistry between them made it even more difficult for Vera to keep control of her feelings. She tried to blame the sherry for her behaviour but knew that it was a poor excuse — she really longed for Stefan to make love to her; become a part of her, drown with her in waves of ecstasy like lovers did in beautiful poetry where everything was perfection.

Stefan caressed her breasts and whispered over and over again, "I love you, I love you."

The chemistry that had set alight such powerful emotions could not possibly be love, Vera argued with herself. Not on so short an acquaintance. They had fallen in love with the idea of love. The excitement of war — glamour of meeting someone who was interested in you — and for Vera, what it felt like holding another man in her arms besides Jack. She wanted to play with fire without getting burned but if she was not careful the flames would engulf them both.

'Beware, beware' the words echoing inside her head were now so loud she thought she had spoken them out aloud.

"I'm sorry, Stefan," Vera pushed him away and could not look at his face, "I'm sorry, but I can't . . . I just can't. Please believe me, I'm very sorry. I want to, but I just can't."

She heard him sigh; the sigh seemed to be a substitute for words. He sighed again as though trying to gain composure and then he held out his hands to her in a gesture of apology.

"I also am sorry. You can forgive me, yes. Long time I have not hold woman in my arms. My Anya . . . you understand . . . not with me for long time . . . I am sorry, Vera, but I would wish to make love with you, because you are so beautiful."

Vera reached for his outstretched hands and clasped them tightly in her hands then she kissed him on the cheek and said, "We must go now anyway. Your transport will go without you if you don't go now."

Vera leaned against a pillar at the front of the Theatre Royal. One or two cars passed by. Shaded headlights on the cars gave out thin streaks of light and reminded Vera somehow of Hallowe'en, when lights were shone out of the darkness to frighten the timid and candles were placed inside pumpkins to terrify the impressionable. For some inexplicable reason the shaded lights made Vera feel very melancholy.

Stefan turned to smile at her then climbed aboard the lorry. Vera could not see his face properly in the darkness and, all at once, it became very important for her to see his face once again before the lorry sped off into the black night. She rushed forward and called out his name, "Stefan . . . goodnight, Stefan. Don't forget Christmas."

Men already seated inside the lorry mimicked her in a friendly way," Goodnight, Stefan . . . see you soon, Stefan . . . yoo-hoo, Stefan."

Stefan leaned down from the back of the lorry and for a few moments their fingers entwined. "My April lady of the night," he whispered the endearment so that she alone could hear.

The lorry lurched forward the engine choking to life then it headed along Parliament Street. Vera watched until the lorry was no more than a swaying black shadow — at

106

last the shadow faded into nothingness as the night embraced yet another secret to her breast.

Jenny tucked her arm inside Vera's arm as they headed towards Canning Circus.

"Been a good night, hasn't it? Poles are very good company, aren't they? . . . they're so romantic."

"I only hope Jack doesn't find out we've been drinking with airmen, that's all." Vera experienced feelings of guilt and slight panic.

"Why not?" Jenny giggled, "we didn't do anything wrong." She giggled again and added, "Well I didn't . . . I can't answer for you."

"I feel awful," Vera continued, "we *are* both married women. You haven't been married all that long either. Don't you feel guilty when you think about your poor Reggie out there in India somewhere?"

"As I've just said, Vera, we've not done any harm. This is wartime . . . you've got to enjoy yourself a bit else you'd go crackers."

"Those poor Polish airmen looked ever so lonely, didn't they?" Vera answered, "and Stefan was such a gentleman, I've never met anybody like him before."

"All they want is a bit of harmless fun. You've got to realise that the poor blokes are all worrying about getting killed. It's no picnic going up in them planes and not knowing when your number's going to be up."

"No, you're right there, Jenny . . . it must be awful for them." Vera felt better and did not feel so guilty, even though the feel of Stefan's mouth was still on her lips and the memory of his body pressing against her still sent thrills tingling all over her own body.

They reached the top of Mitchell Street and prepared to part company.

"Goodnight then, Vera. Sleep tight, love."

"Goodnight, Jenny. Don't forget to come round for a cup of tea tomorrow."

"Can anybody come then?" An air-raid warden stepped from the doorway of a chemists' shop. He shone his torch on their legs.

"Put that light out," laughed Jenny. "Funny how you lot always shine your torches downwards."

"Oh, that's our training, me duck. Don't want the Jerries to see lights shining down here." The warden still kept the light trained on their legs.

"I can't hear no planes," Vera laughed, "you dirty dog. I'll tell your missis on yer. I know who she is."

Now the warden shone his torchlight on their bodies searching out the shape of their breasts.

"Just checking you've got yer gas masks handy, gels. Wouldn't want yer to get gassed, now would we?"

"I know one thing for sure," laughed Jenny.

"And what's that then, me duck?"

"I bet you've always got your stirrup-pump handy."

"Ah . . . and I can squirt it to order an' all, me duck."

Their laughter echoed down the street and made dents in the darkness.

EIGHTEEN

Jack closed the cellar door with his foot and struggled with a large crate which he set down on the kitchen table.

"I'm not on duty till late, Vera. I'll take you in the Oak tonight. Nice drop of port . . . see Christmas in together. Try and forget about the war for a bit."

"Oh, all right then, Jack. But I'm not going if we can't get somebody to sit with the kiddies. Can't ask Annie, not on Christmas Eve, we can't. I did half promise your Jenny I'd go for a drink with her and some mates from the factory. They're going down to Yates's before they finish up at the Oak."

"We'll ask Mrs Cohen to babysit," Jack grinned at her, "poor old duck won't want to spend Christmas Eve on her own. Getting all upset thinking about that lad of hers who the Germans killed."

"You don't know for sure the Germans killed him."

"He was all right till they put him inside one of them camps. Mrs Cohen said he was perfectly healthy and strong till the Jerries got hold of him. Anyway, we'll ask her round here. She can have a drop of port and listen to the wireless. Then she can have some supper with you and our Jenny. While I'm doing my duty looking out for spies and foreign planes."

"While you're having a game of cards and drinking Shippo's you mean." Vera pulled a face at him.

"Wait till you see what I've got you for Christmas," Jack's cheerful mood reached out to her and coaxed a smile to her face.

"Give us a clue then." Vera hugged him around the waist. "Dozen pairs of silk stockings and a crate of bananas, is it?" She bit his ear playfully and added, "I could just fancy a banana."

Jack patted her behind and said, "You'll get a banana later . . . when I come off duty. Just keep the bed warm and I'll pretend I'm Santa Claus."

"Don't get stuck up the chimney," Vera giggled.

"Right then," Jack picked up the crate from the table, "just going to get rid of this little lot. Me and Bert are going down to the Walter Fountain. Got a few things off the black market to shift . . . and some Christmas wrapping paper and mistletoe . . . make sure there's plenty of kissing going on. Should earn a bob-or-two today." He set the crate down again and took out his wallet. "Get a bottle of White Horse and a couple of bottles of Sandemans." Jack counted pound notes into Vera's hand. "We're rich this week. I made a fair bit on them tins of John West salmon and them tins of fruit."

"You'll end up in Lincoln Prison you will, Jack."

"You can bring me a cake with a file in then." Jack picked up the crate again and walked towards the back door. "See you later then, gorgeous. And make plenty of mince-pies."

The door closed behind him and Vera sat down on the sofa in front of the fire. She thought about Stefan and imagined him waiting for her, watching the door and counting the precious moments that would be ticking the time away.

Elizabeth Rose called out from the bedroom but Vera only half heard, her thoughts were still with Stefan. She tried to imagine what his face looked like and could not picture his features at all. But his voice was easy to capture in her mind. 'My lovely lady, my April lady of the night. Many peoples to be killed.' His soft caressing voice that had succeeded in coaxing such feelings of longing inside her. His Polish accent that somehow made him seem like a little boy — unsure and fumbling for the right words.

She longed to see him again, to take him in her arms and hear him speak words of love that thrilled and delighted her senses. Vera longed to taste, just once, the forbidden fruit that would surely be the sweetest taste of all.

Vera knew that she would not be able to see Stefan that evening. Tears trapped at the back of her eyes felt like bruises. She called to Elizabeth Rose, "Come and have your breakfast," and concentrated on real life. Make-believe was for heroines in novels and film-stars at the Windsor picture house — not for housewives living on Independent Street up to their eyes in food rationing and every other kind of shortage — stand to reason there was a shortage of romance as well.

'Hark the Herald angels sing
Glory to the newborn King.'

Half-past nine and the customers in the Oak had oiled their singing voices with plenty of Shippo's and spirits.

'Peace on earth and mercy mild
God and sinners reconciled.'

The door opened and Jenny, Florence and two of Jenny's factory pals pushed their way through the crowd towards the bar.

"What yer having, gels?" Bert took out his wallet. "Have a Christmas drink with yer Uncle Bert."

"Have they got sherry? We'll all have sherry if they have," Jenny answered him and pushed forward again so that she was standing next to Vera.

'With the Angelic host proclaim
Christ is born in Bethlehem
Hark the Herald angels sing
Glory to the newborn King.'

Jack sang out loudly and turned his attention towards Florence and the young girls from the factory.

Jenny leaned closer to Vera and mouthed something in her ear. Vera's face took on the appearance of a carnival mask — her eyes did not move from Jenny's face — her body went taut and her lips trembled as though she could not release words from inside her mouth.

"I'll have to go and see a man about a dog," said Jack before pushing his way through the crowd towards the gents lavatory.

Jenny spoke louder, "It's a terrible shame, isn't it. Such nice lads, all of them. As I was saying . . . soon as we stepped inside Yates's their pals came up and told us all about it. They recognised me from the other times. Their pals said they lost four planes altogether, in the raid. They were all shot down somewhere over Berlin, they said. It's a terrible shame . . . it made me feel awful when they told me . . . I felt as though they were part of our family or something. Well you do, don't you . . . when they're such nice lads . . . and so young . . . all under thirty . . . the rotten war . . . it's such a shame."

So Stefan was dead! Once again Vera tried to remember what he had looked like but still the image of his face would not materialise inside her mind. She could imagine the uniform; the sparkling buttons on the uniform; his cap with the badge; the smell of him — that manly mixture of hair cream, shaving soap and faint whiff of whisky and cigarette smoke.

'More peoples to be killed.' Vera tried to recall the sound of his voice — lock the sound away inside her mind so that she could play it like a gramophone record over and over whenever she wanted to recapture the time they had spent together. 'In war, there is much loneliness, yes.'

'Good King Wenceslas looked out
On the Feast of Stephen
When the snow lay round about
Deep and crisp and even.'

The customers sang out loudly, the spirit of Christmas in their hearts as well as their stomachs.

'On the Feast of Stephen,' Vera repeated the name quietly without moving her lips. 'Stephen . . . Stephen . . . Stefan . . . Stefan . . . Stefan.'

The shy, polite young airman, with the gentle blue eyes, had now gone forever. Would never return to his beloved Poland — to Anya the sweetheart who would never become his bride.

"Ey up, Jack . . . look at your Vera getting carried away with the carols." Annie thrust her face in front of Vera's face. "You sentimental thing . . . you're as bad as our Bert. He always cries when they start singing carols."

'Bring me flesh and bring me wine
Bring me pine logs hither
Thou and I shall see him dine
When we bear him thither.'

The lights flashed off and on and the landlord called 'time'.

"Merry Christmas, duck . . . give us a kiss then."

"Merry Christmas, everybody. Ey . . . put us another pint in here, Jim . . . it's only Christmas once a year."

"How about a small whisky in here, Jim? Keep the cold out."

"I wonder what owd Hitler's doing tonight?"

"He'll be doing the goose-step round his Christmas-tree."

"Bleddy maniac . . . somebody ought to cook his bleddy goose."

"War won't last much longer, mate. Where are they going to get their ammunitions from? Stands to reason, they'll run out of ammunition next year. It'll all be over by next Christmas."

"That's right, mate. Here you are, landlord, better fill us all up so's we can drink a toast to peace."

Vera blinked tears from her eyes and placed a smile on her lips. Later, in the secrecy of her bedroom, she would shed tears for the young Polish airman, but for now, she belonged to the living.

Later that night, as Vera turned out her bedside lamp, the tears did not flow as she had imagined they would. Instead, she thought about Anya, wondered what she looked like, how old she was.

Vera felt guilty about Anya, knew she had encouraged Stefan to be unfaithful to her. Vera's had been the last lips that Stefan had kissed and those lips should have been Anya's.

Suddenly, Vera could see Stefan's face quite clearly. The shape of his cheekbones, his smiling mouth and the aristocratic curve of his jaw.

Vera tried to analyse her feelings of guilt but could not work out why she felt more guilty about Anya than she did about being unfaithful to Jack. I would never have actually allowed Stefan to . . . to go all the way, she told herself, not to have actually . . . well, make proper love.

She tried to hold on to the image of his face, and gradually the guilty feelings disappeared as though someone had scrubbed her body clean. Instead, another feeling took hold of her, a deep sadness that seemed to crush her as though the bedclothes had been sewn down on either side so that she could not move; could hardly breathe.

Never again will I be unfaithful to Jack, she told herself, because this is a punishment, retribution for playing with fire. Nobody should feel as bad as this — not for doing what she and Stefan had done — fallen in love for so short a time.

Vera closed her eyes tightly and went readily into the darkness of private dreams and solitary nightmares.

NINETEEN

Jack set his empty barrow down outside Mrs Cohen's house and knocked at the door.

Mrs Cohen beamed a welcome at him and Chamberlain the cat tried to claw his way up the outside of Jack's trousers.

"Have you got that kettle on, Mrs Cohen? I can't spit a tanner . . . me throat's sore from shouting and bawling."

"Come on in, Jack." Mrs Cohen waved her hands in the air and added, "I've just baked a nice big fruit cake. Used up all that dried fruit and the margarine you got for me last week."

111

Jack sniffed loudly and laughed, "Blimey, close the winders, duck. If the neighbours get a whiff at that lot you'll get me arrested."

They laughed together and Jack flopped down on the sofa whilst Mrs Cohen clattered tea-cups and plates in readiness for tea.

"How's our Jenny going on at the factory? Never thought she'd take to owt like that." Jack tickled Chamberlain's head and the cat, encouraged by the attention, leapt into action. He landed on Jack's knee and repaid the kindness with loud purring and a gentle clawing of Jack's knees.

"She's taken to it very well, Jack," Mrs Cohen called from the scullery, "it's hard work and she moans a bit about having to wear overalls and a turban. And she gets covered in grease. But I think she really enjoys herself. She's got Henry the foreman wrapped round her little finger. Earning a good wage too."

Jack started to cough and the sudden spasm shook his body making Chamberlain leap to safety back onto his rug in front of the fireplace. Bubbles of sweat appeared on Jack's forehead and the veins in his neck became more pronounced as they swelled up blue and sinewy against the paleness of his neck.

"Still got that bad cough haven't you, Jack." Mrs Cohen looked concerned as Jack continued to cough. "You should go to the doctor."

Jack tried to muffle the coughing by placing a handkerchief over his mouth "Can't seem to get rid of it, Mrs Cohen. It's on me chest."

"You should go to the doctor," Mrs Cohen repeated, "all that standing about in the rain and snow . . . you're always getting wet through. Get some medicine and shift it off your chest. Don't want you catching pneumonia." Mrs Cohen poured tea and then poked vigorously at the already roaring fire with the brass poker.

Jack removed the handkerchief from his mouth and Mrs Cohen stared at the patch of bright red which had soaked a corner of the handkerchief.

"You're coughing up blood, Jack. How long has that been going on? Have you told Vera? Does Vera know?"

"No need to worry her . . . and no need to worry you. I'm all right except for feeling tired all the time. It's all that card playing I do when I'm on warden duty. I reckon I'd have been a lot better off in the forces. Much easier riding across the desert in a tank then pushing me barrow up Wollaton Street." He laughed and changed the subject. "Did you hear the latest about Elizabeth Rose? She got hold of the black-lead brush again . . . brushed black-lead into her hair and all over the wallpaper at the bottom of the stairs. She's getting to be a right little devil."

"You go and see the doctor tonight, Jack" Mrs Cohen would not waver from her advice. "Coughing up blood's nothing to laugh at."

Chamberlain leapt onto the sofa and rubbed against Jack's arm as though endorsing Mrs Cohen's advice.

"But you can't shove me into hospital, doctor," Jack fastened the buttons on his shirt, "I've got a wife and two young 'uns to support. And who'll look after me stall? I've got to keep going. Just give me some medicine and I'll be all right. Can't you give me something to clear up the lung without bunging me away inside Newstead?"

"Now I want you to listen very carefully, Jack." The doctor leaned back against his chair and interlocking his fingers placed them on his chest. "If the lung doesn't get

112

treatment straight away . . . and plenty of rest . . . your other lung could become infected and then you'll die. What use will you be to your family then, eh? Not much, will you. The report from Forest Dene showed a large patch on your left lung. You must go to bed and have complete rest . . . it's very serious, Jack."

"But the hospital's miles away. Nearly at Mansfield it is. You might as well send me to China, doctor."

"Your wife can visit at the week-ends. But they don't allow young children in the wards. Plenty of buses pass right by the hospital gates, so don't worry about your wife getting to see you. If you do as you're told and get plenty of rest you could be cured and back home again in about a year."

"A year, a year," Jack's voice grew louder, "I can't be away from home for a year! What am I going to tell, Vera? She's a right worrier, you know, doctor. Since our lads drowned in the Trent she's never been quite the same. I have to watch her very carefully. She can't manage without me for a year."

"She'll manage perfectly, I'm quite certain of that. She would worry a lot more if you didn't seek treatment. You're a very sick man, Jack . . . you must go to hospital right away."

"All right then," Jack said reluctantly and then added, "they send all them posh folks to Switzerland, don't they? How about sending me there? I wouldn't mind a holiday in the Alps. I could practice me yodelling, up there in the mountains."

"You can do all the yodelling you want out at Newstead, Jack." The doctor smiled and sat back in his chair again. "Now off you go. Pack your toothbrush and pyjamas and I'll arrange everything for you."

"What about Vera and the young 'uns? Do you think they could have caught the TB from me? Will you want to check them?"

"Yes . . . all in good time, Jack. Leave that to me." The doctor picked up the telephone and dialled. "Hello . . ah, Sister James. About that bed for Mr Denbey. Yes, that's right, Mr Jack Denbey. I believe Forest Dene telephoned you earlier. Yes, I have the patient with me now. Yes, he can be admitted right away. Thank you, Sister . . . keeping well, are you?" He winked at Jack and added, "Oh, I'm very sorry to hear that. Your knee still giving you a lot of pain then, is it?" Well, take care of yourself . . . and I know you'll take good care of my patient. Thank you again, goodbye for now."

The doctor chuckled and said to Jack, "Bit of a dragon, but a splendid nurse. Keep on the right side of Sister James and you'll be all right."

"What happens if I don't?" Jack asked mischievously.

"Plenty of enemas and cod-liver oil, I shouldn't wonder." The doctor also laughed and added, "So you've been warned, Jack. Plenty of rest and do as you're told."

Vera listened to the words but they seemed to echo inside her head — as though someone was shouting inside a cave. Jenny looked real enough, sitting in the armchair, waving the piece of paper but somehow, to Vera, she seemed unreal. Like a character in a play, mouthing the words because they had been written down to be said out aloud.

"He's dead! . . . I know he's dead . . . they've killed him. I'll never see him again. He's dead, isn't he, Vera? You know he's dead. They say missing, but they know he's dead."

Jenny thrust the telegram from her and putting her arms across her breasts rocked up-and-down as though seeking consolation from the self-hugging, trying to squeeze the pain from her chest and exorcise the horror from her mind.

Vera stared at the telegram. 'MISSING BELIEVED KILLED'. Reggie, just an ordinary lad from down The Meadows. Vera thought about what his short life had meant. A likeable young man who would leave hardly any impression on the world at all. He was nothing more than a memory. Someone who would only live on in the hearts of a few people who had loved him.

Vera could not bring herself to say anything. The tragedy of the situation made her feel so weak she could only stare out of the window. There was nothing to be said. Weak rays of February sunshine tiptoed round the room and then alighted on the dark brown ringlets surrounding Elizabeth Rose's lovely face. Vera reached out and picking up Elizabeth Rose placed her onto Jenny's lap.

"Show your Aunty Jenny how you've coloured that picture." Vera held out the colouring book.

Yellow ducks, pink chickens and purple pigs smiled from the pages.

"The Japs have killed him. It was the Japs."

"Show Aunty Jenny the chuckie-hens."

"There," Elizabeth Rose pointed to the hens, "chuckie-hens."

"He's dead and I'll never see him again. It's just not fair."

"Show Aunty Jenny the moo-cows."

"Moo-cows, Aunty Jenny." Elizabeth Rose pointed to cows that had big, sad brown eyes.

"Yes . . . moo-cows." Jenny stroked Elizabeth Rose's hair. "I feel as though I'm going to die, Vera. I can't get my breath. I'm sure I'm going to die."

"You won't die, Jenny. Something inside you does, but you'll carry on. You'll keep on going because you have no choice."

Vera thought about her boys — floating, floating to the bottom of the Trent — lifeless bodies that would torment her forever.

"Are you going in to work today, love? I would if I were you. It'll help to keep your mind off things."

"Baa-lambs." Elizabeth Rose pointed to lambs that gambolled over a bright green meadow. "Will you paint one, Aunty Jenny?"

Vera wished that she could step inside the pages of the colouring book with her children and close the covers. Protect them and herself from all the misery and heartache; the inheritance of war. But instead, she filled the kettle with water, put more coal on the fire and continued the ritual of living.

How futile everything seemed, Vera thought, the more you struggled to live a normal life the more abnormal it became. Jack in the TB hospital; Reggie killed in some God-forsaken place the other side of the world; air raids, food shortages, blackout restrictions and gas masks. There was only one answer, Vera mused, the whole world was sick with some kind of madness and things were getting worse.

TWENTY

Vera put the parcel down on the small cabinet at the side of Jack's bed then she sat in the chair nearest the french windows.

The end of the bed was hoisted up on wooden blocks so that Jack's feet were higher than his head.

"Well then, Vera . . . what have you all been up to this week?" Jack wriggled about in the bed and tried to get more comfortable. "Getting enough to eat, duck?"

"Oh yes, more than enough, Jack. Your pals down Sneinton Market see to that. Oh, and Bert got hold of some more tinned peaches last Thursday." Vera patted the parcel. "Thought the nurses might like a treat. And there's some stockings. Only a few pairs, so you'll have to ration them out to your favourites. Charge what you like. Bert says five shillings a pair. Some of the barrow-lads have sent you a few bits as well."

"Did you manage to get some fags? I've cadged some from the other blokes so I've got to pay them back."

"Thought you weren't supposed to smoke in here?"

"We're not . . . but the nurses are good gels. Turn a blind eye when we nip to the lavatory for a few gasps. What's the first things they give a bloke when he's been shot? A fag and a mug of strong, sweet tea, that's what."

"But you haven't been shot, Jack, so don't try to come the old soldier with me." Vera tried not to laugh.

Two jolly looking ladies pushed a tea-trolley up the middle of the ward, one nodded and smiled at Jack.

"Good afternoon, Jack. Would you like a nice slice of bread and jam?"

"You know what I'd like . . . I told you yesterday."

The two women giggled and fussed with the tea things.

"Piece of cake, Jack, and two sugars, isn't it? Got to have plenty of energy. Sugar gives you plenty of energy."

"Blimey, I don't know what for. The only exercise I've had is eating and drinking and staring up at the ceiling."

"You're here to rest, Mr Denbey." A nurse approached Jack's bed and stood with arms folded across her breasts. She looked at Vera and added. "I've told him, if he doesn't do as he's told, we'll tie him down."

"I'm like a blooming gipsy, I am." Jack munched on his bread and jam. "They make us sleep with all the winders open. Like sleeping in the middle of a blooming field. I feel like Tarzan . . . out in the middle of a jungle. When I wake up in the morning there's field-mice and rabbits having a dekko at me. A bull tried to get into bed with me the other night when it was raining."

"Don't think you'd find many bulls in the middle of a jungle, Mr Denbey." The nurse smiled at him. "And clean, fresh air is good for your lungs. Make a new man of you we will." The nurse breathed in deeply and stuck out her chest. "He loves being in here, Mrs Denbey. Waited on hand and foot, just like at home." The nurse sniffed snootily and continued down the ward.

"Can you pump me pillers up a bit, duck." Jack wriggled into a sitting position. "Open me parcel, let's have a dekko to see what you've brought." Jack winked at the

115

tea ladies and said, "Give me missis a cup of tea and a bit of cake, gels, and I'll have a look what's going on the black market this week. Might be a tin of salmon."

The women pretended not to be interested but they hovered at the end of Jack's bed, pouring tea for Vera and slipping extra cake onto a plate.

"Ey up, look here," Jack whispered, "if it isn't stockings. What size are you, ladies? No, don't tell me. You'll have to try them on like Cinderella did that shoe. Come on, gels," he held the stockings in the air, "who'll be the first to try them on? I'll help you with your suspenders if you can't manage."

"Ooh, you are awful, Jack."

"Don't know how you put up with him, Mrs Denbey."

Still they hovered, eyes looking longingly at the stockings. Jack handed them both a pair of stockings and said, "Don't let on now . . . careless talk costs lives. No charge to you, gels, but I'll want extra cake tomorrer."

"Oh, bless you, Jack. Don't know what we'd do without you."

"You're a marvel, Jack, I was desperate for some stockings. I've been using graving browning on me legs all week."

"Blimey," Jack chuckled, "if it rains you'll smell like an Irish stew."

Stockings were tucked away inside overall pockets. The tea-trolley trundled on its way again.

"Jack! What are you doing, giving stockings away!" Vera looked annoyed. "We can't live on fresh air, you know."

"No, but I'm supposed to," Jack laughed, "stuck out here in No-man's-land. There's nothing *but* bloody fresh air out here."

Vera took hold of Jack's hand and squeezed his fingers affectionately.

"How are you really feeling though, Jack? I think it's doing you some good being in here. You've put a bit of weight on, I can tell by your face. And you haven't coughed once."

"Yes, I'm feeling tons better. I'm bored stiff mind you. Although the other lads are good blokes. We get plenty of laughs."

Another nurse approached and looked at the chart at the end of Jack's bed.

"Bit of a temperature this morning. I expect he was excited because you were coming to visit, Mrs Denbey." She placed a thermometer inside Jack's mouth and checked the pulse at his wrist.

"How about that for cheek?," Jack mumbled through his teeth, "holding me hand in front of the missis."

"Just you keep quiet, Mr Denbey," the nurse checked the thermometer, "else I'll give you an enema." She laughed and moved on down the ward, shoes squeaking on the polished floor.

"I'm missing you, Jack," Vera continued, "it seems ever so funny sleeping in the big bed all on me own."

"I'm missing you," Jack answered softly, "especially missing having a bit of love. It'd be lovely if you could get into bed with me so's I could hold you. I keep imagining how lovely your body feels when you're in your nightgown. All soft and warm and your lovely breasts pressing against me."

"Ssshh," Vera was embarrassed, "somebody might hear you."

116

"They won't," Jack laughed and looked down the ward, "they're all too busy saying the same as me."

"It'll all be worth it though, Jack, when you're well again."

"Yes, I know, but I'm not used to being so inactive. I like to be out and about, you know that. Look when I worked in the cigarette factory . . . I felt like a rat in a trap. The days drag by in here, it's terrible."

Vera looked out of the french windows, the fresh air drifted clean and pure from the meadows and tree-filled woods.

"Can't believe there's a war going on when you look out there." Vera breathed in deeply. "You can feel the fresh air doing you good."

"I wish you could all live out here instead of bang in the middle of Nottingham. If we lived out here I could get a stall on Mansfield Market. I worry myself to death about the air raids on Nottingham. You'd all be safe out here. The Jerries don't bother to drop bombs on a few cows. I worry they might bomb Nottingham again."

"Well you can just stop worrying," Vera answered him, "we've got plenty of air raid shelters . . . we're as safe as houses."

Jack laughed and answered, "And that's not very safe . . . not if they drop a bomb on them."

"Jack, I've got something to tell you." Vera fidgeted about on her chair. "I've been about a job on munitions. I've got a job working on cylinder-heads with your Jenny. Working on cylinder-heads for Merlin engines. I'm going to do something to help our lads in the RAF. I'll be earning good money, Jack."

"Oh, you are, are you. That's another bomb dropped. And who's going to look after Alex and Elizabeth Rose?"

"Well, I asked Annie and she jumped at the chance. I'll pay her of course, and she said the money would come in handy. Bert can't rake the money in like you can, Jack. Annie's always short of money . . . and you know she worships our Elizabeth Rose."

Jack let go of Vera's hand and hunched down inside the bedclothes.

"It's not a woman's job . . . munitions. A woman's place is at home with her kids."

"Not in wartime, Jack. Things are different in wartime. Don't get yourself worked up. When things get back to normal again . . . when you're back working again, I'll pack it in if you like."

"You're not strong enough to work in a factory. You're just not strong enough. It's man's work . . . munitions."

"Your Jenny manages all right. She loves working on munitions. Your Jenny reckons I'll take to it the same as she did."

"Our Jenny wants to stop interfering. I'm telling you, Vera, I don't think you ought to kill yourself in a factory." Jack hunched down the bed further and resting his head on flattened pillows, stared at the ceiling, showing his disapproval of Vera's plans.

A nurse stood at the end of the ward and rang a hand-bell. Vera kissed Jack on the cheek and said, "Look what else you've got in your parcel. There's some fruit and plenty of books. It's just like Christmas. Nobody'd guess there was a war on, your pals down the market have been more than generous."

"Shan't be able to concentrate on reading, not knowing you're killing yourself working on munitions." Jack would not be placated. "I'm telling you, Vera, you're not strong enough."

117

They parted under a cloud of obstinacy. Like a day that had begun sunny suddenly turning to rain; each one believing that they were in the right.

The bus headed towards Nottingham and was soon passing the gateway which led into Newstead Abbey. Vera sat at the back of the bus, mind filled with the conversation she had had with Jack earlier. She felt tense and a headache was climbing upwards from her neck into the back of her head.

Jack's words echoed inside her head. 'You're not strong enough.' She wondered if Jack might die. Always, there was the dread that he would not get better. There were the stories — people were always full of stories — of how they got you into the TB hospitals and then opened up great holes in your back — snapped ribs and cut pieces of lung away — and people looked like skeletons and could not breathe. 'You're not strong enough', Jack's words returned, 'killing yourself in a munitions factory'.

Vera looked out of the window at the fields on either side of the road. Birds glided and dipped and their outstretched wings reminded her of Stefan. Flying, flying away up into the sky, like aeroplane wings the birds flew towards the sun and then glided downwards again.

Vera remembered Stefan's shy smile and the way his blue eyes had stared into her eyes, sealing a bond of friendship.

'You're not strong enough', again the words of warning. Vera sat back in her seat and thought that she had never felt stronger than she did at that moment. Jack needed her and the boys who flew the planes needed her — and she was ready to give them all she had to give and more.

TWENTY ONE

Music quavering from the loudspeakers competed with the din from clanging, hammering machinery. Men and women, young and not so young, manoeuvred levers and pedals, engrossed, working as though part of a speeded-up dance, they were happy in the team work. Hammering, filing, welding — rivets and screws twisting and turning — faster and faster, making doubly sure everything was sound for the airmen who would eventually fly the planes that would house the huge cylinder heads.

A bell put a stop to the noise and activity. People ran in one direction, pushing and shoving in a friendly tidal wave of overalls, turbans, factory boots and sensible shoes, they made their assault on the canteen.

"Find some chairs, Vera," Jenny's voice rose above the noise, "I'll get the teas and the buns . . . grab two chairs."

"If yer want a bun in the oven, I can help there." A grey-haired podgy man kept pace with Jenny. "Ey up, Jenny . . . how about going to the Victoria Ballroom with me tomorrer night? It's Rube Sunshine and his band. I'll give you a good night out, Jen. Fish and chip supper after, if yer like. Proper sit down supper, with bread and butter and a pot of tea to follow."

"No thanks, Henry." Jenny joined the end of the queue. "I've got to stay in and do me knitting. Khaki scarves for our lads in the Army."

"Do yer good to get out a bit, Jen. Can't stay in moping every night." Henry put his arm round her waist and gave her a squeeze.

"Who says I stay in moping?" Jenny wriggled free.

"A little bird told me. Since you got the, er . . . the bad news about your husband . . . you've been fretting yourself silly. It happens to thousands, Jen . . . you've got to start again. Start enjoying yourself, a young gel like you ought to be enjoying life. How about tomorrer then? I'm a good dancer. Light as a feather, I am, and I know how to spend me money. You'll have a good night with me, I can promise you."

"No thanks, Henry. I've told you, I'm staying in to do some knitting. Two teas and two buns, please." Jenny dismissed him with her back.

"I saw the foreman getting off with you again." Vera bit into her bun with enthusiasm. "Oh, I am hungry. It don't half make you hungry working on munitions. I feel as though I could eat a horse."

"I told Henry I was staying in tomorrer, but I wouldn't mind going out for a drink. If you're game, I'd like to go to Yates's for some jungle-juice."

"Well . . . er . . . Jack wouldn't like it, but we do work hard. A bit of harmless fun never hurt nobody. I'll ask Annie to babysit. Ey, it'll soon be Elizabeth Rose's birthday. She's nearly three. I've asked one of the blokes at Notman's to make me a doll's pram. He's going to use up wood leftovers and scrounge a few bits and bobs. And I've got her a lovely doll."

"Just think, Vera, there's been a war on nearly all her life. Makes you think don't it. The war could go on for years."

"No, you're wrong there. Where are they going to keep getting the ammunition? Can't keep producing guns and planes forever. Mind you, Nottingham's got off light up to now. Makes you wonder whether the Jerries'll have another go at us."

The bell rang once again, the workers sauntered back to benches and machines. Heels dragged and once eager steps switched to slow motion.

"Run rabbit, run rabbit, run, run, run
Don't give the farmer his fun, fun, fun."

The wireless greeted them. Machinery started up and tired war-weary workers snapped to life like supercharged automatons. Down with the levers, up with the levers, turn spanners to the left and wrenches to the right.

"Roll out the barrel, we'll have a barrel of fun."

Voices sang out almost drowning the musical accompaniment from the wireless.

"Now's the time to roll the barrel, 'cause the gang's all here."

Cylinder heads gleamed brighter underneath the splinters of sunlight that pierced through the huge glass roof — monstrous weapons of war that monopolised the scene like pagan idols.

Vera manhandled a box of screws onto the bench then looked round the room. A tingling sensation whispered through the hairs at the back of her neck. Never before had she felt so much a part of everything. An important part of the war effort and she felt quite certain that everyone in the room felt the same way. They were all committed to one cause; the destruction of everything German; nothing could stop the British people now; the bulldog was showing its teeth so they had all better watch out! She remembered something she had read in the newspapers. Hitler had said, 'the British are stubborn'. Huh, he hasn't seen anything yet, she thought, as she prised open the box and reached inside for a handful of screws.

"Now's the time to roll the barrel
'Cause the gang's all here."

Vera sang out loudly and felt prepared to work all day and all night as well if it were required of her.

Jenny felt reckless the minute she took the curlers out of her hair. She felt completely feminine and dainty again. The tough, spanner wielding girl had been discarded, together with the overall and turban and flat, sensible shoes.

The comb teased waves and curls into place and the Drene shampoo she had used earlier fulfilled its promise of giving her hair the look of a film-star's hair. She rolled stockings up over her legs, gently teasing the seams straight, fastening the suspenders carefully. Precious stockings that had to be taken care of and only used for 'Sunday-best' times.

Mrs Cohen looked up from her knitting and nodded happily.

"I'm glad you're going out, Jenny. You've not been the same girl since Reggie . . . since the news came about Reggie. You look lovely, just like Ginger Rogers with your hair done that way."

"I've made up my mind, Mrs Cohen," Jenny knelt down by the sofa and put her hand on Mrs Cohen's arm, "I know I've lost Reggie. I've come to terms with it now. I would have heard something by now if there was a chance he was alive. I know I've got to try and rebuild my life, but I feel as though I can't get going while there's still a war going on. But I work hard at the factory . . . I think I deserve a few laughs now and then. I'm going to enjoy myself a little bit."

"Yes, that's right, you go out and enjoy yourself." Mrs Cohen patted Jenny's head. "Ooh, you smell like a chemist's shop."

"Evening-in-Paris." Jenny stood up. "It'll give the lads summat to think about, sends 'em silly, scent does." She turned her back and asked, "Are me seams straight?"

"Straight as an arrow," Mrs Cohen replied, "and don't forget your gas mask now. And get to a shelter if the sirens go off."

"Yes, and you. No sitting on a stool with Chamberlain on your knee like last time.

120

Just you remember it isn't Guy Fawkes night when they start dropping flares. Nip across to the Mitchell Street shelter if they start. The Smalley family go to that shelter. You'll have a nice sing-song with the Smalleys."

Jenny picked up her handbag and gas mask case. She closed the door behind her and clickety-clacked on her black patent high-heeled shoes up to Independent Street.

"Let's get tiddly tonight." Jenny pushed forwards through the throng. "Plenty of jungle-juice and we'll forget all our troubles."

"All right, I'm game." Vera followed close behind. "I wouldn't mind a packet of crisps as well."

"Ey, steady on, Vera. Where do you think you are, the Ritz?" Jenny held a ten shilling note in the air and attracted the barmaid's attention. "Two large white wines, please."

Women 'dressed to kill' laughed and giggled and made eyes at the men. What a variety of men, Jenny observed. British forces, interspersed with Poles and civilians. All spending money as though they had to get rid of it as quickly as possible.

"My round, Bill. Want a short with your next pint?"

"Drink up there, gels . . . have doubles this time."

"Anybody want a fag?"

"Put them away, Frank. Have one of my cigars. Special black market . . . straight from one of them posh clubs in London."

"They ran out of ale early last night . . . drink up, lads . . . while the going's good."

Clink, clink, clink — forces' pay and factory wages mounted up inside the tills.

Jenny and Vera hurried towards two seats vacated by ATS girls. Jenny nodded towards the balcony and asked, "Shall I go and request a song, Vera? Tell me what you'd like and I'll nip upstairs and ask the trio to play it for you."

"Oh, let me just think a minute." Vera sipped her wine then licked her lips. "Do you like this colour lipstick? It's New Pink by Tangee. If you lick yer lips it makes them look glossy like a film star's lips." She licked her lips again and pouted.

"Hurry up," Jenny stood up, "tell me what you'd like them to play."

"All right then, I'd like 'I only have eyes for you'. Jack likes that one because Ruby Keeler sings it and he likes her."

They sipped their drinks and listened as the violin sobbed 'I only have eyes for you'. Soon, everyone had joined in the song and men and women flirted with each other and pretended to mean every word of the song.

Men gazed into womens' eyes — women gazed back.

Two Polish airmen sitting at the next table to Jenny and Vera did not join in the singing but, smiling and swaying their shoulders in time to the music they stared at the two young women.

The trio played the song again. The singing from the crowd in the vaults swelled upwards towards the balcony and the crowd on the balcony sent it down again.

One of the Polish airmen leaned across the table and said to Jenny, "Very nice . . . you enjoy to sing. I enjoy to sing."

"Oh, that's nice," Jenny looked at Vera and giggled, "he enjoys to sing." She leaned towards Vera and added, "It's that man again. Don't you think he looks a bit like Tommy Handley?"

Vera looked at the smiling officer and answered, "I think he looks more like Cary Grant."

"No he doesn't," Jenny shook her head, "his nose is much broader than Cary Grant's. He looks more like Herbert Marshall."

The trio started to play the opening bars to 'I'm forever blowing bubbles'. The crowd started to sing again, louder and louder.

Jenny smiled at the Polish officer who had spoken to her. He moved his chair closer and Jenny noticed that his eyes were the same colour as Reggie's had been. They also had the same mischievous glint in them; expressive eyes that gave away secret thoughts.

"I'm Jenny . . . this is Vera."

The officers were encouraged and moved nearer.

"I am Stanislaw Kowalski. My friend is Henrik Stolarski."

"Whatski?" Vera grinned at them.

"Ooh, a couple of rumskis," Jenny laughed, "out for a larkski."

"Pardon?" The officers smiled and looked puzzled.

"We'd better call you Laurel and Hardy," Jenny laughed again and finished her drink. Both men reached for her glass.

"Allow me, to please replenish your drink." Stanislaw got there first. "What would you like for drink?"

"Thank you," Jenny smiled at him, "we're drinking white wine. That's jungle-juice straight out of the barrels."

Vera and Jenny retreated to the 'ladies'. Hair was combed and recombed. Noses were dabbed with powder-puffs and lips were made more glossy with further applications of Tangee lipstick.

"Dab some of this behind your ears, Vera." Jenny pulled the rubber stopper from the Evening-in-Paris perfume bottle, "bit of scent gets 'em going."

"I don't want to get anybody going." Vera dabbed perfume behind her ears. "They're nice looking though, aren't they. Did you notice they're officers? They're wearing eagles on their tunics. Don't get many officers in Yates's, do you. Oh, don't they look marvellous in their uniforms. I love those caps and those eagles with the two silver chains hanging down."

"I'll have Stanislaw and you can have Henrik." Jenny checked the seams in her stockings.

"I don't want either." Vera looked flustered. "Not with poor old Jack being stuck out at Newstead. I feel guilty enough as it is, just sitting with them. I'll have a laugh and a joke but that's all."

"Right then," Jenny closed her handbag and adjusted her gas mask strap, "a laugh and a joke it is then. You're a good wife, Vera. Our Jack's a damned lucky man."

Jenny paid extra attention to Stanislaw, and Vera did likewise with Henrik. The officers seemed pleased with the selection.

Conversation was difficult because of the background noise of loud voices and singing but much smiling was indulged in and eye-signalling, with a considerable amount of hand gesturing done for extra emphasis.

Soon, it was closing time. Friends parting, music fading and laughter dying — strangers forming new friendships as the evening ended.

They walked to the end of Long Row. Jenny and Vera stopped walking and hesitated.

"May we see you to your homes?" Henrik was polite and showed concern. "Blackout is not nice for ladies alone."

"We don't live far," Jenny pointed towards Derby Road, "past the Cathedral to the top of the hill and down Alfreton Road and we're home. Me and Vera take care of each other. And anyway, haven't you got to get back to your camp?"

"We have passes," Stanislaw smiled at her and added, "we stay at hotel on Shakespeares Street. You could be guests . . . come to hotel to have drink and sandwich perhaps."

"Time is not late," added Henrik, "nice lounge to sit and talk . . . and ladies can have nice drinks. Then we could take you to your homes safely in blackout. We would be pleased to escort you."

Vera and Jenny looked at each other. The wine had weakened their resistance. Temptation beckoned in the forms of two handsome officers. Vera was the first to back away.

"You go if you like, Jen. But I must get back to the kiddies. No need to see me home," she addressed Henrik, "I'll be all right. You go and have your drink"

"I won't this time either," Jenny moved closer to Vera, "but we could meet you some other time if you like. How about the Palais, next Saturday? Can you get passes for next Saturday?"

"Perhaps we are lucky to see you for dance at Palais. We meet you outside, at what time is convenient?" Stanislaw looked pleased. "Is good to dance . . . nice music and dancing."

"Half past eight then," Jenny decided, "we'll be working till six. That'll give us time to have some tea and get ready."

"Half past eight we see you," agreed Stanislaw.

"All right then. Outside the Palais. It's a date," Jenny smiled at him, "don't be late."

"I'm not going, Jenny. Whatever would Jack say. Somebody's bound to see me. It'd be awful . . . Jack having TB and stuck in the hospital. People'll talk about me if I go dancing at the Palais. You'll have to go on your own. Or else you can ask Florence to go with you."

"People won't talk about you. It's wartime . . . funny things go on in wartime. I daren't go on my own. You'll have to come with me."

"Do you like Stanislaw then? Are you a bit sweet on him?"

"I am a bit. He's very good looking, isn't he. Oh and that uniform . . . they do look marvellous don't they in their uniforms."

"Don't get too keen, Jenny," Vera frowned, "doesn't pay to get too keen."

"Yes, I know . . . but you must admit they are gorgeous. Florence says the Poles are ever so generous. Plenty of money and they spend it like water. Oh, you'll have to come with me to the Palais. You love dancing . . . you'll really enjoy yourself."

"I'll have to think carefully about it. I haven't been to the Palais for ages."

They reached the top of Mitchell Street.

"See you at work tomorrer then. Goodnight, Vera."

"Goodnightski," Vera giggled, "Sleep tightski."

"I wouldn't mind holding Stanislaw tightski," Jenny replied.

They parted company still giggling.

Jenny switched on the kitchen light and was surprised to see Mrs Cohen sitting on the sofa.

"What are you doing, sitting in the dark. Did you nod off to sleep?"

Jenny kicked off her shoes and walked to the front of the sofa. Chamberlain lay across Mrs Cohen's lap — body stretched out — eyes closed and head to one side.

"It's because of the blackout," Mrs Cohen mumbled as Jenny sat down beside her on the sofa.

"What was the blackout? What do you mean, love?"

"Chamberlain." Mrs Cohen stroked the large, handsome tomcat head. "They didn't see him, because of the blackout."

A cold feeling trickled downwards through Jenny's spine. Reaching out she stroked the cat's body, fingers searching, gently exploring, she prayed to hear the familiar purring. Chamberlain did not move — body locked in death he withheld his affection for the first and last time.

"It must have been a car . . . they can't see hand in front of them with those shades on the headlights." Mrs Cohen stroked the magnificent head of her only treasure and a sigh escaped from her broken heart. "I went to look for him when he didn't answer my calls. Somebody had put him in the gutter, on Denman Street. The car must have broken his neck. Can't see much blood . . . only a little around his mouth." She stared at Jenny and said, "I feel just like I've lost a baby. Isn't it silly, Jenny . . . I know he's only a cat, but I feel heartbroken. He loved me you know . . . you could tell he loved me."

"I know he did, love . . . he thought the world of you. And we both loved him, didn't we. He wouldn't feel any pain you know. Not with a broken neck . . . it would all happen ever so quickly."

"I'll have to find a little box to put him in. We'll get somebody to bury him in the back garden."

"Yes, I'll see to that for you. I'll ask one of the men from the factory to see to it." Jenny stood up and added, "Better think about going to bed now. You can't sit there all night." Jenny held out her arms. "Let me have him . . . we can put him on the rug in front of the fire. He liked it there. Give him to me and you get off to bed."

"No," Mrs Cohen looked down at her lap, "I'm going to nurse him for a while. You go to bed. You've got to be up early for work. I'll be all right here. I just want to love him for a while . . . he'd like me to nurse him . . . he loved sitting on my knee."

There was nothing more to be said or done, thought Jenny as she climbed the stairs, we each have to bear our own heartaches. No amount of words or hugs can take away the pain when something terrible happens. Only time with its healing balm of forgetting and forgiving could be of any use. Sorrow stayed for as long as we let it remain.

She pulled the bedclothes over her face and tried to recapture the happiness she had felt earlier and wondered whether it was 'on the cards' that she would encounter the handsome Polish officer once more.

'Then like my dreams they fade and die'. The tune would not leave her brain. All dreams fade and die, she thought, as sleep threw the first blanket of drowsiness over her mind. She thought about Chamberlain again — one moment full of life, leaping off walls, chasing windswept paperbags, scampering up trees — and then suddenly, he was lying in some gutter, a lifeless little bundle of fur.

Jenny decided that from now on she would live her life to the full, just like Chamberlain had done. I'll cram nine lives into one, she smiled to herself, then drew her legs up like a child does and hurried into the land of dreams.

TWENTY TWO

Jenny and Vera walked more slowly as they approached the corner facing the Palais.

"Have a peep, see if they've turned up." Vera held back.

"Yes, they're there," Jenny sounded breathless, "waiting at the bottom of the steps. It's them all right. Don't change your mind. We're only going to have a few dances with them. Oh, I feel ever so excited . . . my heart's all of a flutter."

They approached the steps and smiled shyly at Stanislaw and Henrik. The officers also seemed shy, but their smiles also held genuine delight at seeing Jenny and Vera standing there.

"Good evening . . . so pleased to see you," said Stanislaw.

"Good evening," echoed Henrik.

Both men gave a polite bow.

"Good evening," Jenny and Vera said together, still shy.

Henrik bought four admission tickets. They agreed to meet at the bottom of the stairs after visiting the cloakrooms.

A few minutes later, Vera and Jenny parted company as the officers whirled them round the dance floor to the music of a quick-step.

Stanislaw held Jenny in the polite way, leaving a space between their bodies. His movements were rhythmic and he held his lithe body well, guiding Jenny round the floor with style and skill.

The band was good with a perfect blending of saxophones, trumpets, clarinets and drums. The dance ended then the musicians started up another quick-step and the dancers were away again, whirling, swirling, one-two-three-four-five, 'Heaven, I'm in heaven', crooned the vocalist as he stood at the microphone and looked out over the crowded dance floor.

After a few minutes the music ended with a loud roll on the drums. Dancers left the floor, some staying with the same partners others scattering and searching for new romantic encounters.

"Perhaps you would like to be seated and I will bring drinks." Stanislaw ushered Jenny towards the stairs which led up to the balcony. "You find seats and I will go to bar. What would you care to drink, please?"

"I'll have a gin and orange, please . . . not too much orange." Jenny headed for the balcony and found two seats in the corner near the band. The bandleader raised his arms into the air and the musicians started to play a fox-trot.

Vera and Henrik danced by and Jenny looked on with amusement. Vera was smiling at Henrik and obviously enjoying herself. Jenny felt responsible for Vera's safe-keeping. Vera's friendship meant a lot to Jenny — and she knew she could always trust her — a loyal friend was worth their weight in gold, Jenny thought, as she leaned over the balcony and tried to catch Vera's eye to make her laugh as she danced by.

"I have for you, gin and orange," Stanislaw intruded into her thoughts, "not much orange for your liking."

He sat opposite her, Jenny looked at him and liked what she saw. The intelligence housed in his handsome face made him even more desirable to her. Jenny liked a man she could learn things from. She had a lot to thank her married man in London for, she thought, and then concentrated on looking at Stanislaw once again. She noticed his hair for the first time. Now that he had removed his cap he looked different. Light brown hair growing thick and wavy from a high, broad forehead. Once again Jenny noticed the similarity to Reggie. He too had had thick, wavy, light brown hair and eyes like dark treacle toffee with just a hint of green and overflowing with mischievousness.

"Cheerio," Jenny raised her glass then sipped at her drink, "ooh, I can feel that going down! How many gins are in there, you devil!"

"Nice drink to make you feel good. You will dance on air . . . like fairy in woods." Stanislaw beamed a smile at her and raised his glass. "Cheery-ho," he mimicked her politely, "thank you."

"Cheerio," Jenny repeated then sipped down more gin and orange. "Ooh, it's making me hair curl."

"Your hair is beautiful," Stanislaw answered, "one of things I notice . . . shining hair. I notice colour of sun in your hair. Like straw with fire burning quickly." He leaned across the small table, gently touched her hair and stroked a curl which was nestling over her right ear. "You are most beautiful in room."

"That's what you say to all the girls." Jenny was pleased.

"I say to you only. Is truth for you." Stanislaw sat back in his chair and gazed at her, unashamed of his staring he did not look away from her face for a long time.

"Where do you live then?" Jenny leaned closer, "which part of Poland?"

"I come from most beautiful city. Is called Krakow . . . is in southern Poland. After war I take you to meet family if you wish. You would like to be in Krakow, yes?"

"Hold on a bit. You don't just up and go somewhere. I'll have to ask me dad."

"Pardon?" He was puzzled, did not understand her humour.

"I mean, I hardly know you," Jenny spoke more slowly.

"We could know each other much better . . . if you permit."

"Where are you stationed at?" Jenny changed the subject. "Are you at Hucknall?"

126

"At Swinderby, which is not far."

"It's far enough from here. How do you manage for transport? Do you come into Nottingham by lorry?"

"Sometimes lorry perhaps. We find ways to bring us here." He laughed and added, "Some men have bought bicycles . . . they travel many miles from other camps, Hucknall, Newton, and other places. They find way to see beautiful ladies in Nottingham." He gestured towards the dance floor and added, "Nottingham ladies have reputation for beauty . . . Polish men appreciate such things . . . you understand." He laughed again.

Jenny looked at him and once again experienced the excited feeling she had felt when standing on the corner of Parliament Street looking across the road to where he was standing. She had experienced the feeling many times before when meeting her married man and also, but with less intensity, when meeting Reggie. The thrill trickled slowly down through her breasts — down and down until the familiar tingling began deep inside her stomach — spreading and surging through the most intimate part of her body.

The band played a waltz. Lights were dimmed and the multi-coloured hugh glass globe hanging from the ceiling began to slowly twist and turn. Splinters of light searchlighted down and rested for a second on each face of the waltzing dancers below.

Stanislaw gently pulled Jenny closer. One, two, three, one two, three. The heat from his body made her feel faint. Closer and closer, faces touching, cheeks burning, they danced round the floor oblivious to other dancers.

The eagle pinned to his tunic pressed into her — thrust its way through the delicate satin of her blouse as though it were alive — a real eagle pecking into the soft flesh of her right breast.

The band played another waltz and then another, Stanislaw still held Jenny tightly — almost as though they were part of some exotic love ritual — the dancing an excuse to partake in body exploration in public.

Music drifted into silence and the spell was broken.

"I get more drink . . . if you would please go back to seat." Stanislaw ushered Jenny towards the stairs once again.

"Jenny! . . . Jenny!" Vera waved from the balcony, "two seats up here."

Jenny used the intrusion to try and talk herself into facing reality. She and Stanislaw hardly knew each other. She argued silently with herself, 'you've only met him twice, take care, take care', but she knew deep down that she did not want to go against destiny, fate had thrown two lonely people together, and you couldn't do much about that.

"Are you enjoying yourself, Jenny?" Vera asked.

"Yes, are you?" Jenny replied.

"Henrik's a lovely dancer. Can do all the dances."

"So's Stanislaw. All the twiddly bits when we do corners."

Stanislaw and Henrik returned with more drinks. Drinking and talking they got to know each other a little more.

Time danced away to the beat of the waltzes, quick-steps and fox-trots. The 'last waltz' created a quiet sadness on the dance floor as lovers and casual acquaintances alike held onto each other and swayed underneath the gently whirling glass globe.

Stanislaw held Jenny closer than she had ever danced with any other man. She no longer tried to resist the feeling of longing that persisted since they had first danced together. Eyes closed, arms draped around his neck, she welcomed him into her mind and body and gave out signals that she needed to be loved.

"You come back to hotel?" he whispered into her ear, "we have drink and can talk together, yes?"

"Yes," Jenny answered him, "I'd like that."

"Annie'll be worried if I don't get back home." Vera had made up her mind.

"Just for an hour, Vera. The hotel's only on Shakespeare Street. We can have a couple of gins and a few laughs . . . needn't stay long."

They reached the counter inside the cloakroom and handed over tickets for their coats.

"Sorry, Jenny . . . but I must think about the kids. I've got full responsibility now that Jack's in Newstead. You go and enjoy yourself. You'll be all right with Stanislaw. He looks like a gentleman. He'll walk back home with you no matter how long you stay at the hotel. Henrik's walking me home. I said he could walk with me as far as Canning Circus. Don't want any of the neighbours to see me."

"Nobody'll see you in the blackout."

"I've made my mind up, Jenny. They're very nice blokes though, aren't they. Certainly like to spend their money on us. I've had shorts all night."

"So have I . . . no shortage of shorts here," Jenny laughed.

The lounge of the hotel was already filled with people when Jenny and Stanislaw arrived. Polish officers leaning, relaxing, smoking cigars and drinking. Young women smiling, reclining on chairs and sofas, sipping vodka, gin and whisky.

Factory girls, all sorts of girls out for a good time — a brief respite from the hard slog at factory bench or whatever other war work they had chosen to do.

Stanislaw found a seat for Jenny then pressed a bellpunch. Shuffle, shuffle, an elderly man carrying a silver tray underneath his arm entered the room.

"Large gin and orange and a large whisky, please," said Stanislaw.

"Right you are, Sir. Any sandwiches . . . got some nice cheese." He was obsequious and yet disinterested. Ears and eyes not working properly, the right combination for the night porter of a hotel that allowed lady guests into its lounge late at night, thought Jenny, as she watched him shuffle away.

Louder and louder the laughter and conversation filled the lounge.

"Perhaps you would like to see my room?" Stanislaw blew a tiny cloud of cigar smoke towards the ceiling and looked nonchalant, "is much quieter . . . perhaps you would wish to be quieter?"

"All right," Jenny answered, "I'd like to have a look at your room. We can take our drinks up there."

The bedside lamp had a gold brocade shade with tiny gold bobbles round the edge. The bed was large; covered with a gold satin quilt it was the focal point of the bedroom.

Stanislaw placed his overcoat across the back of a chair together with his cap then holding out his hands gestured for Jenny to hand over her coat. He switched on the bedside lamp and turned out the main light.

Jenny sat on the bed and sipped at her drink.

"It's a nice room, Stanislaw," she nodded towards the thick gold brocade curtains that shut out the night, "quite elegant in fact."

Stanislaw sat on the bed beside her and put his arm around her waist. He nuzzled her ear and said softly, "I desire you, Jenny. Perhaps you would permit!"

He caressed her breasts with the tips of his fingers, so gently that she could hardly feel their touch, but her breasts responded at once, nipples erect and thrusting against the delicate texture of her green satin blouse.

He took her glass and placed it on the bedside cabinet. Leaning, gently pushing, he eased her downwards, downwards onto the luxurious satin quilt.

"Your hair catches light, Jenny," he said her name for the second time.

The beauty of her titian hair was highlighted against the backcloth of gold satin. Stanislaw stroked her hair and leaned closer. Jenny looked up into his eyes and saw the desire there that had now replaced mischievousness.

Once again his fingers caressed her breasts then he quickly removed her blouse and placed it on the chair at the side of the bed.

"I take off for you?" He undid the buttons at the side of her skirt, "it will not make creases." He slid the skirt down over her hips then removed her shoes almost in the same movement.

Jenny did not move, but watched him — watched as though under the influence of a hypnotist — thrilled by his caresses she began to breathe more quickly — excited beyond the limits of self control she lay outstretched on the bed and luxuriated in the feelings of lust and her craving animal instincts.

Stanislaw's movements were slow and deliberate. Undressing, he revealed his own nakedness with no trace of shyness. Proud of his manhood he hid nothing from her gaze — his magnificent body, muscular and youthful, towered over her.

Jenny concentrated her mind on the moment — as though about to partake of a delicious feast — savouring instead of devouring — making everything last.

Stanislaw secreted a small packet underneath the pillows and said, "I take care . . . you will not have baby . . . I promise."

Kissing and caressing, he removed the remainder of her clothing. Jenny looked round the bedroom. Gentle light not quite reaching the corners of the room created sinister shadows — like huge creatures listening and waiting they did not move. A mirror sparkled, reflecting the flower filled vase which stood before it on the mantelpiece. Flowers in the vase seemed to reach out towards the mirror, growing, growing towards the glass. Jenny stared at the twinned beauty of the flowers then looked once again into Stanislaw's eyes.

Very gently, he lowered himself onto her naked body. Searching, finding, he joined their bodies together with one thrusting movement and then pushed harder and harder until she cried out — the cry held no pain, only ecstasy shrilled from her half-open mouth. He clutched at her shoulders, fingers digging into her flesh and then, as his movements became more urgent, much faster, he began to moan softly in Polish.

129

Jenny clung to him and arched her back, thrusting her body upwards to meet his, she released all frustrations and, a little of the heartache that she had endured for such a long time.

The flowers reflected in the mirror were the first thing Jenny saw when she opened her eyes.

Then, glancing sideways and still half-asleep, she looked at the light brown wavy hair and the face in repose on the pillow next to hers.

"Reggie!" The name was catapulted from her lips on a gasp. Wide awake now she sat up and in a moment realised her mistake.

"Jenny!" Stanislaw opened his eyes and smiled at her. "Are you all right, Jenny?" He stroked her face. "I was dreaming . . . so sad was my dream . . . of funeral and lonely church." He snuggled closer and placed his head between her breasts and was silent, as though listening for her heartbeat.

"It's good luck to dream of death." Jenny stroked his hair and added, "In my grandma's dream book it says if you dream of a death it means a birth. It's always the opposite to what you dream."

"Ah," he smiled up at her, eyes brimming with mischief once again "a birth perhaps then. In that case, I try never to dream of birth . . . I do not want to hear of death."

"I'll have to think about getting home now, Stanislaw. Mrs Cohen will be worried about me. And I've got to go to work in the morning."

"I walk with you to your home." Stanislaw sat up.

"All right then, thank you . . . but give me another cuddle first." Jenny pulled him towards her. The shock of thinking that she had seen Reggie had filled her with a great sadness. She wanted good memories of her evening spent with Stanislaw — no melancholy or guilt — she deserved a few good times and here was her chance. This would be the beginning of lots of good times.

Stanislaw pressed up closer and the nearness of her naked body aroused desire in him once more.

"No," Jenny whispered, "just hold me, Stanislaw . . . just hold me for a while."

The colours of the flowers in the mirror seemed to become brighter. Jenny observed the delicate petals and dark green leaves; shadows on the wall still listened and waited but did not seem so menacing; Jenny held Stanislaw tightly in her arms and pretended that he was Reggie; then she held Reggie in her arms and pretended that he was Stanislaw.

She closed her eyes and tried to erase all thoughts and pictures from her mind — but could still see the beautiful flowers quite clearly — all mixed up with the smiles of Reggie and Stanislaw.

TWENTY THREE

Jack looked round the kitchen and could not get used to how small everything seemed. After the spaciousness inside Newstead coming home to Independent Street felt like stepping into a doll's house, he thought, then looked out of the window at the rows of grey slated rooftops on the terraced houses opposite and felt more oppressed.

The house did not feel welcoming, Jack sighed, without Vera bustling and fussing — making the house into a home with her cooking and cleaning and constant tea mashing. He decided to nip round to Bert and Annie's house and see Elizabeth Rose. She would be shy, he expected that, a year made a big difference to a child. But Jack had been adamant; Alex and Elizabeth Rose had not been allowed to visit him in the hospital. TB hospitals were out of bounds for children at the best of times, but Jack had not even agreed to see them when he was almost cured — sometimes, children were allowed to stand outside the wards and wave to sick parents through the french windows. Jack had exchanged many letters with Alex but even so, he knew they would have to get to know each other all over again.

Jack pushed open the back door and called, "Are you there, Annie . . . it's me, duck." Jack stepped inside the scullery and peered into the kitchen.

Annie and Elizabeth Rose were on the sofa in front of the fire. The fire danced and crackled giving a cheerful atmosphere to the room. A dance band on the wireless provided soft background music. They were both fast asleep. Annie, mouth open, sat slumped with arms folded across her chest — Elizabeth Rose was curled up like a cat, feet hidden from view beneath a red pleated skirt; hair still worn in ringlets she lay with her head resting upon a cushion: vulnerable and beautiful the sight of her made Jack's heart lurch with emotion. He held his breath for a few seconds and drank in the magic of the moment.

This is what it's all about, he thought, the year spent in the sanatorium, the boredom, frustration and worry, this was what he had stayed alive for, to see his children again and to be with Vera.

Jack smiled to himself as he looked down at his sleeping child. A little bit of Vera and a little bit of me, he observed, and an even bigger bit of Grandma Denbey. He looked at the jutting Denbey chin and the slight tilt of the Denbey nose. How his mother would have loved her.

"Ey up, Jack," Annie opened her eyes, "how long have you been standing there then? Sit yer down while I make some tea. You're looking like a king, Jack. Done yer a bit of good out there at Newstead. They reckon the air out there's worth a guinea a bucketful." Annie stood up and kissed Jack on the cheek. "Vera's working till six," Annie rambled on, pleased with the company, "Alex'll be home from school soon. He likes to listen to Childrens' Hour. Stay and have some tea with us. We're having beans on toast and I've made a treacle tart."

"Cup of tea'd go down nicely, Annie." Jack sat in an armchair and continued, "Vera's been telling me about your Bert's contacts for black market stuff."

"Oh, I know," Annie chuckled, "he'll end up in Lincoln Prison before he's much older." She did not look too worried, Jack noticed.

"That's where we'll all end up, duck." Jack lit a Woodbine.

"Clothing coupons fetch the most. Can't get clothing coupons for love nor money, if you're not in the know. Cyril England from the pawn-shop's earning a fortune in second-hand clothing. People snatch his hand off for owt that's going."

"The lads from down Sneinton Market have seen me right while I've been in Newstead. I'm going to look after them now I'm back. Salt of the earth them lads are, Annie."

"Not going out with the barrer just yet though, are yer, Jack? Don't want you catching a chill, else you'll be back where yer started."

"I'm completely back to normal. Don't want wrapping in cottonwool. I'm dying to get back earning me living again. I want Vera to pack up that factory job." He made the popping noise with his mouth, the noise he made when he was annoyed. "No need for Vera to slog away on munitions now . . . she can pack it in now I'm back."

Annie poured tea and said nothing.

"Jack!" Vera rushed over to Jack and gave him a hug then she kissed him on the lips. "You got here all right then."

"Looks like it." Jack was sarcastic. "You smell like a motor-bike engine."

"Ey . . . like what?" Vera took off her coat and the turban made from a headscarf. "Of course I do . . . I'm working in grease and muck all day long. Good honest toil, Jack . . . keeping our lads flying." She smiled at Alex and Elizabeth Rose. "Int it nice to have yer dad home again."

"Yes," they answered together, not sure.

"I'll get something to eat." Vera walked towards the scullery.

"I've had summat at Annie's house." Jack sat down.

"Cup of tea then? I could drink a gallon of tea, I could."

"All right then . . . always got room for a cup of tea."

His homecoming was not as Jack had expected and he felt cheated. He could not bring himself to be pleasant. Vera seemed different — much stronger, more self assured and in control of things. It made him feel uneasy.

"Do yer want to nip across to the Oak, later on?," Jack said casually, "I've forgot what a good pint of Shippo's tastes like. We'll go early before the barrels run dry."

"I don't get paid till Friday, Jack." Vera cut a thick slice of bread and made herself a Bovril sandwich. "And I am a bit tired. I've been up since before six. Had to do some washing before I went to work this morning."

"I've got some money." Jack's mood blackened. "Didn't expect you to pay."

"All right then. I'll come across for an hour. Have to put some curlers in me hair though."

"Put your turban back on," Jack grinned at her, "I don't mind."

"Oh yes . . . and I'll keep me overalls on as well," Vera laughed then bit into her sandwich again.

"That's it, ladies and gentlemen . . . no more ale till tomorrow . . . if you're lucky." The landlord covered the beer pumps with tea towels. "Whisky and gin'll be here tomorrow as well. I've got a drop of port if anybody'd like some . . . and some brandy." He winked at Jack and added softly, "Black market the brandy is, Jack, but it's a drop of good. Stay behind . . . I think I can squeeze a drop more Shippo's out the barrel. Nice to see you back again, mate. Bleddy bad luck, that TB. I'd sooner have the screws like me missis than that TB. Laying in hospital for a bleddy year . . . it's enough to send you barmy, mate."

The landlord measured out ports and brandies for eager drinkers then after a while stopped serving. "You've drunk me dry," he shouted, "you've drunk enough to sink a bleddy battle ship. See you all tomorrer . . . if the brewery send me owt." He closed and bolted the doors.

A dozen people besides Jack and Vera waited expectantly as the landlord removed the tea towels and pulled on the beer pump.

"Don't see why bleddy strangers should drink all me ale," he roared, "come from all over they do . . . soon as one pub runs dry they scuttle like a plague of rats to the next. Folks queuing with their jugs and bottles . . . half of them I've never set eyes on before." He handed Jack a pint of Shipstones. "Take good care of me regulars, I do." He laughed heartily and added, "You're the chosen few. Ha-ha-ha . . . the bleddy chosen few." He handed pints to three sailors and asked, "How's yer mam then, me lad? Still charring for that Doctor Newton, is she?"

"Put that light out!" There was a loud banging on the 'snug' door at the back of the pub.

"Oh, there's the bleddy coppers come for their pints. Let 'em in somebody, else I'll lose me bleddy licence."

Jack put his arm around Vera's waist and whispered in her ear, "Feel all right, do you, duck? Still feeling tired?"

"Not bad, Jack," she smiled at him, "the drink's made me feel a bit more human. I felt a bit edgy earlier on."

Jack kissed her on the cheek and answered, "I'll make sure you get a good night's sleep."

"Ey up! . . . look at bleddy Clark Gable there," chuckled the landlord, "he's been away for a year you know," he addressed everyone, "first night back."

"Blimey," one of the policemen raised his pint mug and grinned, "like the first night out after being in prison."

"Or coming home after being shipwrecked on a desert island," added one of the young sailors.

Vera blushed and sipped her drink for something to do.

"Hope we don't get an air raid tonight," Jack joined in the fun, "I've got better things to do than sit in a damp shelter."

"Don't bother about that, Jack," said the landlord, "put some bleddy ear-plugs in yer tabs then you won't hear owt."

"I'm sorry, Vera," Jack put his head on Vera's shoulder, "there's still nothing happening."

"I told you, Jack, don't worry about it. It's the excitement of coming home after all this time. Or it could be the drink. You're not used to drinking . . . it's bound to have an effect on you."

Jack sighed and did not move.

"Honestly, Jack . . . it'll be all right next time. When you've had a good night's sleep." Vera struggled to stay awake. It had been a long day for her and she still felt

133

edgy. Jack was acting like a child again — needing comfort and sympathy, drawing on her strength he could not accept that his body had let him down yet again. First the TB and now his lovemaking.

"The TB's ruined me, Vera. I'm not the same man." It was as though he had been reading her mind.

"It's nothing to do with that," Vera stroked his hair, "the doctor told me you were completely cured. You know he was telling the truth. I'm going to sleep now, Jack. I've got to be up at half-past six. It'll be all right next time, you'll see." She closed her eyes and fell asleep.

Jack wished he could be back inside the hospital. Among the nurses who smiled a lot and had time for him. Gentle hands and kind voices — they had seemed like part of his family. He could have made love to Vera if she had been like those lovely nurses in Newstead. Soft and feminine, smelling of talcum powder and scented soap. No greasy overalls and turbans on the nurses, he thought sadly.

He turned onto his back and placed his hands down between his legs, a position he had often taken when needing comfort as a small boy. He cupped his hands over flesh that felt like warm velvet — as though protecting the softness that earlier, had let him down so badly.

Imagining, pretending, Jack once again entered his secret world of make-believe. Lustful images and fantasies of women he had never met, doing things to him that no decent woman would ever contemplate whirled round and round inside his head. The softness between his legs responded; slowly, but definitely happening, he felt the familiar throbbing as he grew harder — not quite hard enough but it was almost there.

He turned onto his side and put his arm across Vera; pressing closer he stroked her soft belly; Vera did not respond: locked inside her own fantasy world she breathed deeply, oblivious to Jack's needs.

Jack kept his hand on her belly until he also grew sleepy. It was going to be all right, Jack thought, then unable to resist the power of alcohol, he too fell fast asleep.

TWENTY FOUR

Jack looked down at the tiny black face of the kitten which was wedged inside the front of his jacket and stroked one of its ears. He banged on Mrs Cohen's front door and was surprised when Jenny answered his knock.

"Ey up, Jenny . . . what you doing at home? Run out of engines, have they?" He followed her through to the kitchen.

"Didn't feel too well this morning when I woke up. Too much Polish vodka last night. Stanislaw got me a bottle from the officers' mess last Saturday and I've polished the lot off. I'm going out to dinner with him tonight again as well," she pointed to the curlers in her hair, "got to get glamoured up. Going to the Palais first."

"Oh, are yer now. Well when you get inside that officers' mess, see if you can get some bacon and a few jars of jam. And a bottle of vodka for your poor old brother would be very much appreciated. Ey, and see if you can get some butter and cheese."

"Hang on a minute, Jack," Jenny laughed, "I'm going to have me dinner . . . I'm not going on a tour round the quartermaster's stores."

"Get owt you can, Jen. It'll go like lightning on the black market."

"Meeowww." The kitten demanded attention just as Mrs Cohen walked in from the scullery.

Jack placed the kitten in Mrs Cohen's arms and said, "You needn't keep it if you don't want, duck. But there's seven of 'em and they've got to get rid of them all. It'll have to be drowned if you don't want it. Our Rupert won't let another cat within a mile of our house so we can't have another."

Mrs Cohen sat down on the sofa and placed the kitten on her lap.

"I said I wouldn't have another pet, Jack. Too much heartbreak when they die. No other cat can replace Chamberlain." She stroked the tiny head and startled eyes stared into hers.

"Oh well then," Jack winked at Jenny, "get the bucket out . . . I'll do the job for yer. Put plenty of water in the bucket."

Mrs Cohen picked up the kitten and held it close to her breasts.

"I'll drown you if you come near it. What a thing to suggest." The kitten was home and dry, Jack thought, and wondered if the saying had originally referred to kittens and buckets filled with water.

"Is this romance of yours serious then?" Jack lit a Woodbine and inhaled the smoke.

"You shouldn't smoke, Jack . . . not with your lungs." Jenny looked concerned.

"I don't take the smoke right down. Just swirl it round in me mouth." Jack inhaled again and puffed out his cheeks. "Now then, what about this officer of yours? Don't try and change the subject. Going to be a wedding is there? We could do with another booze-up. Plenty of vodka and whatnot."

"Never you mind," Jenny grinned at him, then all at once looked very sad. "Doesn't do to get married . . . not when there's a war on. Might get married after the war . . . and even then I don't know."

Everyone was silent. Precious thoughts hugged to hearts. Outside a March wind threw itself around in a temper and the only tree in the tiny back garden bowed down in surrender.

"Meeowwww."

"There there, Kitty," Mrs Cohen fussed over the bundle of fur, "would you like some milk. By the way, Jack, is it a he or a she?"

"Can't see owt hanging down, Mrs Cohen," Jack exploded with laughter, "I reckon it's a she. You could call her Kitty."

"No . . . give it a posh name," Jenny curled her legs underneath her and cosied down in an armchair, "how about, Emerald? Look at those lovely emerald peepers."

"Black cats bring you luck." Jack rested his head on the back of the sofa and closed his eyes. "How about, Lucy? Sounds like lucky."

"I like, Gipsy," answered Mrs Cohen, "they bring good luck."

"They give you bad luck as well . . . and spit at you if they don't like you," Jenny added.

"So do cats," replied Mrs Cohen, "so that's settled then . . . Gipsy."

"You don't want me to drown it then?" Jack teased her.

"She'll be our good luck charm," Mrs Cohen ignored him, "and you can just go and mash some tea, Jack. I can't move because Gipsy's gone to sleep on my knee."

"Blimey . . . her luck's working for you already, duck." Jack took the kettle from the hob. "Now don't be catty . . . and I'll make you both a purrrfect cup of tea."

They all laughed and looked down at the kitten who had begun to charm them even as she slept.

Jenny caught the trolley-bus at the corner of Forest Road. She had decided to wear her navy blue bouclé coat with the fox-fur collar and underneath she wore her pale blue Shantung silk frock with the tiny mother-of-pearl buttons at the throat and wrists. A headscarf covered her hair, protecting curls from the still angry March wind.

"Palais," the conductress yelled from the bottom of the stairs. "Keep yer 'ands on yer ha'pennies, gels," she laughed raucously. "And watch them lads in the forces. They put extra polish on their boots so's they can see up yer frocks when they're dancing with yer."

Passengers alighted from the trolley-bus smiling and chuckling.

Stanislaw was late and it was windy on the corner where the Palais stood. Jenny pulled her headscarf tighter and peered up the road. One by one, men appeared from blackout gloom and headed towards the dance-hall. Sometimes, a shadowy figure looked like Stanislaw but each time Jenny was disappointed as the shadow materialised into someone else.

Stanislaw was nearly an hour late! Jenny decided to wait for him inside the Palais.

The doormen stepped forward as she entered the foyer.

"I'm meeting someone inside," Jenny explained, "my fiance's been delayed." She took off the headscarf and shook titian curls loose over her shoulders, then she dazzled the men with a friendly smile and coquettish gleam in her eyes.

"Right then, love," one of the men stepped towards her, "if you get let down I'll see you home."

"Watch him, duck . . . wife and ten kids at home. Isn't that right, Elsie?" The other doorman nodded towards the ticket seller."

The band was playing a waltz as Jenny found a seat on the balcony. Sipping at gin and orange, she watched as dancers glided by, then glanced now and then towards the entrance where Stanislaw would appear. She could imagine the expression on his face; eyes searching for her, apology written all over his face because he had let her down. No matter, she smiled to herself, it would soon be all right, when they were in each other's arms. She could almost feel his arms around her — feel the warmth of his body — smell the manliness of him.

"Good evening," a voice from behind addressed her. "Good evening, Jenny. It is Jenny, is it not?"

"Oh, hello." Jenny recognised the Polish officer's face but could not recall his name. He was one of the men from Swinderby.

"I hope that you are well," he continued, "please . . . may I sit?"

"Yes, of course, I'm just waiting for Stanislaw."

The officer stared at her and did not sit down. He looked uncomfortable and his mouth opened as though he were about to say something, but he did not speak for a while. At last he asked, "May I fetch for you another drink?"

"Thank you. It's a gin and orange."

The officer hurried away and Jenny leaned over the balcony and looked for Stanislaw once again.

After a while the officer returned with her drink accompanied by two more officers. They sat down and one of the officers leaned closer to Jenny. "I am so sorry . . . but I have learned you do not know about . . . about Stanislaw."

"Know what? Don't tell me he couldn't get a pass again."

"He . . . he was on mission . . . three nights ago. Flying across Channel . . . laying mines I think . . . you understand! There were German planes also . . . many dog-fights . . . some planes were lost. German planes . . . English planes . . . many pilots did not come back. I . . . er . . . Stanislaw did not come back. Many pilots died bravely that night."

"No! . . . oh, no!" Jenny held onto the edge of the table and tried to breathe normally. "Oh, no . . . he can't be dead! You've made a mistake. Not Stanislaw! He promised to be here tonight. He wouldn't break a promise. It can't be Stanislaw. I would have known. They would have let me know. He can't be dead . . . he can't!"

"Swinderby . . . they have your address perhaps?" the officer spoke softly, "next of kin to be informed . . . telegram will go to Poland. Perhaps they do not have your address. Stanislaw was good officer."

Jenny tried to concentrate on what the officer was saying but the words seemed jumbled.

"Stanislaw was good fellow to have for friend," the officer continued, "everyone is sad for his death." He put his hand on Jenny's arm and added, "All are sad for you. We know of your great friendship with Stanislaw. Pleased for him always we were, that he had such a friendship."

Jenny stared in front of her — everything looked like a smudged painting — as though an artist had painted the dance hall and then wiped a cloth across the wet canvas and merged the colours on the painting into one great blur of colour. She tried to stand and felt hands supporting her, guiding her, but still the painting looked smudged.

The band played a tune and the human puppets on the dance floor whirled round in time to the music; the technicolour splinters of light from the glass globe danced with them.

A smiling cloakroom attendant handed Jenny the coat with the fox-fur collar. The doorman uttered words that had no meaning and opened the foyer door for her.

The March wind beckoned her into the dark night — ran cold fingers through her hair and tugged at her coat.

Stanislaw was dead! Stanislaw was dead! Reggie was dead! The whole world was dead!

On and on she walked through her nightmare not caring or knowing where her feet would take her. She walked to the end of Parliament Street and headed for the General

137

Hospital. At last she reached the wall at the top of the flight of steep steps. Climbing onto the wall, she peered out into the darkness and imagined what everything looked like below. The houses, streets, canal and river, just the same — flowing, flowing down to the sea; bodies in the sea; fishes in the sea; nothing in the sea; Stanislaw in the sea, eyes lifeless, heart no longer beating, the heart that had beaten in tune with hers when they had made love.

"Stanislaw!" Her cry was carried by the wind, up and up, then died away as though gobbled up by the dark sky overhead. "Stanislaw!" She knew he could not hear her — and knew that he would never answer.

"Now then . . . what's all that about then?" A man's voice intruded into her despair. "Are yer all right then, duck?" A torchlight was shone onto her face. The man held out his hands and helped her down from the wall.

"Yes," she answered him in a whisper, "yes I'm all right, thank you."

"Don't sound like it, duck. Somebody been upsetting you, have they?"

"My . . . my young man's been killed. I've only just heard. He was Polish . . . a pilot," Jenny's voice sounded matter of fact. "You half expect it to happen," she continued, "but when it does happen, it comes as a shock." She gasped and added, "I don't know what I'm going to do. I just don't know."

"Where do you live, lovey? I'm on fire-duty at the hospital but they won't miss me for a while. I'll walk to your house with you." The warden tucked his arm inside Jenny's arm and steered her away from the wall.

"I . . . I live on Independent Street." Jenny needed Vera and Jack more than she had ever needed anyone. Vera would say all the right things and Jack — well, he would just be Jack. Mrs Cohen was a lovely lady, just like a mother in fact, but she wasn't family, not real flesh and blood, thought Jenny, right now I need to be with family.

She concentrated on making her legs walk properly. Legs that felt like cottonwool and jelly attached to leaden feet.

The warden knocked on the front door and Jack appeared.

"Thought you'd gone dancing . . . changed yer mind then?"

"She's heard bad news, mate. I've just brought her home for yer. Got to get back . . . on fire-duty at the General. I'll say goodnight to you then." The warden let go of Jenny's arm and walked away from the sadness.

"What's the matter, Jen?" Jack led the way into the kitchen. "It's our Jenny," he said to Vera, "she's heard some bad news or summat."

Jenny flopped into an armchair and the fox-fur collar shrugged up over her neck and chin.

"It's Stanislaw . . . he's been shot down. He's dead, his pals said. The Germans shot him down, somewhere over the Channel, they said. He was on a mission. He didn't come back."

Jack and Vera stared at Jenny then looked at one another. Jack was the first to speak, "Well, just try to think of it this way, love. You had some lovely times together didn't you. You made his last few months really mean something. His number was up, Jen. You can't beat fate no matter how you try. His number was up, Jen."

Jack opened the sideboard cupboard and took out a bottle of brandy. He poured three large brandies and after offering Jenny a glass sat on the edge of her chair and put his arm around her shoulders.

"It's this bleddy, sodding war. Thousands and thousands of people killed . . . and all for what!" He took a drink of brandy. "Lousy stinking Germans . . . they all ought to rot in hell."

"Oh, Jack," Jenny started to cry, "I feel devastated."

"I know . . . I know. That's right . . . you have a good cry. I tell you what we could do . . . we could ask them at Swinderby to let you have one or two of his belongings. Something you can have for a keepsake. Perhaps they'll send you a photo . . . summat like that."

"Yes, Jack'll make enquiries for you," Vera added, "see if you can have a keepsake. There's bound to be something inside his locker. You haven't got a photo, have you? Jack'll try to get you a photo. You ought to have a keepsake, seeing as you were his girl."

"I have got something," Jenny spoke in a whisper," I have got a keepsake."

"There then . . . that's something," Vera said, "you'll want a keepsake. Something to remind you of Stanislaw."

"You'll be all right, Jen," Jack added, "just get over the next few months. We'll help you all we can you know that. Just get over the next few months . . . they're the worst."

"I'm having his baby!" Jenny huddled down and pulled the fox-fur collar closer to her face. "That's my keepsake."

TWENTY FIVE

Mrs Cohen placed the baby back into Jenny's arms and said, "And aren't you a lovely little girl then. Never seen so much hair on a newborn baby. We'll have to call her curlylocks."

"It's good to be back home, Mrs Cohen." Jenny stroked the baby's hair and sighed. "They were very good to me up at the City Hospital but I couldn't get any proper sleep. Always people rushing around and babies crying . . . I feel exhausted."

"We'll soon get you built up again. Plenty of rest and some bowls of chicken broth and some beef stews . . . you'll be fighting fit in no time."

"Thank you for looking after me, Mrs Cohen. I don't know what I would have done without you. Some landladies would have thrown me out when they knew I was expecting."

"I'm not some landladies," Mrs Cohen answered, "it will be lovely to have a child running about the house again." She smiled down at the baby. "Now then, you must decide on a name. She'll have to be registered. Are you going to give her a Polish name? Stanislaw would have liked that."

"No . . . not Polish. Something pretty and feminine . . . I don't know many Polish names anyway. I'll think of something today."

"What surname are you going to put on the birth certificate? You could put Reggie's name on the certificate . . . as the father."

"No, I daren't do that. The Army knows I'm a widow. They'd find out sooner or later. She'll have Reggie's surname but I'll put Stanislaw down as the father. I'm not ashamed, Mrs Cohen . . . I loved him."

"I know you did." Mrs Cohen sighed. "What a good husband he would have made. Such a gentleman and so generous."

"I think I'll call her Louise. It sounds nice and French."

"Oh yes, that's nice. I like that."

"Mrs Cohen . . . are you sure you want to look after her when I go back to work? It'll be hard work you know, all those nappies to change and then there's the feeding times."

"It'll be a pleasure," Mrs Cohen's smile was genuine, "never thought I'd hear a child's laughter in this house again. My Sammy was no trouble at all. Such a good baby, right from the minute he was born."

Her eyes shone with happiness. "Such a beautiful boy."

"We'll be able to manage all right, once I start earning again. Not much hope of getting help from the Polish Air Force, they said at the hospital. You have to have proof . . . they want to know your life-story before they'll consider helping. I can't prove Stanislaw was the father. I'm not going to grovel on my knees, not if I can manage. And I insist on paying you for looking after the baby."

"I'm not short of money." Mrs Cohen touched her on the arm. "We all help each other in wartime and hard times. And I'm getting a few shillings from your Jack now he's back working the stall again."

"Anybody there?" Jack's voice interrupted them. "Just heard some good news." He walked into the bedroom. "The Italians have just surrendered. I'll bet owd Hitler's crying his bleddy eyes out." He sat down on the edge of the bed. "Here y'are . . . got a present for your two. Ey, won't be long before the war's finished now." He placed a carrier-bag on the bed and fished about inside. "Here y'are . . . two lovely jars of home-made strawberry jam . . . tin of John West salmon, and some new-laid eggs." He put both hands inside the carrier-bag and pulled out something large wrapped in newspaper.

"Oh, Jack!" Jenny sat up and said excitedly, "a chicken . . . a lovely chicken."

"Don't get too excited," Jack poked at the chicken, "it might be a bit tough. I think it died of old age."

"I'm sure it will be beautiful, Jack." Mrs Cohen picked up the chicken. "We'll get some lovely broth from the bones. Just what your Jenny needs to build her strength up."

"Are these any good to you?" Jack fumbled inside his wallet and threw a book of clothing coupons onto the bed. "Thought you might like to get summat for the baby. A nice shawl and a few bibs so's she don't slavver down me best suit."

"Thanks a million, Jack." Jenny squeezed his hand.

"Well, I've got to do me bit. First time I've been a monkey's uncle."

"She's no monkey," laughed Mrs Cohen, "she's an angel."

"And that's what you can be, duck," replied Jack, "be an angel and make us all a cup of tea."

Mrs Cohen laughed and hurried downstairs.

"And I will be a monkey's uncle if this war's still on at Christmas. Now the Italians have jacked it in there's a good chance Hitler'll call it a day. I tell yer one thing an' all . . . I'll be glad when Vera packs her job in at the factory."

"Trouble is though, Jack, you get used to the money. Annie takes good care of Alex and Elizabeth Rose, and the money certainly comes in handy every week."

"Yes, I know, but Vera's always tired out. It's making an old woman out of her. I even have to get me own dinner ready."

"Oh, now we're getting down to it. You miss being waited on, hand and foot. All your homely comforts."

"No, I just like her to be there. I'm making enough to keep us going . . . me black market racket's earning plenty. She ought to stay at home . . . looking after us all like a proper wife."

"You're lucky you've got each other. Look at me, what a mess I'm in." Jenny cuddled the baby to her breast and added, "but I wouldn't part with a hair on her head . . . not now."

"What yer going to call her? Proper little carrot-top, isn't she. You ought to call her Ginger . . . after Ginger Rogers."

"Louise . . . I'm calling her, Louise."

"Why don't you name her after Mrs Cohen? She'd be over the moon if you did."

"All right then, how about Louise Rachel?"

"Beautiful. Did you hear that, Louise?" Jack tickled the baby's chin and started to sing, "Every little breeze seems to whisper, Louise."

"Here we are then." Mrs Cohen set the tray down. "Help yourselves to biscuits."

"What do yer think to, Louise Rachel, then?" Jack dipped a Lincoln cream in his tea and grinned.

"Yes, I've decided to name her Louise Rachel," added Jenny.

Mrs. Cohen's eyes filled with tears as she replied, "My cup runneth over. Oh, I knew a black cat would bring me good luck." She wiped her eyes on her pinafore and looked proudly at Louise Rachel.

TWENTY SIX

Jack was wrong, as usual; the war continued after Christmas; Hitler and his fellow madmen did not want peace. Newsreels at the picture houses told the world what he really wanted. World domination at any cost was Hitler's crazy goal. His own country was being destroyed but he did not seem to care.

In Hamburg alone, thousands upon thousands of men, women and children had reportedly been sucked to their deaths into terrible firestorms — flames of hell which had been caused by incendiary bombs, the newsreels had revealed — but still the maniac would not surrender.

The cream of his own nation disappearing forever — young men being shot out of the skies, blown out of the water and shelled to pieces on land.

Italy had declared war on Germany — like rats deserting a sinking ship they changed sides but still the crazy captain would not give up the helm — steering the ship through death and destruction Hitler seemed to enjoy and thrive on war.

In Nottingham, as in the rest of England, the people endured with stoicism and good humour. Public houses took it in turn to open their doors as beer barrels stood empty down cellars and shelves behind bars looked bare and forlorn.

Queues of people were to be seen everywhere; at the food shops especially, women patiently stood in line, rations books at the ready they laughed and joked and talked about what they would eat when the war came to an end.

"I'm going to eat bananas till I look like a monkey."

"I like oranges. I'll eat the peel as well."

"Give me a big joint of beef and I'll show you. I'm a beefeater, I am . . . like them blokes who guard the crown jewels. Oh, all that lovely dripping you get, that black jelly in the bottom of the cup. Ooh . . . what I wouldn't do for some black jelly."

"Chocolate's my favourite. I'm going to gorge meself on chocolate till I look like a big slab of Cadbury's Milk."

"I like big chunks of cheese. That strong cheese that makes yer tabs laugh when you chew it. Even the mice are fed-up in our 'ouse. The bit yer get on yer rations int enough to feed the mice."

People queued outside the cinemas. Desperate to escape the realities of life they clambered to see the film stars who oozed glamour and lived fairy-tale lives of make-believe.

Everything suddenly became very important. It was important to get enough food; enough fuel; enough clothes; enough dancing: enough loving.

Then it happened! They had been promising long enough — the words and rumours reaching across the seas and skies.

'THE YANKS ARE COMING!'

After the war had dragged on interminably for nearly five years the 'Yanks had arrived.'

Jack sat in the cafe at the side of Sneinton Market and discussed strategy with other stallholders and barrow-boys.

"I tell yer, we can make a packet out of the Yanks. They come into Nottingham like bleddy stampeding cattle after our gels. And they've got money to burn. You can sell them owt. They even buy my home-made brylcreem and most of them have got crew-cut hair."

The other men laughed and looked interested.

"What else, Jack?" asked a stallholder, "what about that whisky you was telling us about?"

"Yes, I got a load of black market Johnnie Walker. You can sell it to the Yanks for double the price. Or do a swap for a load of their fags. Lucky Stripe and Camel . . . ugh . . . smells like camel dung but people grab yer hand off for them."

"Things are looking up, mate," said another stallholder, "it's about time we made some real money. Scratching about for petrol . . . and when yer do get out to the factories there's nowt at the end of it."

"Try and get hold of them there nylons," Jack grinned at him, "the women go crazy for a pair of nylons. I nearly got killed in the rush when the word got round I'd managed to get a dozen pairs."

"Where's the best places to get down to bargaining, Jack?"

"Oh, the Palais . . . Victoria Ballroom . . . Black Boy . . . George Hotel . . . Flying Horse . . . you name it, the Yanks are in there . . . flashing the money around."

"There'll be some fights, Jack. Our lads'll be jealous if the Yanks take all the best gels." A barrow-boy shook his head and whistled. "And yer know what the women are. They like a man with plenty of money."

"That's their lookout," answered Jack, "I'm out to make some money meself. There's a hotel up Mansfield Road making a fortune out of the Yanks. Charging them double the price for bed and breakfast and making a packet on drinks and sandwiches. The Yanks smuggle gels galore up the fire-escape when it gets dark, but the management turn a blind eye. The locals call the hotel, 'French Letter Mansions'."

"There'll be a lot of little Yanks running about after the war, Jack."

"Ah . . . and they'll all have crew-cut hair . . . and chewing-gum stuck in their gobs."

Jack ordered mugs of tea for everyone then handed round a packet of Lucky Stripes and grinned. "What's that saying they've got round? . . . that saying about the Yanks?"

"Overpaid . . . oversexed . . . and over here," answered a stallholder.

Jack blew cigarette smoke into the air and added, "And . . . overcharged."

The men thumped on the tables and roared with laughter.

"You'll never guess what, Jack?" Vera placed two carrier-bags on the kitchen table and stood with hands on hips. "I'll give you three guesses. I'll bet you can't guess."

"Hitler's marrying Old Mother Riley?"

"No . . . but you're warm. It is a wedding."

"Our Jenny's marrying Henry the foreman?"

"No . . . you're way out . . . one more guess."

"Oh, I don't know. Go on, tell me."

"Florence is getting married to Chuck. Her Yank from Texas. His family's got a ranch, in Fort Worth I think she said it was."

"Blimey . . . is she in the pudding-club then? That was quick."

143

"Don't think so. She's getting married at St Michael's. And she's having Elizabeth Rose for bridesmaid."

"We'll be invited to the do then. Good old Florence. She'll be going out to Texas after the war. I can just imagine Flo galloping across the prairie with Roy Rogers after her."

"They're having tables of food set out on Independent Street. And free ale . . . till it runs out. And a gramophone so's we can have dancing."

"Trust Florence to find a bloke with plenty of money."

"Yes, Florence says he comes from a very well-off family. That's why they're having a white wedding. So's he can send the photos home to Texas. It's like a fairy-tale. Imagine going to live in America."

"Don't get jealous now," Jack teased her and caressed her breasts. "Get up them stairs and I'll make you saddle sore if that's what you want."

There was a knock at the door then Florence appeared with Elizabeth Rose.

"Show them your frock, love." Florence looked smug.

Elizabeth Rose lifted the skirt of her pink satin dress and whirled round and round.

"I'm going to hire the frocks from Mrs Calladine off Boden Street. She let me borrow this one so's we could show you how it looks. Twenty five shillings to hire my bridal gown and you should see it, Vera. Satin brocade with a great, long train. It was Chuck who insisted on a white wedding. He's ever so romantic." She chewed on gum and added, "I've got hold of some clothing coupons so I'll be okay for my trousseau. Oh, I'm really looking forward to the do. Dancing in the street and tables all set out ever so nice."

"Could you do with a few pork-pies and one or two tins of salmon?" Jack looked smug now.

"Oh, that'd be marvellous, Jack. Thanks ever so much."

"Don't mention it, duck. You can send me one of your cattle when you get to Texas."

"Don't know where you spirit the food from, Jack. You're a wonder."

"There's still plenty the British can do that the Yanks can't. Even though they reckon everything in America's bigger and better."

"I wouldn't say that, Jack," Florence giggled, "not everything."

"Glad to hear it, duck," Jack grinned, "very glad to hear it."

Florence looked radiant. Vera and Jenny both agreed that it appeared to be a genuine love-match between Florence and Chuck. Either that or Florence was a damned good actress, thought Vera, as she watched the newly-weds dance by — cheek to cheek and oblivious to everyone else.

"Wonder how many cattle his family own," said Jenny.

"Thousands, I expect," answered Vera, "they have thousands in those cowboy films."

"You care to dance, honey?" a tall American soldier smiled at Jenny. "I sure would be honoured if you'd dance with me."

"Will you hold Louise for me?" Jenny passed the baby to Vera.

The soldier's body was full of rhythm. He steered Jenny towards a space in the middle of the road and gyrated his body with great enthusiasm, gum-chewing mouth moving up and down in time to the music.

"Sure is a swell party, er . . . what's your name, honey?"

"Jenny," she answered after whirling round underneath his arm. "What's your name?"

"William the third."

"Blimey . . . I didn't know your dad and grandad were kings."

"Ha-ha-ha . . . you're cute, Jenny. My daddy is called William the second so, I'm William the third. Say, how'd you like to go dancin' sometime? We sure go swell together."

"Might do . . . all depends."

"On what?"

"What shift I'm on at work and whether I can leave my baby."

"Oh gee . . . I didn't realise you were married, Jenny." He looked disappointed.

"I'm a widow. My husband was killed by the Japs."

"I sure as hell am sorry to hear that, honey. Damned awful Japs . . . sure want teaching a lesson."

"Where are you from? Do you come from Texas, like Chuck?"

"Hell no . . . I ain't no cowboy. I'm a city guy. My home's in Detroit. My daddy owns a large steel factory. I come from Detroit where they make all those big cars, honey." He clapped his hands and jumped into the air then he swung Jenny round and round again.

"Ooh, you're making me dizzy." Jenny laughed and held onto him. "I've never danced like this before."

"Just go along with the music, honey, and hang in there." He clicked his fingers and chewed on the gum furiously. "Doo-doo-bedoo . . . doo-doo-bedoo. Gee, I sure love weddings. Ha-ha-ha . . . 'specially when some other poor guy is giving up his freedom."

"You're not married then?" Jenny jumped into the air and clapped her hands.

"No, sireee. Say, you sure pick up the steps mighty quick. You and me could really go places."

"Yeah . . . we sure could," Jenny replied, and thought, and that doesn't include bed.

Jack sat on the doorstep and drank heartily from his pint mug. The cool beer made him feel good, he looked up at the sky and shielded his eyes.

The late afternoon sun crouched down behind white clouds and hid for a while. Then suddenly, like a quivering red beach-ball it shrugged the clouds to one side and emerged once again — painting the surrounding clouds orange, it reached out still further with its rays and turned part of the blue sky into a silver, draped curtain. A technicolour sky — a gift from God.

"Happy the bride the sun shines on." Jack smacked his hands together. "Having a good time, William?" He nodded towards Jenny's dancing partner. "Thirsty work, dancing. I've got some damned good whisky if you'd like to buy a bottle."

William kept on dancing but shouted back, "Sure thing, Jack. Put me down for a dozen bottles."

145

"One born every minute," Jack turned to Bert, "we'll sell him some of our special. The whisky with a nice blend of cold tea."

"He'll enjoy that, Jack, "Bert chuckled, "very distinctive flavour, Johnnie Walker and cold tea."

The party continued until blackout time then one by one the revellers drifted away. Children were tucked up into bed — old women sought the comfort of warm hearths. Jack, Vera, Annie and William the third, all headed for the Oak. Mrs Cohen switched on the wireless and settled down to an evening of looking after the children. Florence and Chuck locked the back door and closed out the rest of the world.

TWENTY SEVEN

Jack and Bert pushed the barrow towards the Walter Fountain. They had no trouble selling things now — people pushed each other out of the way — eager to buy they bought Christmas wrapping paper, sprigs of holly, mistletoe, coloured crepe paper, apples, pears, home-made dolls and animals made out of material leftovers and a few of Bert's 'specials' — carved wooden boats and aeroplanes painted bright blue, red and green.

"Come on now, ladies, get yer crepe paper. Just what you need to dangle from the ceiling." Jack weighed apples and shouted to the crowd, "And don't forget yer mistletoe, ladies . . . make sure you're kissed this Christmas."

A group of American soldiers pushed forward.

"We sure wanna get plenty of that kissin'", laughed one of the soldiers, "pass some mistletoe over here, you guys."

"I'm gonna be puckering up my lips all over town," added another.

"Hand over those boats and planes," called another as he held out a fistful of pound notes, "I've got lots of nephews who sure would like to get their hands on those toys."

"Yo wait yer turn, mate. Get in the bleddy queue like the rest on us." A woman looked over her shoulder and glared at the Americans. "We tek our turn over 'ere." She held out money to Jack. "I'll have one of them boats, duck . . . some of yer crepe paper and a sprig of that mistletoe."

"Gee, honey . . . save your dough," one of the soldiers grinned at her, "come over here . . . I'll give you a smackeroo without standing underneath any mistletoe." He put his arm around her waist in a friendly gesture.

The woman shrugged him away and said, "Yo can kiss my arse, duck."

"Not here, duck," Jack handed her the mistletoe, "you'll get us all arrested." He winked at the Americans and added, "Got summat you might like, lads." He beckoned them closer. "Whisky . . . black market . . . only a few bottles left. See to them, Bert . . . look after our lads from overseas."

146

The soldiers parted with their money as though it was too hot to handle. Each carrying a bottle of Johnnie Walker, wrapped inside newspaper, they swaggered past Woolworths, gum-chewing and laughing, looking like victors hurrying away with spoils of war.

"Bleddy Yanks," grumbled an old man, "they think they own the place. They can afford to buy owt . . . bleddy load of swanks."

"Don't get jealous, Grandad," Jack lowered his voice, "we've put cold tea in with the whisky."

"Huh . . . you ought to have peed in it," retorted the old man."

"That's a good idea," laughed Bert, "they'd never know the difference if it were my pee."

The barrow was soon empty. Jack and Bert trundled their way through the city centre.

"Well, Bert . . . what do yer reckon then? How long do yer think owd Hitler's going to last out for?

"Can't be for much longer, Jack . . . 'specially now they've liberated Paris. But we can't grumble, can we. Made a nice little packet out of our rackets. I've never been so well off in me life."

"That's true, Bert . . . but I'll still be glad when it's all over. Everything back to normal again. Might be able to rent a shop on Hyson Green when the war's over. Nice little hardware shop . . . people always need bits and pieces from hardware shops."

They reached Mitchell Street and Jack let go of the barrow.

"Take the barrow back for me, Bert. I'm going down to see our Jenny and Mrs Cohen. Our Jenny's meeting her Yank later on. Him in the Airborne Division. He's bringing some of his mates to the Oak. Promised me some cartons of Lucky Stripes."

"Try and get some of that there chocolate, Jack. I'd like to get our Annie some for Christmas. Sweeten her up a bit . . . might let me have some hanky-panky if I get her some chocolate."

"Thought you were past it, Bert! Thought blokes your age only talked about it."

"Well you thought wrong, dint yer. Show me a pair sticking out like chapel hat-pegs and I'm like a rampant bull." He banged his chest with clenched fists. "And I love a nice bum on a woman."

They parted company, Jack striding down Mitchell Street whistling, 'Keep young and beautiful', Bert pushing the empty barrow towards Cyril England's pawn-shop whistling, 'God rest ye merry gentlemen'.

"Ey up there, Bert." Cyril England greeted him. "I've got that little summat you were asking about." He lowered his voice and added, "That little surprise for your Annie."

Bert followed Cyril through the scrap-yard at the back of the pawn-shop and into a small office. Cyril held a fox-fur into the air and stroked the fox's sad looking face.

"It's yours, Bert . . . if you can get me them petrol coupons you promised and some more clothing coupons. And I've got a nice little racket going with the forces' ration books." He grinned and continued," Got loads of orders for your Johnnie Walker an' all. Some Canadians are having a party down Mitchell Street on Christmas Eve. I've promised them a dozen bottles. See what you can do, mate. Not too much tea in the whisky though . . . they're not daft, them Yanks and Canadians. Don't want me bleddy

147

'ead bashing in." He stroked the fur again. "Your missis would make a right fuss of you if she found this in her Christmas stocking."

Both men laughed — drawn closer by surreptitious dealings they enjoyed the corruption and excitement — like a double act on the music halls facing up to the challenge of a hostile audience.

"It's a lovely fur, Cyril. I'll do my best with your order. Is the fur pinched, just as a matter of interest?"

"No . . . some old gel cocked her toes up last week and her son's flogging all her stuff."

"Oh, don't let on to our Annie it's a dead woman's fur."

"Don't see as it makes much difference. And you know what they say. You can't take it with yer."

"You're right there, mate. There's no pockets in shrouds."

"I've worn many a dead man's suit. Never fancied the shoes though . . . not dead mens' shoes."

"Oh blimey, Cyril . . . you're morbid today, aren't yer?"

"No, I'm not. I'm happy as a sandboy." He put the fur back into the drawer of his desk. "Our Edna's just got herself engaged to a Yank. He's bought her a ring with a diamond as big as your eyeball. His family's got a great big ranch out in San Antonio."

"Blimey," laughed Bert, "don't any of that lot live in proper houses like the rest of us? Half the American Forces are bleddy cowboys if you ask me. They all reckon they're rich and live on ranches."

"Land of opportunity, Bert. There's millions to be made in America. Everybody's rolling in money in America."

"Better stay put till you're sure, Cyril. And your Edna might get home-sick for Radford. Can't imagine her on a horse somehow."

"Our Edna'd ride on a bleddy rhinoceros, Bert . . . if she thought there was plenty of money at the end of it."

"So would I, mate," Bert laughed as he pushed the barrow towards Brassey, "and so would you. I'll be back for that fur tomorrer. Keep it in mothballs."

The people of Radford once again enjoyed Christmas; pubs and hotels were filled to capacity as revellers jostled each other for that last drop of port and that final pint of Shippos; publicans stood behind bar counters, smiling benevolently as tills jingled a merry tune and filled up with money.

There were no air raid sirens sending people scuttling for safety down damp cellars and shelters; no enemy aircraft raining down bombs and incendiaries; no terrifying news on the wireless filling hearts and minds with paralysing fear.

Instead, there was laughter, singing, enough food, nearly enough drink and Churchill — smiling and waving his two fingers in the air doing his Victory Salute, Churchill puffed on his cigars and promised peace, quite soon.

After the Oak had closed its doors Jack and Vera opened theirs. Overflowing with people the little house on Independent Street welcomed Jenny, Mrs Cohen, Bert, Annie, Florence and her new husband, the old couple from next door and, it seemed to Jack, half the Airborne Division from Wollaton Park.

148

Upstairs, a sleeping Alex, Elizabeth Rose and Louise Rachel were oblivious to the celebrations downstairs.

"Say . . . let's have some carols," yelled a sergeant who had Jenny on his knee, a glass of whisky in one hand and a fat cigar in the other. "How about? . . . er? . . . " he kissed Jenny on the cheek and forgot about the carols.

"Jack!," Vera looked annoyed, "two of them Yanks have been down the cellar and peed on the coal!"

"Shouldn't worry about it, duck. It'll damp down the dust."

"They think they're back home, Vera," Bert chimed in, "they all live on ranches yer know. There int no lavatories out on the prairies. Mind you . . . they have to watch out for cactus," he roared with laughter.

"Well I think they're dirty, doing that on our coal."

"Have another drop of port and stop worrying, Vera." Jack reached for a port bottle. "And how about a few sandwiches and some pork-pies? Let's show these lads we're grateful for all they're doing to help us win the war. It's no bleddy picnic yer know . . . being parachuted from a plane in the middle of nowhere . . . in the middle of the night." He turned to the Americans and said, "Drink up, lads . . . if you haven't got bad heads in the morning, I'll eat my hat." Jack was now at the merry stage.

"Good King Wenceslas looked out on the Feast of Stephen." The couple from next door led the carol singing and everyone joined in.

Like a beautiful tapestry coming to life, depicting human warmth and happiness, young and old, English and American, they sang together about Christmas, crisp snow, compassion and God — and forgot all about cruelty, destruction and death.

TWENTY EIGHT

Jack listened to the wireless and experienced the excited feeling from his boyhood once again. The fluttering inside his stomach when he had dived from the top board at the swimming pool. He leapt from his chair and rushed outside.

"Hitler's dead! . . . Hitler's dead! . . . Hitler's dead!!" People chanted the good news, faces creased with smiles, voices breaking with emotion.

"Committed suicide . . . the bleddy coward."

"Good riddance to bad rubbish."

"Won't be long now then. Soon be all over."

"Hitler's dead!"

"Hitler's dead . . . and that Braun woman. Good riddance."

Later on that evening, as he lay next to Vera in their bed, Jack felt more aroused than he had ever felt before. Not even his lovemaking with Gloria Goodliffe had

149

inspired such a depth of longing and passion that he now felt. He thought back to his illness, the TB that could have ended his life.

He reached for Vera's hand — she would soon be packing in her job at the factory — no war, no munitions. Now that Hitler had committed suicide the war would speed towards peacetime once more.

He thought about the future. The lorry would be running again, petrol would be no problem after the war. There would be no black market after a while but then he could concentrate on that shop down Hyson Green. Mrs Cohen was always encouraging him to have a shop of his own. Exciting plans for the future overwhelmed him — his body felt super-charged like a dynamo.

"Vera," he pressed closer and kissed Vera on the mouth, "don't let's take precautions tonight. I want to feel you . . . you know . . . without using anything. Take your nightie off, love. I want to feel your flesh next to mine. It won't matter if you catch . . . I'll look after you."

Vera took off her nightgown and placed it on top of the quilt. Darkness hid her shyness, the blackout curtaining shut out all light.

Her breasts nestled against Jack's chest; he lowered himself further down the bed and kissed her soft flesh. He loved the smell of her body; freshly washed with scented soap and powdered with talcum powder; a feminine, womanly smell that made him desire her so much his body ached and seemed to burn with fever.

The hardness between his thighs made him desperate to enter her body. The old familiar pounding inside his head made him feel intoxicated. His mind was full of well-being and his heart felt generous. Instead of entering her body straight away he held back, caressing every part of her — wanting to please, he stroked and fondled her until she cried out for him — pulled him closer with lustful urgency and writhed beneath him.

He struggled to hold back. The excitement of entering her body without taking precautions almost made him let go straight away.

After a while he felt Vera's body shudder beneath him. Her signal excited him beyond the limits of self control. He gushed out his own passion and collapsed on top of her like a puppet whose strings had been cut.

"Hitler's dead! . . . Hitler's dead! . . . Hitler's dead!" Voices calling out in the night. "Won't be long now then, mate . . . soon be over and done with. Fancy owd Hitler committing suicide. I'd have slit his throat if they'd let me get at him."

"And me, mate . . . I'd have loved to have put a bomb underneath his arse."

Jack smiled in the darkness and moved gently on to his side. Still inside Vera's body he held her tightly to him — they fell asleep locked together in mutual contentment and love.

Jenny and Vera sat inside the Windsor picture house and looked forward to the new Bette Davis film. Lights were dimmed and red velvet curtains swished open to reveal the large white screen. Vera had looked forward to seeing the film for days — Bette Davis had never made a bad film as far as Vera was concerned — she was the most talented and beautiful woman that had ever graced the screen at the Windsor.

"This is the Pathe Gazette News," said the voice of the commentator. The cockerel on the screen crowed and stared down at the audience with its cold, beady eyes.

Images came onto the screen but seemed unreal; as though someone was playing a grotesque and obscene joke on the audience. A collective gasp echoed around the picture house, but the dreadful images would not go away.

Men staggered about in front of the cameras — men that did not look like human beings. Skeletons walking in slow motion — dull eyes staring out of skulls they smiled weakly, showing teeth that looked too large for their mouths.

Jenny reached for Vera's hand and squeezed it tightly, neither of them spoke.

The cameras ventured further inside the prison camps. Skeletal bodies piled high — no clothing to give their deaths dignity they lay in twisted, obscene mounds awaiting burial.

Russia, Poland and Germany. One by one the terrible secrets of the prison camps were revealed to the rest of the world.

The voice of the commentator droned on and on but no narration was necessary as the cameras recorded forever the suffering and horror.

Towards the end of the news-reel Churchill appeared on the screen, puffing at a large cigar and doing his famous Victory Salute he smiled as he inspected a regiment of soldiers; the giant leader of men; the British bulldog; a Saviour.

The audience applauded and cheered as they usually did whenever he appeared on the news-reels but this time his presence was not powerful enough to eradicate the images that had gone before.

Vera and Jenny dabbed at their eyes with handkerchiefs and tried to rid their throats of the lumps that had formed there.

Bette Davis swaggered down a magnificent staircase. Dressed in a beautiful ball-gown, hair immaculately groomed, she filled the screen with her loveliness and outstanding personality. But still the images of the starving men would not leave Vera's mind.

"God forbid, Mrs Cohen ever sees those prisoners," Vera whispered.

"I can't believe what I saw," Jenny whispered back.

Bette Davis smiled and flirted, white-gloved hands making graceful gestures as she arranged flowers in a vase, large eyes expressing more than words could ever say.

Vera admired the exquisite satin of the ball-gown and then once again the images of the starving men attacked her mind.

Hanging on to barbed wire fences for support the human skeletons stared out of expressionless skulls and clung to life — and Vera's mind.

TWENTY NINE

Jack put the kettle on the gas-stove, went back into the kitchen and switched on the wireless. A man's voice droned on — something about the Germans — surrendering as expected — men had signed documents — it would be a day for celebrations.

He pulled his pyjama trousers up over his waist and sat down on the edge of the sofa. He became wide awake as the news sank into his sleep-fuddled brain. Rushing towards the stairs he shouted as he reached the bedroom, "That's it, Vera! . . . the war's over! They've just announced it on the wireless. You can stay in bed, duck. Today's a holiday . . . nobody'll go to work today."

Vera sat up in bed and pushed back tangled curls from her face.

"Are you sure, Jack? Is it really true?"

"Yes . . . yes I'm sure. It's just been on the wireless. Today's VE Day. The bleddy Jerries have packed it in at last."

They hugged each other, laughing and shouting, Alex appeared, he yawned and rubbed at bleary eyes.

"Good news, me lad. It's VE Day. Me and yer Mam'll take you down to the Market Square later on. There'll be singing and dancing . . . and I'll bet there'll be fireworks and brass bands."

"I'll have a drop of whisky in me tea," said Vera, "this calls for a bit of celebrating. Oh, it feels just like Christmas."

"Better than Christmas, duck," Jack stood up, "I'll just go and mash that tea."

A few minutes later they sipped tea and listened to Independent Street coming to life. Every voice held excitement and emotion.

They would all 'live to fight another day'. Jack kissed Vera on the cheek and hugged Alex and Elizabeth Rose.

"Don't be soppy, Dad," said Alex as he snuggled closer to Vera. "You don't have to kiss big lads like me. I was nearly old enough to join the Army."

"God forbid," Vera cried out and hugged him tighter, "God forbid."

"Too late now, me lad," Jack cuddled Elizabeth Rose, "I don't reckon there'll be any more wars after this little lot. People will have learned some commonsense at last. There'll be no more lunatics like Hitler and Goering."

"I liked it when they sent all those bombs over, Dad. It was ever so exciting in the air raid shelters. People liked going in the shelters and having a sing-song."

"Oh yes," Jack winked at Vera, "it was good fun . . . so long as the bombs missed yer."

The people from Independent Street flooded from their houses like a gurgling storm-water filled river. Gathering up more people as it noised along — the swell of laughing and shouting surged towards Canning Circus and down on its way to the city centre.

"See me do the conga
Aye-aye-aye-aye-conga
Dee-dah-dee-dah, dee-dah."

"Come on, Bert . . . get a move on, Annie," Jack called over his shoulder.

"We're right behind you, mate. And I've got the necessary." Bert held up a bottle of whisky and a bottle of port.

"Roll out the barrel
We'll have a barrel of fun."

Men and women kissed each other, hugged each other, laughed, cried and then kissed each other again.

"I want you to remember VE night all your life, me lad," Jack shouted to an excited Alex. "You don't get many nights like this in your life."

"I will remember it, Dad," Alex shouted back, "I will . . . I will."

A bonfire was lit and a mighty roar was sent skywards by the crowd. Church bells rang out their messages of victory and peace. Ding-dong, ding-dong, ding-dong, they rang out from all over the city and the sound made Jack's blood race faster with excitement.

A group of servicemen began to chant a song to the tune of Colonel Bogey.

"Hitler, has only got one ball
Goering, has two but they're both small.
Himler, is somewhat similar
And Doctor Goebbels has got none at all."

"Ooh, the rude lot," Annie linked arms with Vera and grinned, "Isn't it marvellous, Vera. I thought the war would go on till we were all wiped out. I thought we'd all be killed or took prisoner."

"Goering, has two but they're both small."

"No chance of a drink in the city pubs, Annie," shouted Vera, "we'd never get near the bars."

"Have a swig of this, gels," Bert held up the bottle of port, "no glasses I'm afraid, ladies." He bowed low and added, "You'll have to swig out the bottle."

"Himler, is somewhat similar."

Vera and Annie took it in turn to drink from the port bottle.

"Just what the doctor ordered," said Jack, after gulping down a mouthful of whisky. "Rule Britannia, Britannia rules the waves," he shouted to the crowd and waved the bottle in the air.

"And Doctor Goebbels has got none at all." The group of servicemen sang louder but they were soon drowned out by other revellers.

"Roll out the barrel
We'll have a barrel of fun."

More people surged into the Market Square. Servicemen climbed onto the statues of two lions which stood at the foot of the Council House entrance — others tried to shin to the top of gas-lamps.

"Oh, knees up Mother Brown
Your pants are coming down."

Ding-dong, ding-dong, ding-dong, ding-dong. The night roared on and still the people did not tire of dancing and singing. They linked arms and swayed from side to side — intoxicated by the celebrations and the importance of the news they held onto each other and let their emotions run free. Kissing and hugging as though it were their last chance the revellers shut out the horrors of war from their minds — shouting and singing they would not allow the dead to take part in the celebrations — even though the dead had made those celebrations possible.

THIRTY

"I thought the horrors of war couldn't get any worse, Bert." Jack and Bert sat huddled over the *Evening Post* which was spread out on the kitchen table.

"Well I say it serves them right," Bert answered. "Bleddy murdering, torturing swines. They deserve all they get."

"What's the matter now?" Vera rubbed at the fire-place with a blacklead brush. "Who are you on about now?"

"The Japs," Jack sipped at his cup of tea, "they've had a bleddy great bomb dropped on them. The Yanks have dropped a bomb on Hiroshima and it exploded and wiped out everything . . . women, children, buildings . . . everything. It says in the paper here, that the bomb has got two thousand times the blast power of any bomb ever used before. It says here, that at least sixty per cent of the city was wiped out and that it left a mountain of smoke seven and a half miles high."

"Oh, I can't believe that, Jack. Do you realise how high that is? You can't believe everything you read. 'Specially not about the Japs." Vera rubbed harder with the blacklead brush.

"It's right . . . seven and a half miles of dust and smoke. I don't like the bleddy Japs, but you can't help feeling a bit sorry for the women and children. Imagine if the Japs dropped one of them atom bombs over here. You'd have to be in a bleddy good air raid shelter . . . that's all I can say. Bleddy atom bombs . . . oh, it makes yer blood go cold."

"Look how the Japs treated their prisoners though, Jack." Vera rubbed at the fireplace with a clean brush. "I don't feel sorry for monsters like that. They ought to drop a few more atom bombs over there."

"Don't you see, Vera . . . if they've invented a bomb as powerful as that, anybody could invent one. The Japs could blow us all to smithereens."

"Stop worrying, Jack. The war's over. The Japs won't mess about now." Bert poured tea into his saucer and made a loud sucking noise.

Bert was right. After a second bomb had exploded on another of their cities the Japanese government surrendered unconditionally.

Jack walked past the cemetery at Canning Circus. So the war really was over now. He stopped to light a cigarette and stared all around him. Gas-lamps flickered cheerily up and down the streets, shop windows showed off goods which were bathed in electric light. Buses and cars beamed their approach through the fading light of evening all headlamp shades now removed.

Jack tried to remember the words of the King's speech — the one broadcast on the announcement of war. Something about light, the King had said to his people. Jack screwed up his face and searched his memory.

'I said to the man who stood at the gate of the Year
GIVE ME LIGHT that I may tread softly into the unknown."

Jack could not remember all the words. He walked down Alfreton Road past all the brightly lit shops. The world was at last 'treading softly, and safely, into the unknown.' Into a future full of peace and commonsense.

Life was good, he thought, and then for some inexplicable reason wondered what Gloria Goodliffe was doing at that very moment.

THIRTY ONE

Jack and Vera heard shouting above the dance music from their wireless.

"Jack! . . . Vera! . . . Jack! . . . Oh, God! . . . Oh, God help me!" Jenny rushed into the kitchen, eyes wild, hair dishevelled, mouth opening and shutting as she continued to shout, "Oh! . . . oh! . . . I can't believe it! I can't believe it!" In her hand she waved a telegram.

"Now then, whatever's the matter?" Jack stood up and held out his arms to her. "Come and sit down. Tell us what's wrong. They can hear you shouting at Ilkeston. Come and sit down."

"It's Reggie! . . . he's alive! He's sent me a telegram. He's alive, Jack! He's coming home . . . coming home to me," she continued to shout, "the Japs didn't kill him. He's been a prisoner all this time. They didn't kill him." She collapsed into an armchair and stared wide-eyed at Jack and Vera. "I can't believe it . . . my Reggie's alive. Here's the telegram," she waved it again, "it must be true."

"Well, well, that's the best piece of news I've ever heard in all me life." Jack poured three whiskies. "Good owd, Reg." He raised his glass and added, "Three cheers for Reg."

They drank the whisky and were silent for a while.

"What about Louise then?" Vera was the first to speak, "what will you tell him about Louise?"

"What about her?" Jack looked annoyed. "These things happen in wartime. Our Jenny thought he'd been killed. You can't blame Jenny. Reg'll understand when she explains."

"Yes, I expect he will," Vera sounded doubtful. "He'll take to her all right. She's a lovely little thing . . . he'll understand."

"I don't expect him to take to her," Jenny's voice was subdued and anxious. "I don't suppose he'll want anything to do with me when he finds out. But I'm ever so thrilled that he's alive and well."

"When's he coming home?" Vera picked up the telegram. "Oh . . . it'll be November. Coming home by boat. That makes it about nine weeks time. We'll have a big do for him on Independent Street."

"He won't want me, Vera . . . not after what he's gone through. The terrible time in those Jap camps . . . and when he finds out I . . . when he knows what I did . . . and he wasn't even dead. He was alive and I went with another man." Jenny's face was full of misery. "I'm so ashamed."

"Stop counting your chickens before they're hatched," Jack tried to reassure her, "he's a nice bloke . . . you'll be all right when things settle down."

"Maybe," Jenny answered him and then picked up the telegram and kissed it. "But even if he doesn't want anything to do with me, I'm still over the moon that he's alive and well."

"Perhaps he won't be well, Jenny," said Vera, "but at least he's still alive."

'Bonfire night, stars are bright
Three little Angels dressed in white.'

November the fifth was given the full treatment by the people on Independent Street. Shouting and laughing they let off fireworks for the first time since the war had started.

Flames shooting upwards, sparks flying in all directions, young children screamed and held back, older children poked about in the ashes for blackened potatoes, threw jumping-jacks at one another and leapt about like March hares.

"So it'll be the eighteenth then?" Jack sat on the front doorstep with Vera and Jenny either side on chairs.

"Yes, the eighteenth," Jenny answered.

"We've got everything ready," Vera sounded excited. "Plenty of flags and whatnot. All the neighbours are going to decorate their houses and windows. So bring him up here as soon as you can."

"There'll be plenty to eat and drink," Jack added, "that's my department. The blokes from down Sneinton Market are going to see him right. We'll soon build him up and make him strong again."

"Expect he'll be all right now, Jack." Jenny looked frightened. "They'll have given him plenty to eat on the boat."

"Course they will, duck." Jack stood up and walked over to the bonfire. He picked up a piece of metal that was lying near the bonfire and poked at the fiercely burning effigy of Hitler.

"Now then, Adolf," he shouted so that everyone could hear, "this is the second time you've had your arse on fire. I bet he's roasting nicely down in hell now." He addressed the crowd, "Bleddy swine."

"Hooray . . . hooray . . . smash him up, Jack."

"Bash his bleddy brains in, Jack."

"Hooray . . . there he goes . . . there he goes."

Everyone joined in the shouting and then they began to dance round and round the bonfire.

"Aye, aye, aye, aye, conga
See me do the conga."

Jack threw the piece of metal at Hitler's effigy and joined in the dancing. Annie put her arms around Jack's waist and called out, "Come on, Jenny . . . come on, Vera . . . aye, aye, aye, aye, conga."

Jenny joined on the end of the snake and thought she knew how it would feel to be an effigy on top of a bonfire. Body on fire, brain scorched with flames of guilt, she longed to be engulfed in the fire so that her misery could be extinguished, swiftly and forever. Instead, she swayed her hips and held on to someone's waist. Held on to life and laughter and wished that she were dead.

Reg stared at the pretty little girl who sat in front of him on the hearthrug playing with a black cat. Titian hair, just like Jenny's and the same captivating smile; she was her mother's image in miniature; a beautiful, living, breathing reminder of Jenny's unfaithfulness.

Jenny sat beside him on the sofa, body tense she sat upright, fingers nervously fidgeting with her skirt.

"So what did you say happened to the father then?" Reg's voice was quiet, too quiet. "Was he married then? Was he married did you say?"

"No, not married."

"And he was killed then?"

"Yes, killed. He was a pilot. He was shot down, they said."

"You would have married him then . . . seeing as he was single?"

Jenny looked at Reg's face. He was still staring at Louise. She observed once more his thin, yellow face — skin stretched tightly across his cheekbones — his scraggy neck and the prominent Adam's apple. He was not the Reggie she had known and loved. He was a stranger.

"Yes . . . I think perhaps I would have married him. You see, we both thought that you were . . . er . . . dead. I had the telegram you see. Killed, they said . . . I thought

157

you'd been killed. Oh, Reg, it was terrible. I thought I'd never see you again. They told me you were dead."

"Didn't waste much time did you. Soon got yourself fixed up. Didn't wait to find out for sure. Jumped into bed with a Pole, didn't you."

Jenny's heart shuddered and she struggled to hold back the tears that smarted her eyes. It was not going to work. No-one could blame Reg. Going through torture and hell for all those years and coming back to find out his wife had had a baby with another man. She had lost him.

She struggled for words — something that would make everything all right again — but the words would not come. There were no words that could heal so deep a wound.

"They gave you a lovely homecoming, didn't they. Been planning it from the minute I got your telegram." Jenny smiled at him.

Louise tired of the cat and turned her attention to Reg. Arms outstretched she attempted to climb onto his knee. Reg lifted her onto the sofa, stood up and went over to the door which divided the kitchen from the front room. He opened the door and called out, "Are you there, Mrs Cohen? You can come into the kitchen again now. We've had our little talk."

Mrs Cohen smiled at him and replied, "Is everything all right then? I've put a hot-water bottle in your bed. Please don't mind what people say about Louise, Reg. Everybody's got troubles of their own." She stroked Louise's head and added, "And she's such a beautiful little child. No trouble at all. The war is to blame, Reg." She kissed him on the cheek. "We'll look after you . . . Jenny and me. We can all look after each other. The war has been such a terrible thing. Put it behind you now."

"I won't be staying, Mrs Cohen. I'm going back to my Grandma's house down The Meadows. Give myself time to sort things out."

He reached for his kit-bag and with one last look at Louise, closed the door behind him and walked out into the night.

THIRTY TWO

Jack and Bert sat near the fire in the smoke-room at the Dog and Partridge. An icy wind beat a tattoo on the window and each time the door opened Christmas garlands hanging from the ceiling jiggled up and down and smoke from the coal-fire swirled about like ghosts searching for someone to haunt.

"Thought we'd be a lot better off now the war's finished, Jack."

"Yes, how wrong can you be. Things are shorter than ever, Bert. Mind you, we're doing all right on our clothing coupon racket." Jack looked at the clock above the fire-place and added, "Hope owd Reg turns up. Poor bogger's still as thin as a lat. It'll take

158

some doing, getting his weight back on again. I saw his grandma on the market last Monday and she said he's got summat wrong with his stomach."

"Might not turn up then." Bert stood up and went over to the bar for more drinks.

Reg brought his drink over from the bar and pulled his chair nearer the fire. Hands outstretched he leaned towards the warmth then turned to smile at Jack and Bert.

"I feel the cold . . . it's being used to all that hot sun."

"Let me get you a whisky, mate." Jack stood up.

"No thanks, Jack. Me stomach's a bit delicate. I'll just stick to me glass of Shippo's."

Bert gulped down the remainder of his pint and pulled his scarf tighter around his neck.

"I'm off then . . . let you have your chinwag in peace. Our Annie's doing stew and dumplings for us dinners. Can't keep a man from his dumplings." He laughed and left the pub.

Jack and Reg talked of inconsequential things. Then it was time to get down to business.

"So I thought you might like to manage the pot-shop for me." Jack leaned forward. "I know you're convalescing for six months on full pay . . . and you need to, mate . . . get yourself well and strong again. But I reckon you'll be ready to start work by May."

"Sounds about right, Jack. I still feel as weak as a kitten but six months should be about right."

"I'm paying rent on the shop from the first of January." Jack sounded excited. "There'll be plenty to do, shopfitting and stocking all the shelves."

"Sounds good, Jack. You're a born businessman, you are. If you can get your hands on the right merchandise you should be on a winner. People always need pots and bits of hardware."

"I need a man I can trust. Somebody who won't have his thieving hands in the till all the while. You see me right and if we make it pay I'll make you a partner. The money's there for the rent and the stock. I've got plenty saved and Mrs Cohen will always chip in. Mrs Cohen put the idea in me head in the first place. She'll back me all the way."

"I was thinking of going back to being a mechanic."

"Oh, you want to forget that, Reg. Too much like hard work. Come and work for me and you can put your demob suit on every morning and go to work all poshed up. I'll get you an assistant. A young gel just left school . . . or a young lad if you'd prefer."

"I'm really grateful, Jack. I'll make you a good manager."

"I know you will, else I shouldn't have asked yer. Bert can still take the barrer out. Plenty to be made from the barrer. Blimey . . . I'll soon be needing a bleddy accountant to manage me money." Jack laughed and moved closer. "Now then . . . about that other business? . . . what was it you had in mind?"

Jenny hurried along The Ropewalk — head down, shoulders hunched, she pulled her coat closer and tried to keep out icy blasts of wind. She trod carefully so that her high-heels would not slip on the frosty pavements.

After a while she looked up and noticed that the lights in the wards at the General

159

Hospital had been dimmed. Visiting time was over — nurses would be observing their patients in the gloomy half-light. Jenny sighed and thought, some patients would see another Christmas Day, others would see their last Christmas Eve.

The Council House clock struck nine o'clock. The chimes sounded extra loud in the crisp, silent air.

Her heart was beating faster — her throat was dry with anxiety, the next few minutes would affect the rest of her life. She had never felt so afraid and the feeling would not go away.

She turned the corner at the end of The Ropewalk and saw the gas-lamp flickering above the flight of steep steps at the end of Park Terrace. A train snaked its way through the darkness, lighted windows flashing signals.

A shadow at the top of the flight of steps moved slightly. Then the shadow was still again. The shadow became a man. A huddled, sad looking figure the man stepped forward and held out his hands in a gesture of welcome.

"Jenny! . . ." Reg spoke in a whisper, "Jenny!" He moved forward once again and she ran to him and put her head upon his shoulder. She could not look at him — dare not meet his gaze.

"It's all right, Jenny. It's all right, love. I've been a fool. It was you who kept me alive all those years. The thought of you . . . holding you close to me . . . loving you. I stayed alive just for you . . . and then I let you go."

"Oh, Reg . . . you don't know what it was like. I thought you were dead. All those years . . . thinking you were dead. It was hell. I thought I'd lost you forever." Still she did not look at him.

"The little gel," he moved so that she could see his face, "she's lovely, really beautiful. Ey . . . I've always wanted a little gel. And come to think of it you know . . . she looks a bit like me. Although she's got your hair. A right little Ginger Rogers, isn't she."

"Do you remember the last time we came up here?" Jenny could not bring herself to talk about Louise. "You carved our initials on the wall."

"Yes," he traced his fingers along the wall, "here they are. They're here look . . . RB and JD. Thought owd Hitler's bombs might have destroyed the wall but they didn't. Well, here we are as promised. We arranged to meet here no matter what. And I've kept my promise."

He lifted Jenny on to the wall and climbed up beside her.

"What a view. Look at all those lights. You can see for miles." He put his arm around her waist and with the other hand gently tilted her head to one side so that he could kiss her lips. "I thought about this view again and again. The houses in The Park and the lovely gardens and trees. I used to imagine I could see the River Trent . . . see the reflection of the sun on the water . . . see the canal and the barges all loaded up."

The wind blew more fiercely and Jenny said, "We'd better go now, Reggie. Don't want you to catch pneumonia."

He helped her down from the wall and answered, "I could face anything now, Jen. As long as you're there to look after me, I could."

As usual, the little house on Independent Street was crammed full with people. Vera and Jack; Bert and Annie; the old couple from next door; Florence and her new

160

husband; Mrs Cohen; Maisie and Grandad Alf; two barrow-boys from Sneinton Market and their ladyfriends; Alex, Elizabeth Rose and Louise.

Reggie and Jenny stepped inside the kitchen and everyone turned to greet them.

"Ey up, here's the lovebirds."

"Come on, me duck . . . find yourself a glass, Reggie."

"Let Reggie get near that fire . . . feels the cold, he does."

"Have this seat, mate, and I'll pour yer a whisky. Bit of good it is an' all. Nice drop of black market."

"Come on, Reg, have one of these chicken sandwiches."

"What did you reckon to that there atom bomb then? That taught those bleddy Japs a lesson, didn't it! Slant-eyed swines . . . they ought to have dropped a load more after what they did to our lads."

"Now then, now then . . . shurrup about the Japs. It's Christmas and we're here to enjoy ourselves. Let's have a sing-song."

"Ey up, Chuck . . . when are you taking Florence to that there ranch of yours? I can just imagine her in the saddle."

"What do yer reckon to me demob suit then?"

"You look like Humphrey Bogart after he's shrunk six inches. Yer turn-ups are hanging on the floor."

"Ohhhhh . . . roll out the barrel
We'll have a barrel of fun."

The noise grew louder as everyone relaxed and enjoyed themselves. Jack edged nearer towards Jenny and Reg.

"Everything all right now, you two?" He winked at them.

"Yes, everything's sorted, Jack," Reg answered him, "we've decided to make a go of things."

Reg lifted Louise into his arms and gave her a kiss on the cheek then he asked, "What's Santa bringing you for Christmas then?"

"Looks like she's got everything she needs." Jack grinned at him. "And just you wait till I start that chain of shops. We'll have everything then. Owd man Woolworths'll be trembling in his shoes."

Church bells began to chime — Christ was being born all over again — into a better world — a world that had learned its lesson, Jack hoped, a place with a happier future.

Everyone stood still and listened to the bells. Ding-dong-ding-dong-ding-dong-ding-dong. Nineteen forty six would be the very best year. Peace all over the world at last and this time, Jack mused, it would go on forever.

'Silent night, holy night
All is calm, all is bright.'

The past six terrible years now belonged to the history books, thought Jack, best forgotten and done with. He imagined driving a brand new, shiny Wolseley up the path of a smart detached house at Trowell — a house with a fish-pond at the front and an orchard at the back — an orchard full of fruit trees where ragamuffins from Sodom

161

could do a bit of scrumping with Jack turning a blind-eye just like that kind farmer had done when Jack had been a boy.

The church bells were silent once more. Jack moved back furniture, wound up the gramophone and said, "Right then, you lot . . . who wants to have a dance with me . . . don't all rush at once, gels."

The revellers laughed and reached out with their hands for someone to dance with — then reached out with their hearts for that brighter, happier future.

THE END